The Ballad of

Book 1: Fugue

Written by
Jean-Marie **Omont**   Patrick **Marty**   Charlotte **Girard**

Illustrated by
Golo **Zhao**

Created and Edited by
Patrick **Marty**

Localization, Layout, and Editing by Mike Kennedy

www.lionforge.com

FUGUE (PRONOUNCED "FYOOG")
NOUN

1. A SHORT MELODY OR PHRASE THAT IS INTRODUCED BY ONE INSTRUMENT AND THEN REPEATED BY OTHER INSTRUMENTS IN AN INTERWOVEN TUNE.

2. A STATE OF LOSING ONE'S SENSE OF IDENTITY, OFTEN COUPLED WITH FLIGHT FROM ONE'S USUAL ENVIRONMENT.

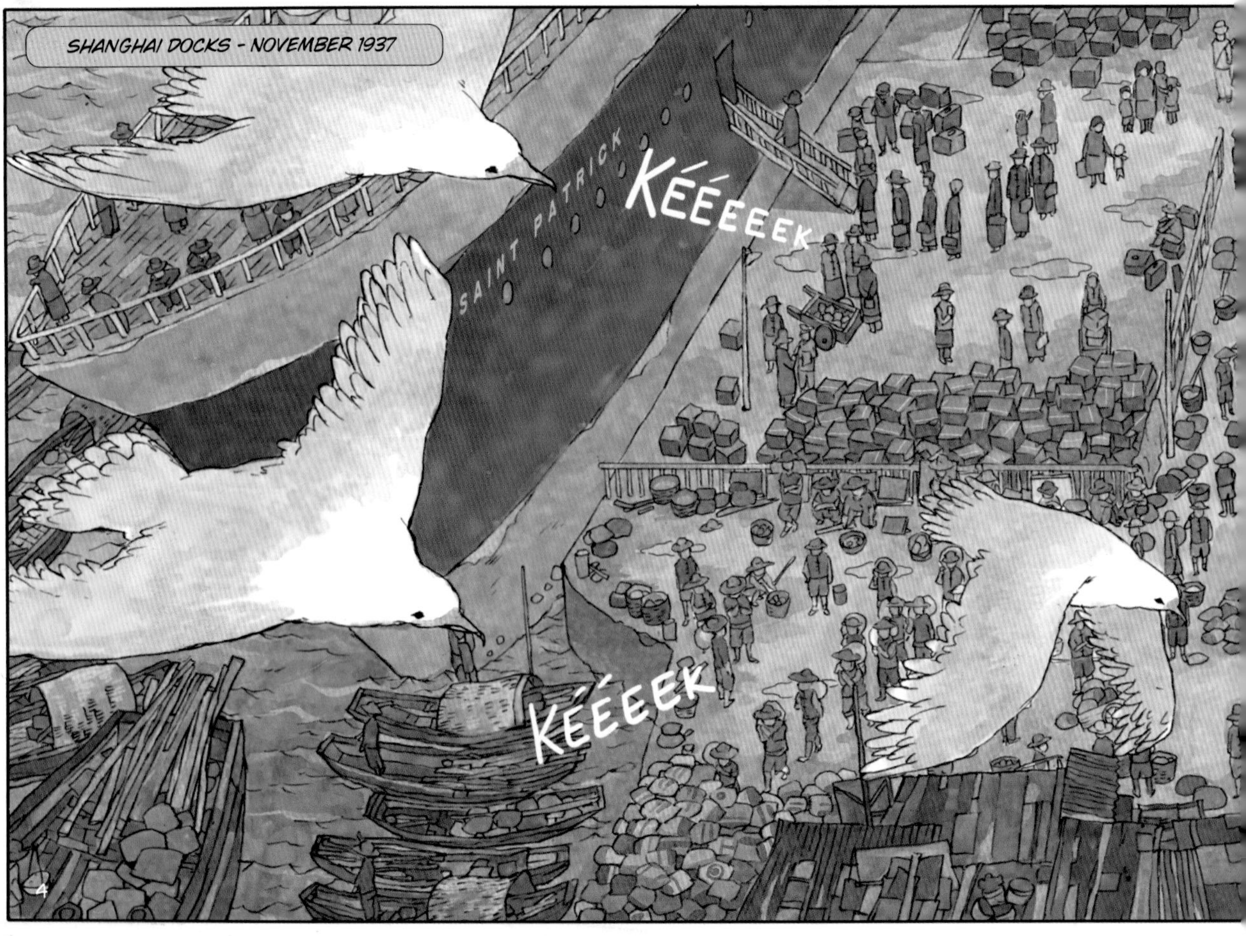
SHANGHAI DOCKS - NOVEMBER 1937
SAINT PATRICK
KÉÉEEEEK
KÉÉEEEK

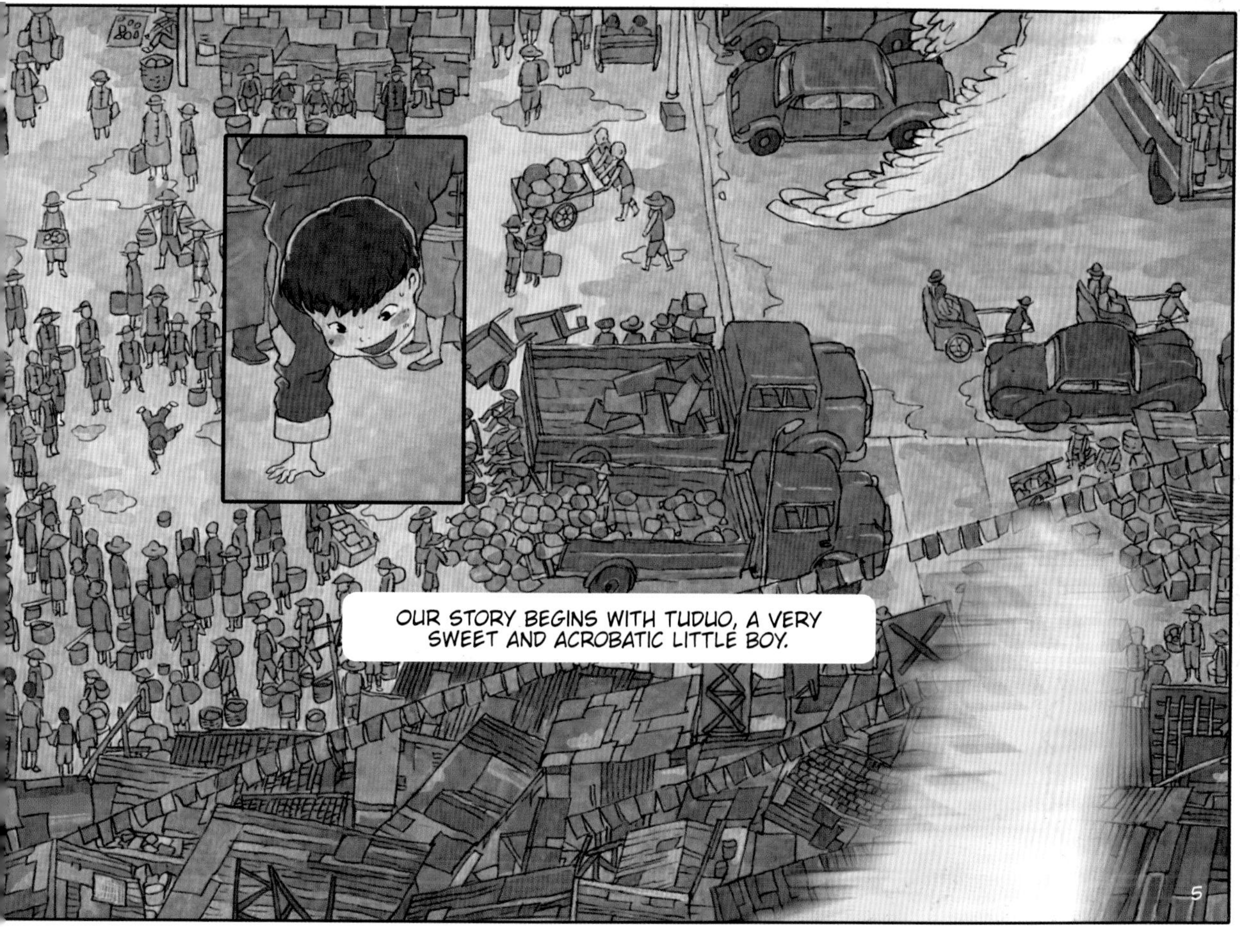
OUR STORY BEGINS WITH TUDUO, A VERY SWEET AND ACROBATIC LITTLE BOY.

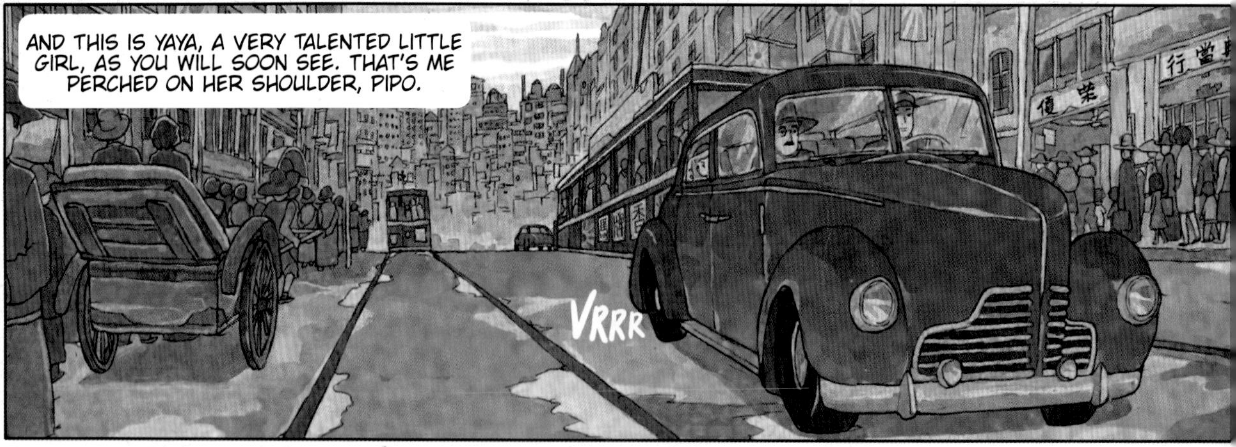
AND THIS IS YAYA, A VERY TALENTED LITTLE GIRL, AS YOU WILL SOON SEE. THAT'S ME PERCHED ON HER SHOULDER, PIPO.
VRRR

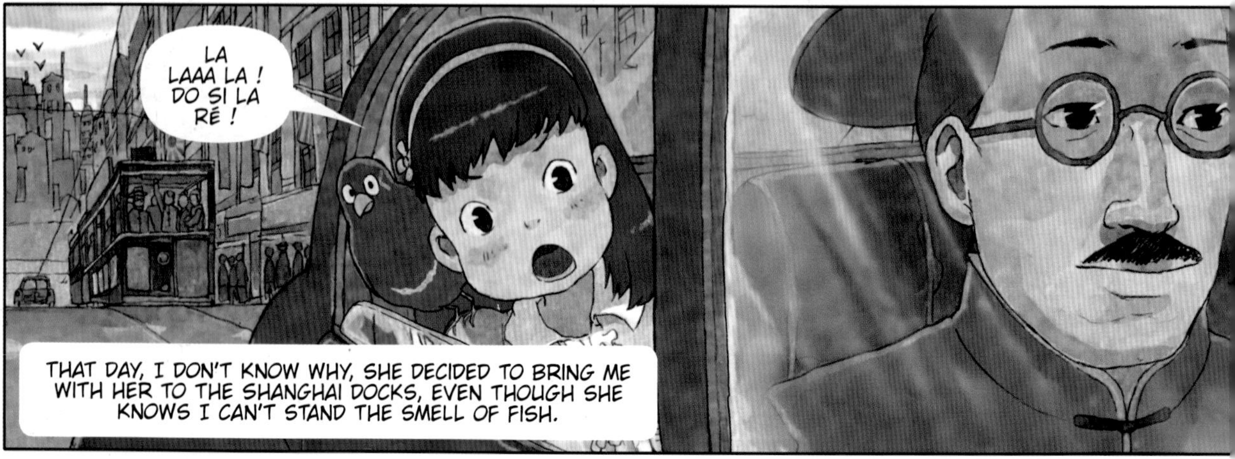
LA LAAA LA ! DO SI LA RÉ !
THAT DAY, I DON'T KNOW WHY, SHE DECIDED TO BRING ME WITH HER TO THE SHANGHAI DOCKS, EVEN THOUGH SHE KNOWS I CAN'T STAND THE SMELL OF FISH.

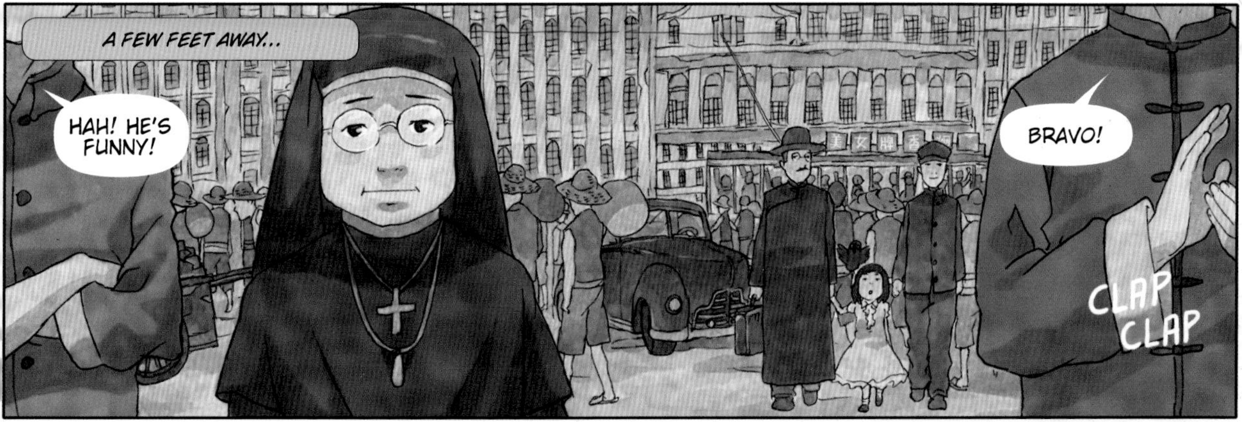
A FEW FEET AWAY...
HAH! HE'S FUNNY!
BRAVO!
CLAP CLAP

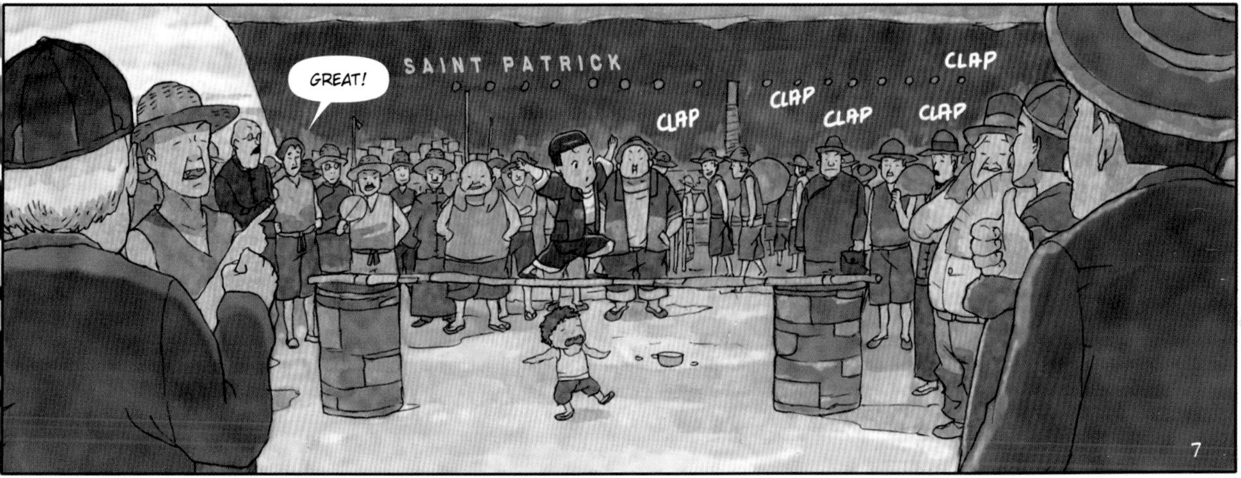
SAINT PATRICK
GREAT!
CLAP
CLAP
CLAP
CLAP
CLAP

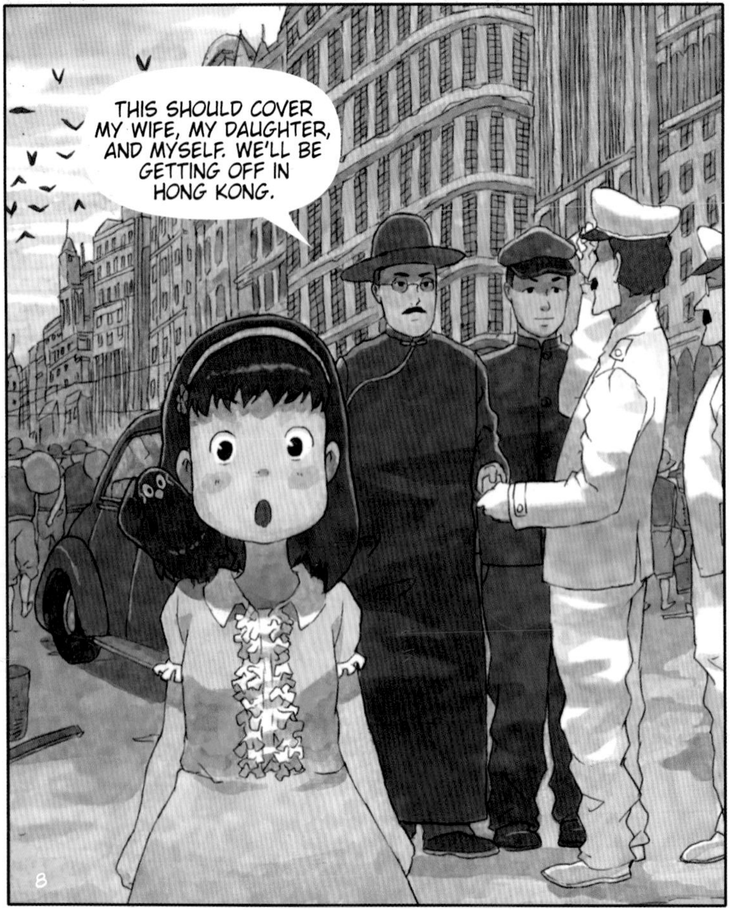
THIS SHOULD COVER MY WIFE, MY DAUGHTER, AND MYSELF. WE'LL BE GETTING OFF IN HONG KONG.

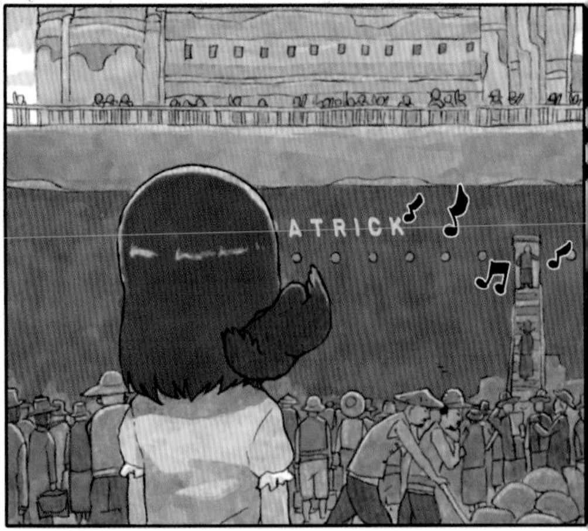
ATRICK

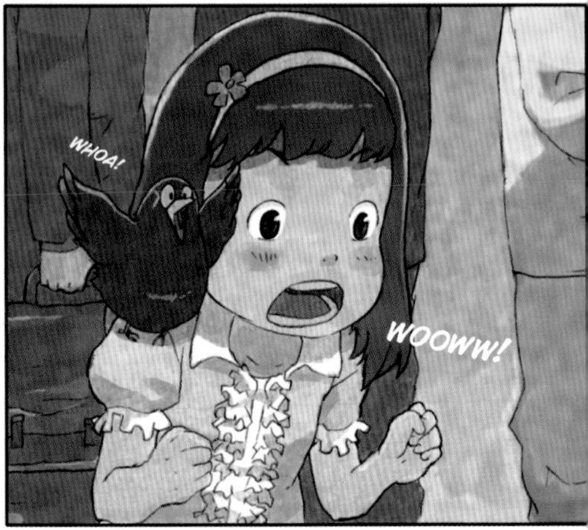
WHOA!
WOOWW!

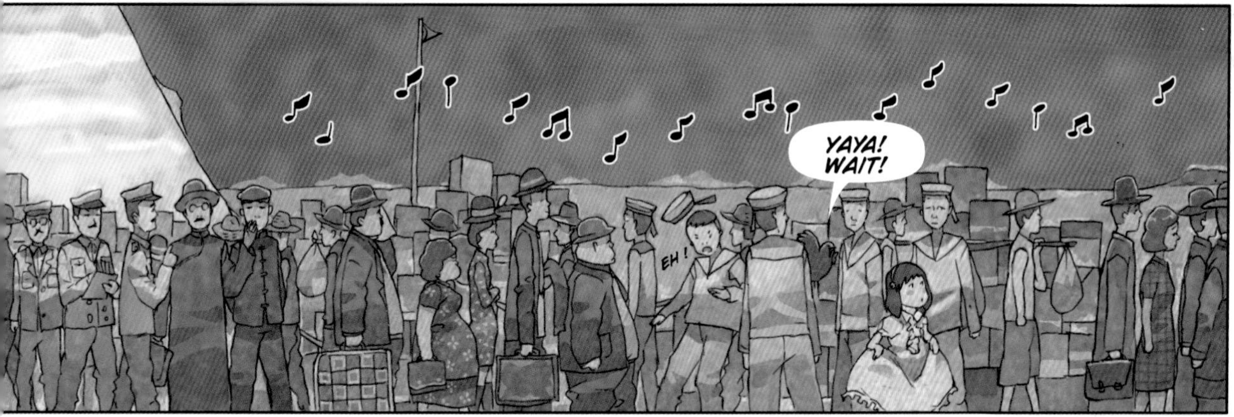
EH!
YAYA! WAIT!
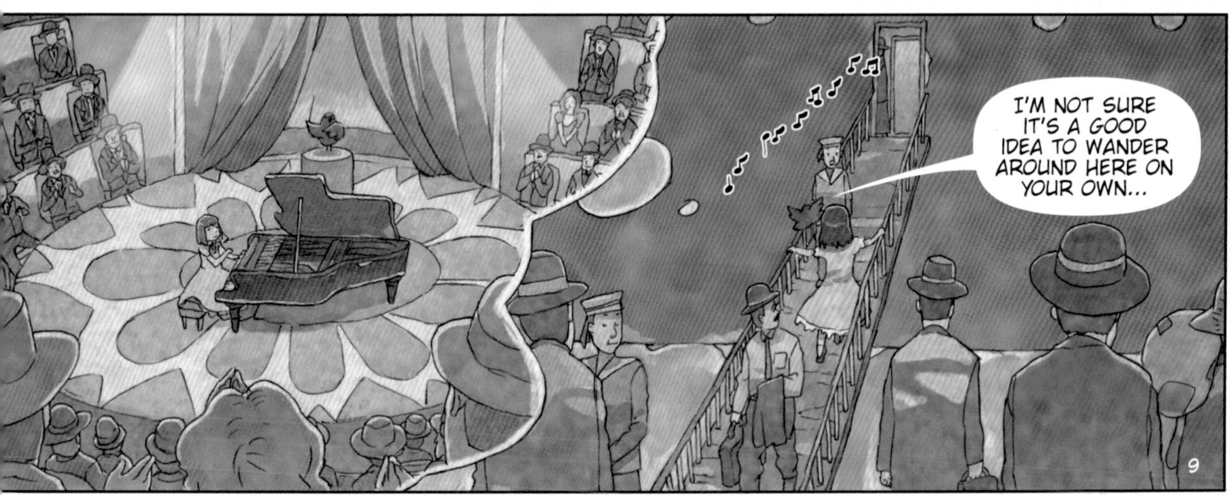
I'M NOT SURE IT'S A GOOD IDEA TO WANDER AROUND HERE ON YOUR OWN...

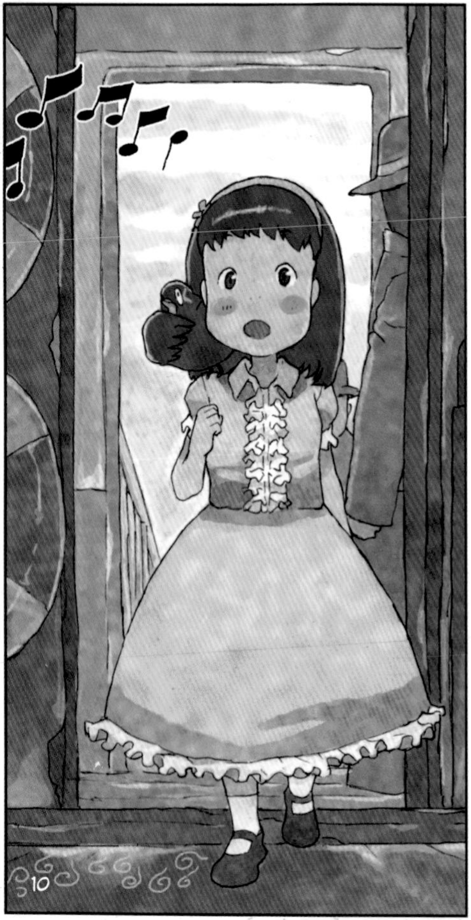

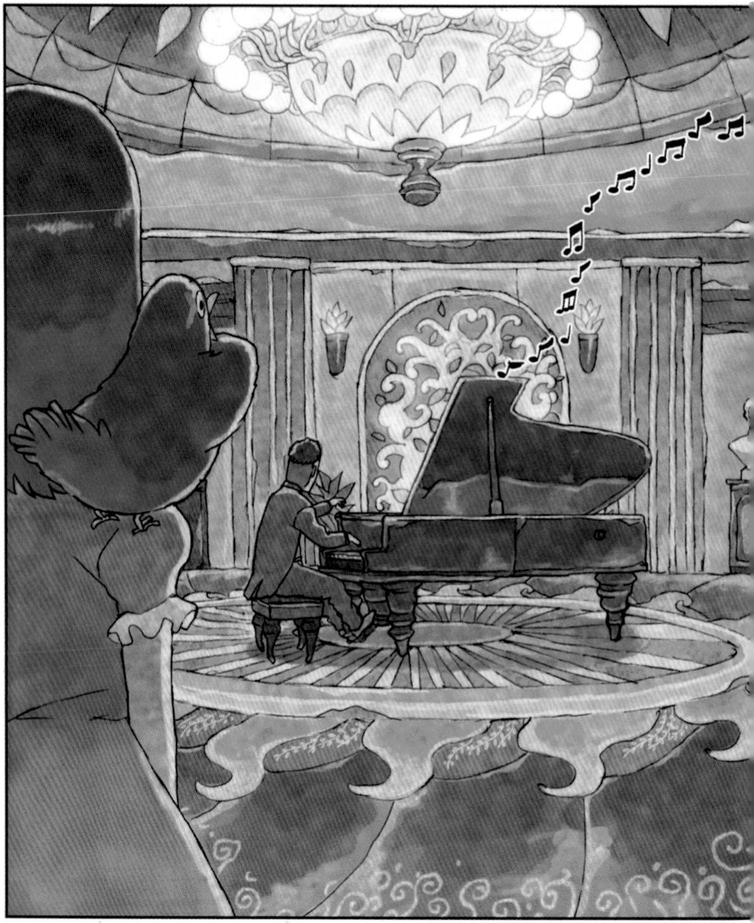

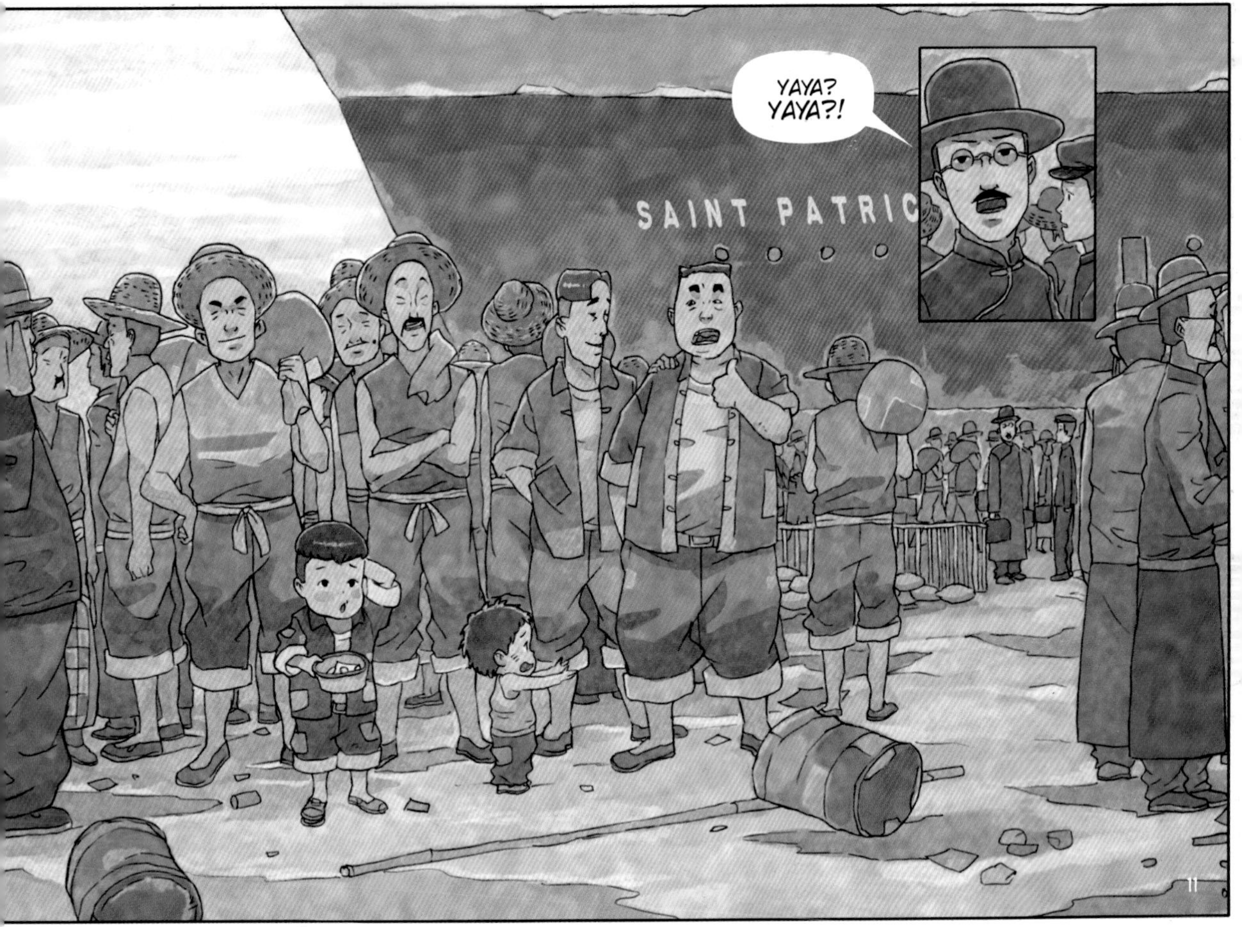
SAINT PATRIC
YAYA? YAYA?!

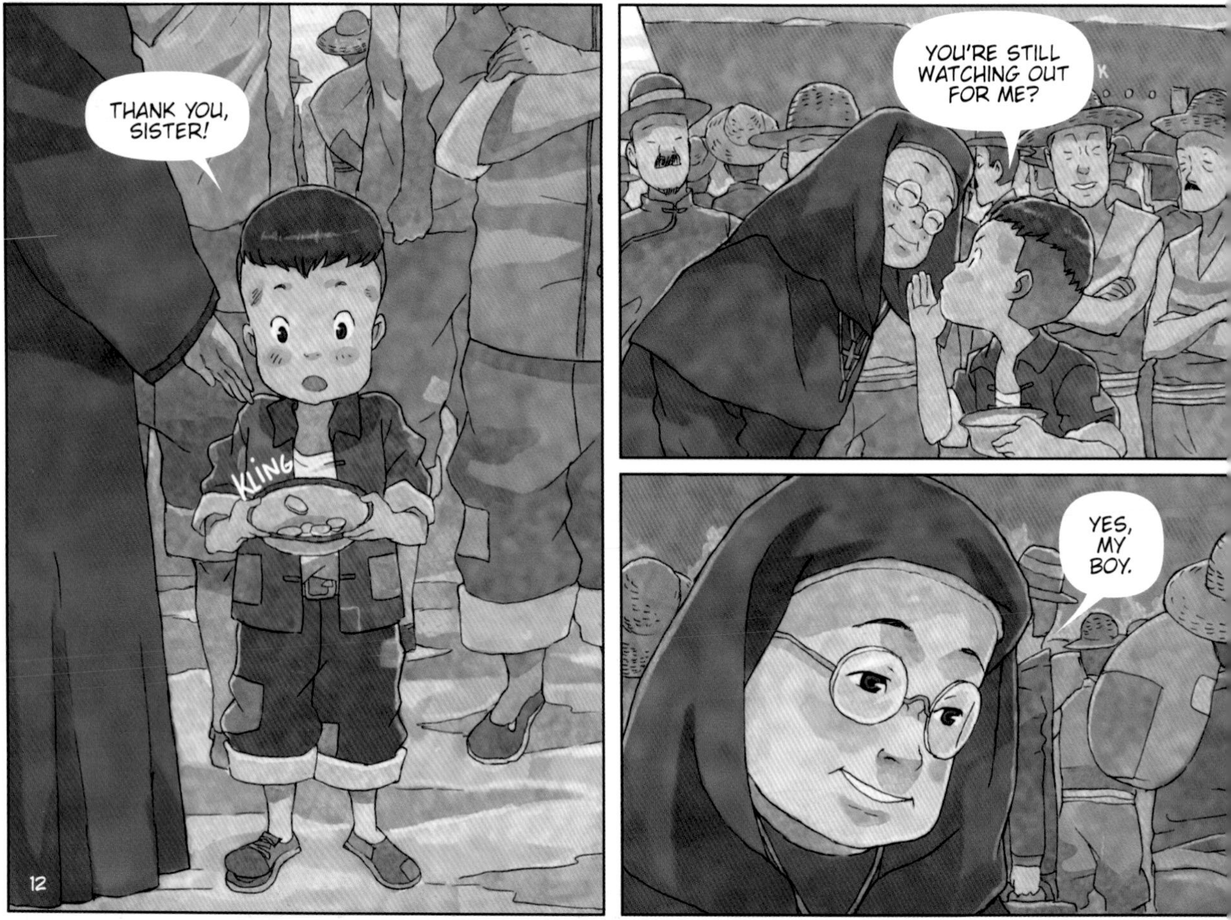
THANK YOU, SISTER!
KLING
YOU'RE STILL WATCHING OUT FOR ME?
YES, MY BOY.

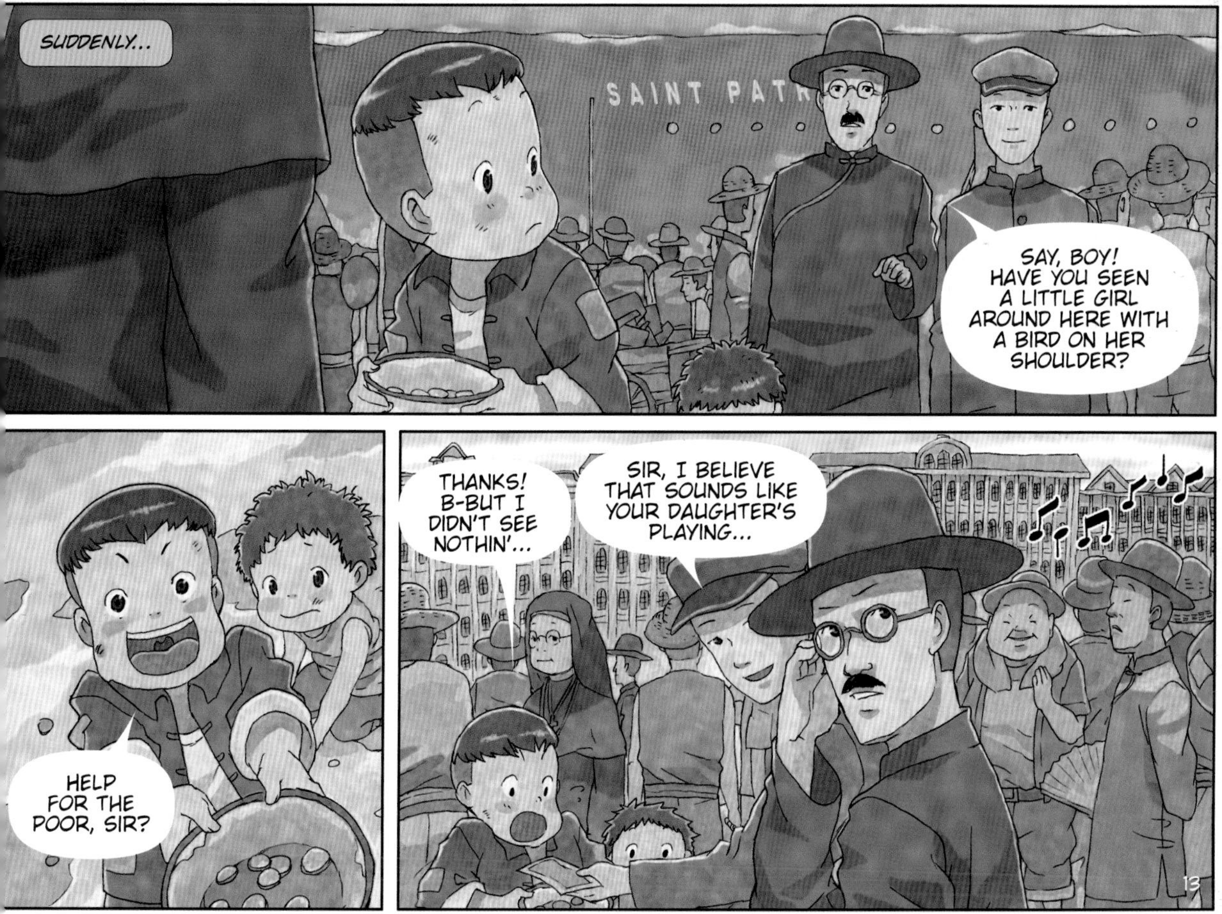
SUDDENLY...
SAINT PATR
SAY, BOY! HAVE YOU SEEN A LITTLE GIRL AROUND HERE WITH A BIRD ON HER SHOULDER?
HELP FOR THE POOR, SIR?
THANKS! B-BUT I DIDN'T SEE NOTHIN'...
SIR, I BELIEVE THAT SOUNDS LIKE YOUR DAUGHTER'S PLAYING...

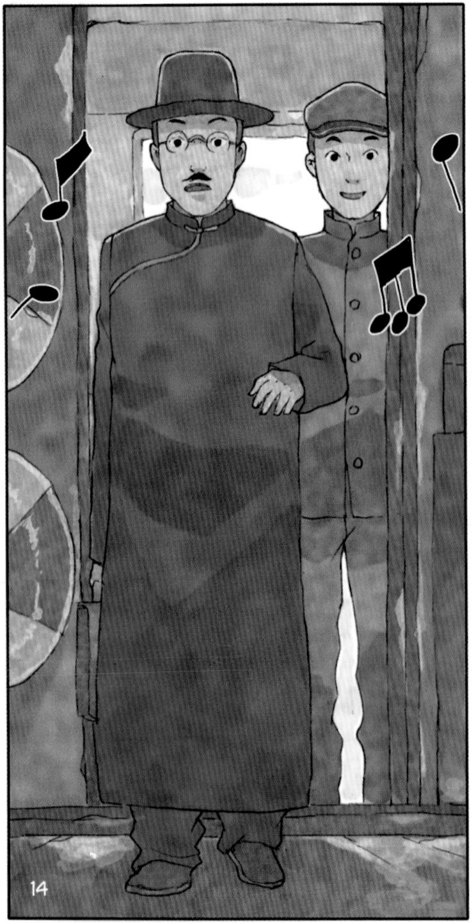

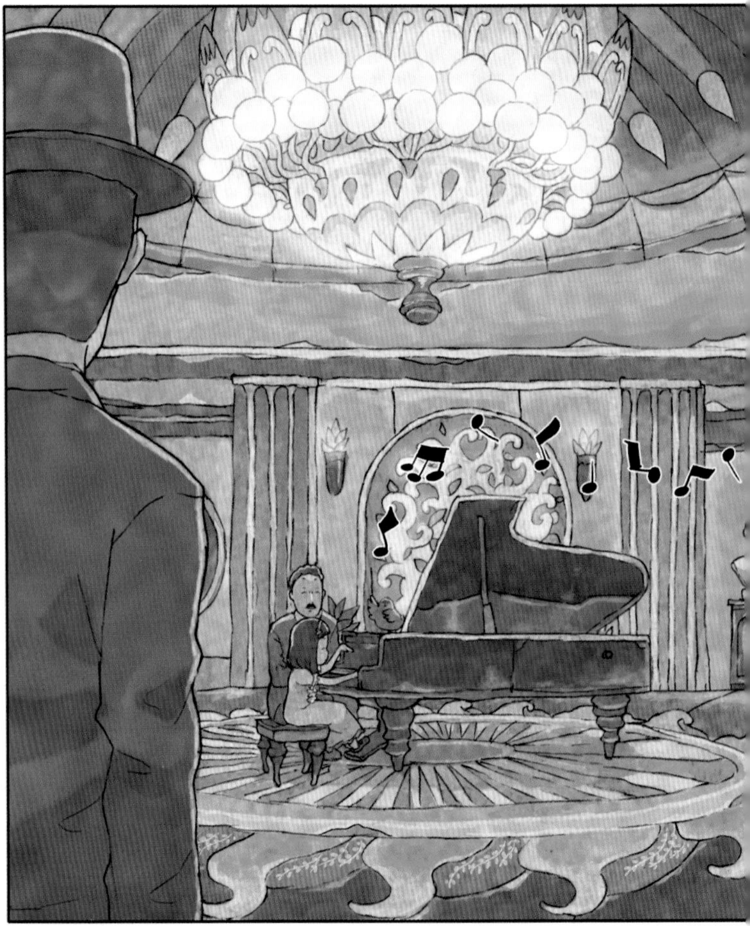

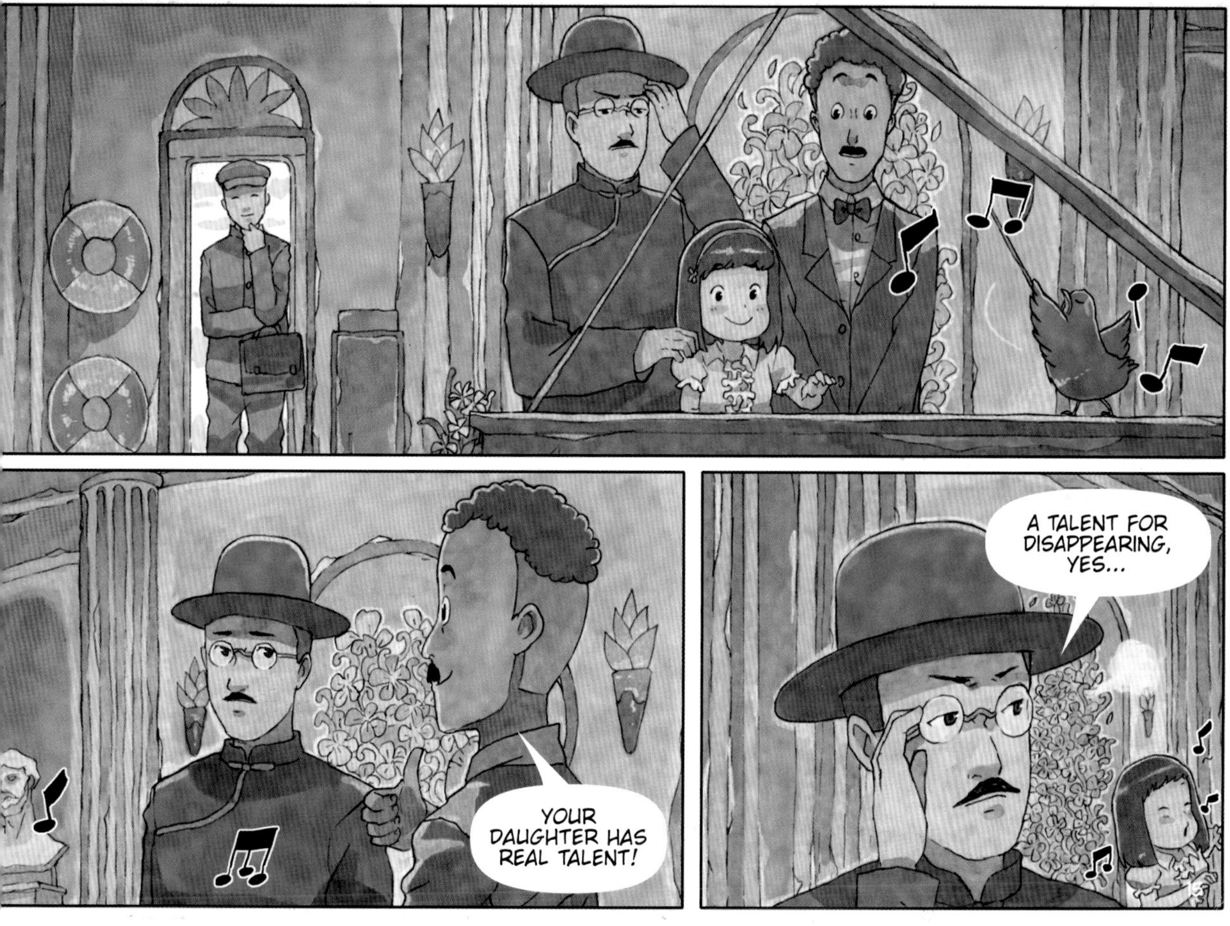
YOUR DAUGHTER HAS REAL TALENT!
A TALENT FOR DISAPPEARING, YES...

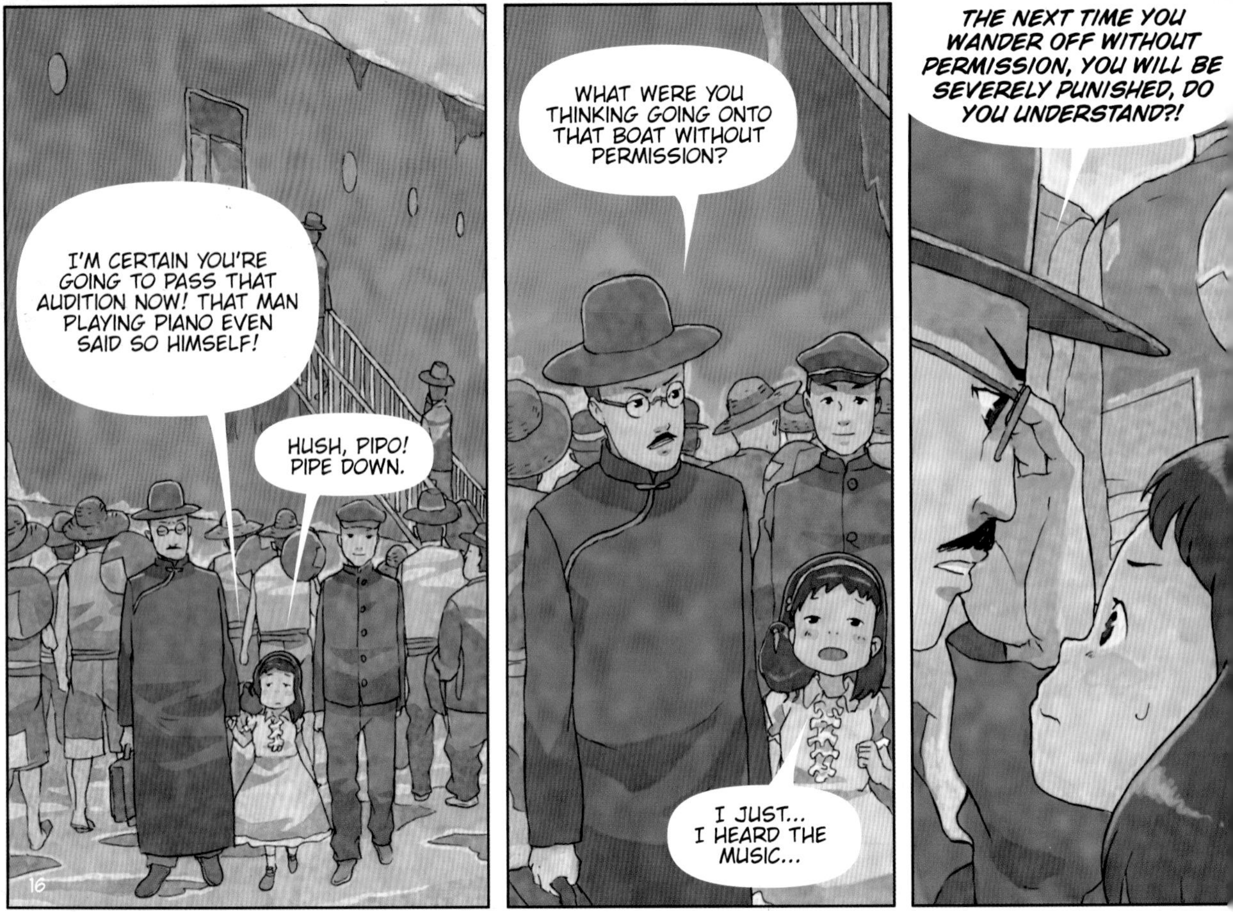
I'M CERTAIN YOU'RE GOING TO PASS THAT AUDITION NOW! THAT MAN PLAYING PIANO EVEN SAID SO HIMSELF!
HUSH, PIPO! PIPE DOWN.
WHAT WERE YOU THINKING GOING ONTO THAT BOAT WITHOUT PERMISSION?
I JUST... I HEARD THE MUSIC...
THE NEXT TIME YOU WANDER OFF WITHOUT PERMISSION, YOU WILL BE SEVERELY PUNISHED, DO YOU UNDERSTAND?!

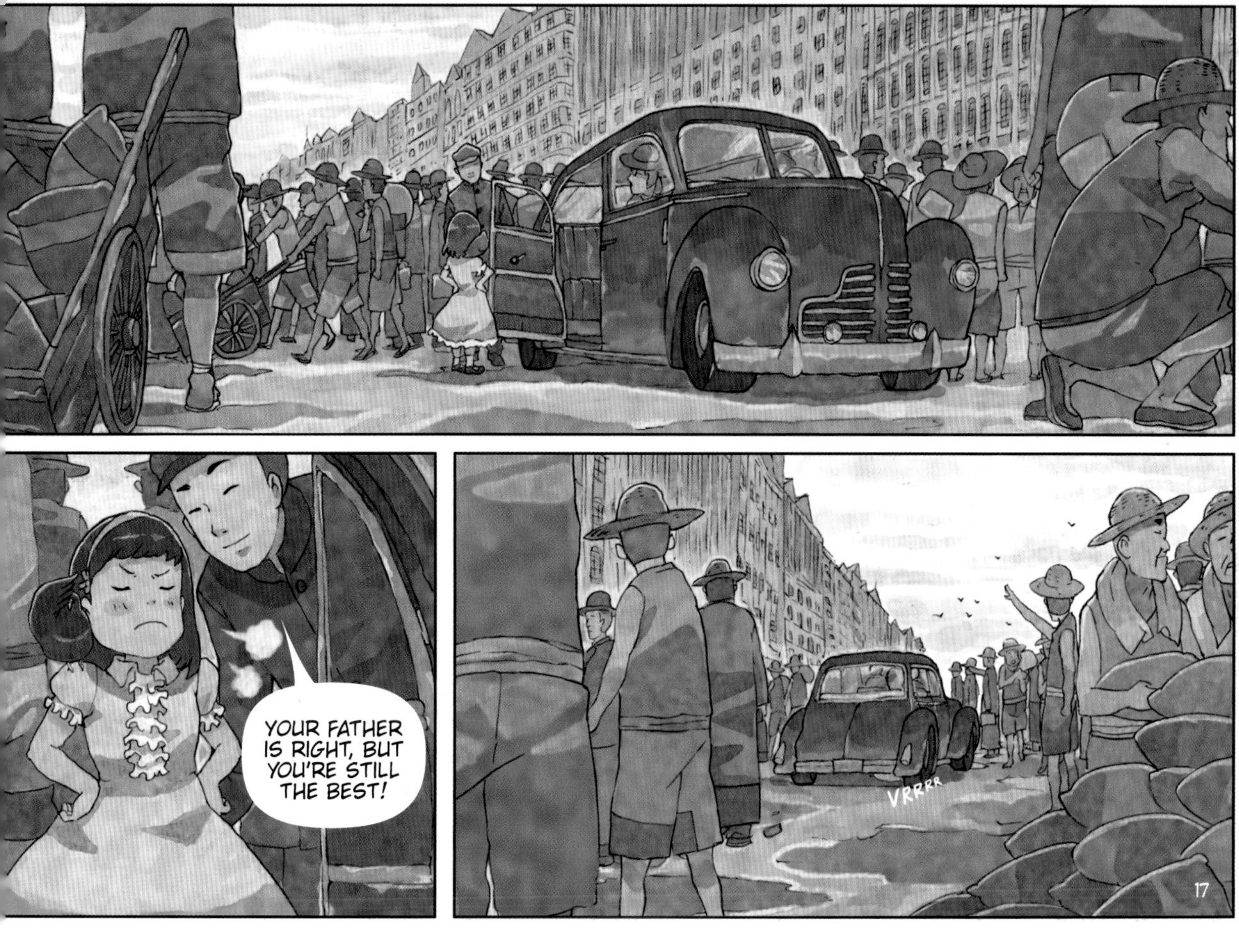
YOUR FATHER IS RIGHT, BUT YOU'RE STILL THE BEST!
VRRRR

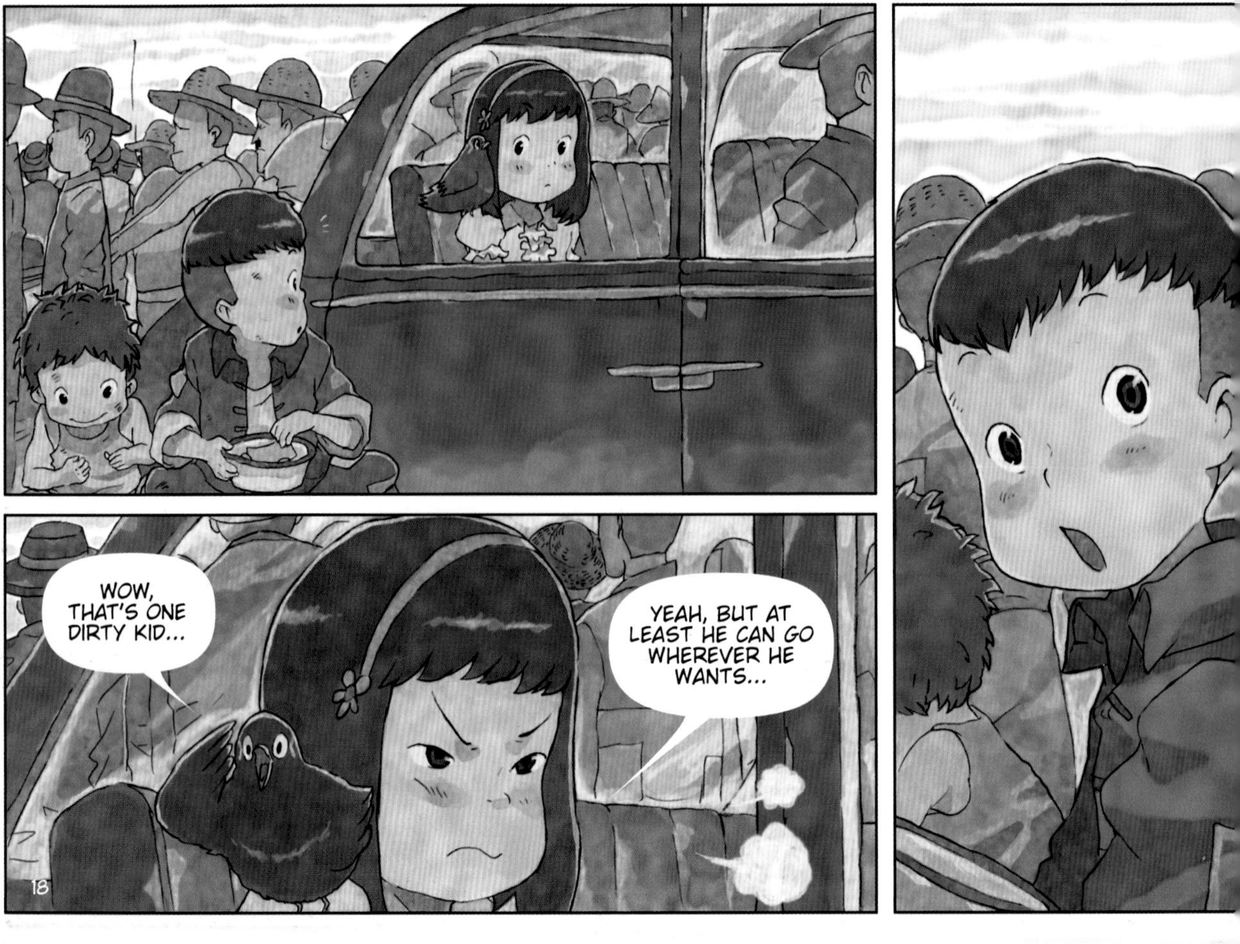
WOW, THAT'S ONE DIRTY KID...
YEAH, BUT AT LEAST HE CAN GO WHEREVER HE WANTS...

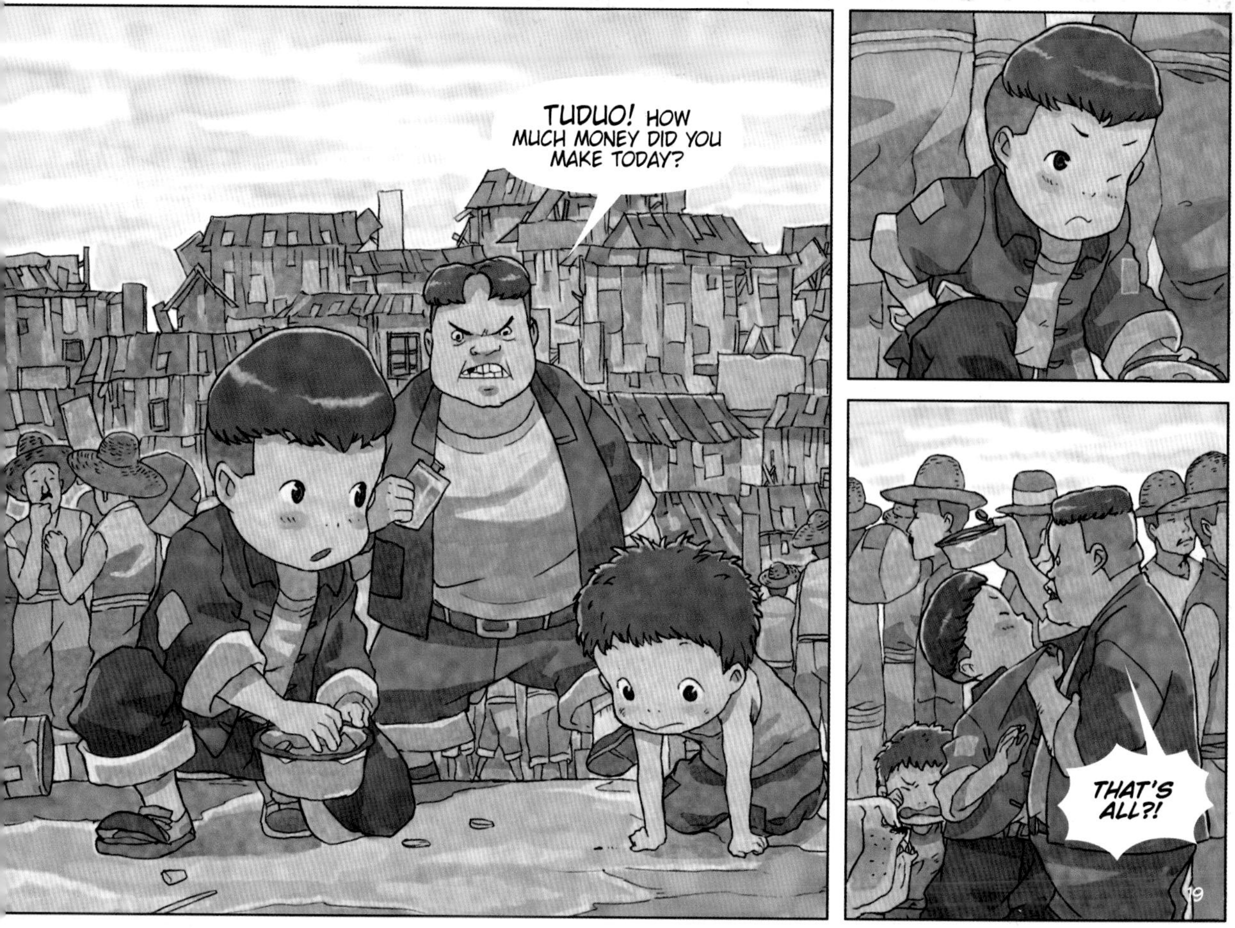
TUDUO! HOW MUCH MONEY DID YOU MAKE TODAY?
THAT'S ALL?!

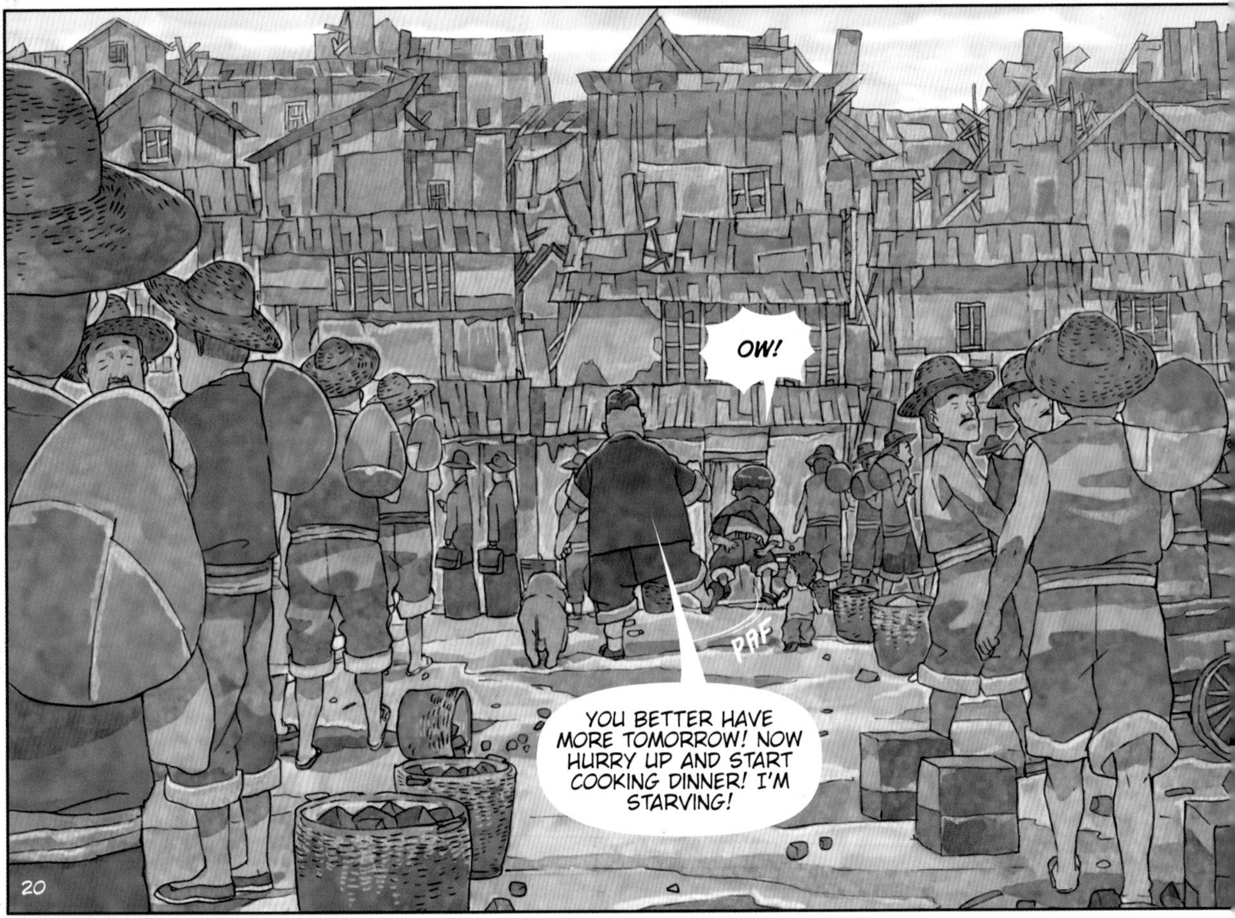
OW!
PAF
YOU BETTER HAVE MORE TOMORROW! NOW HURRY UP AND START COOKING DINNER! I'M STARVING!

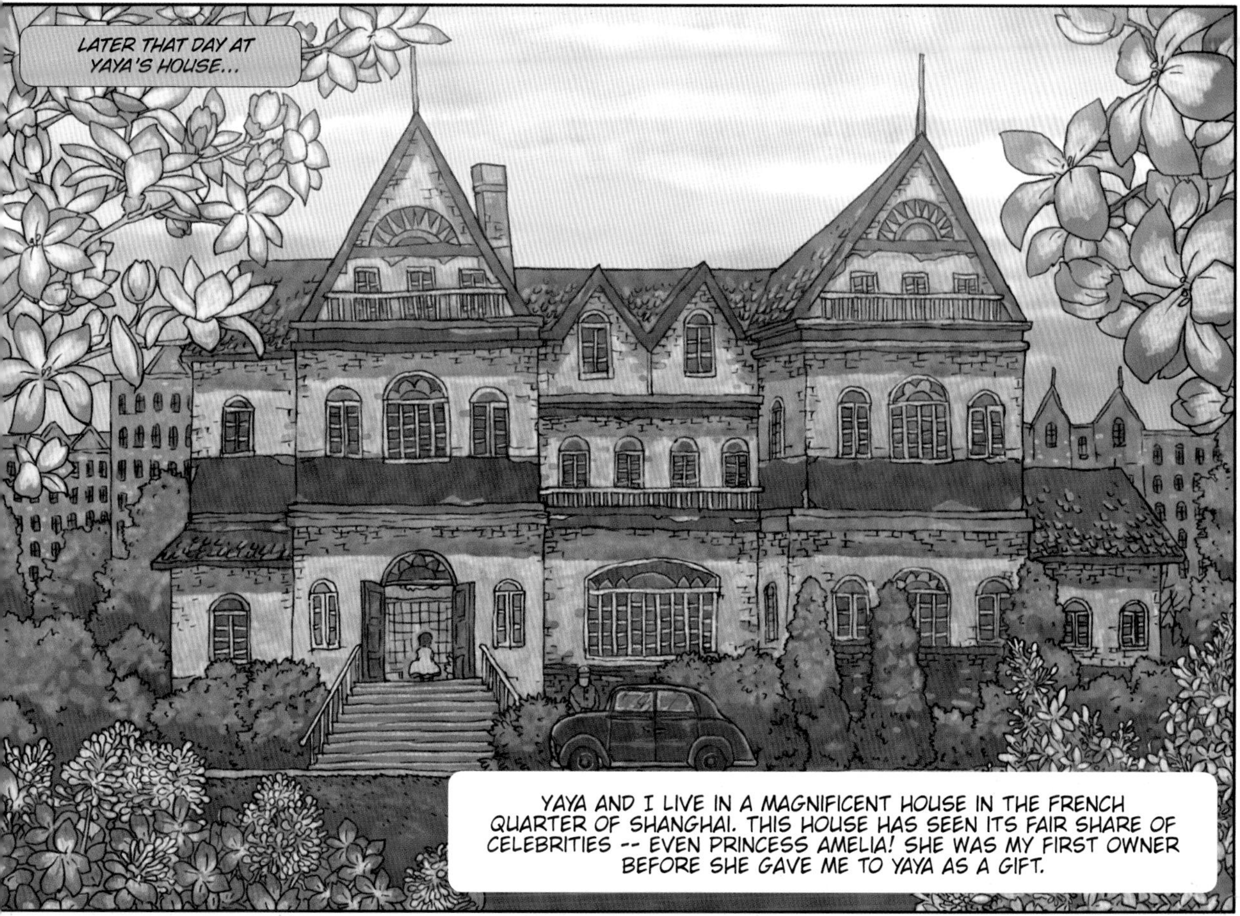
LATER THAT DAY AT YAYA'S HOUSE...
YAYA AND I LIVE IN A MAGNIFICENT HOUSE IN THE FRENCH QUARTER OF SHANGHAI. THIS HOUSE HAS SEEN ITS FAIR SHARE OF CELEBRITIES -- EVEN PRINCESS AMELIA! SHE WAS MY FIRST OWNER BEFORE SHE GAVE ME TO YAYA AS A GIFT.

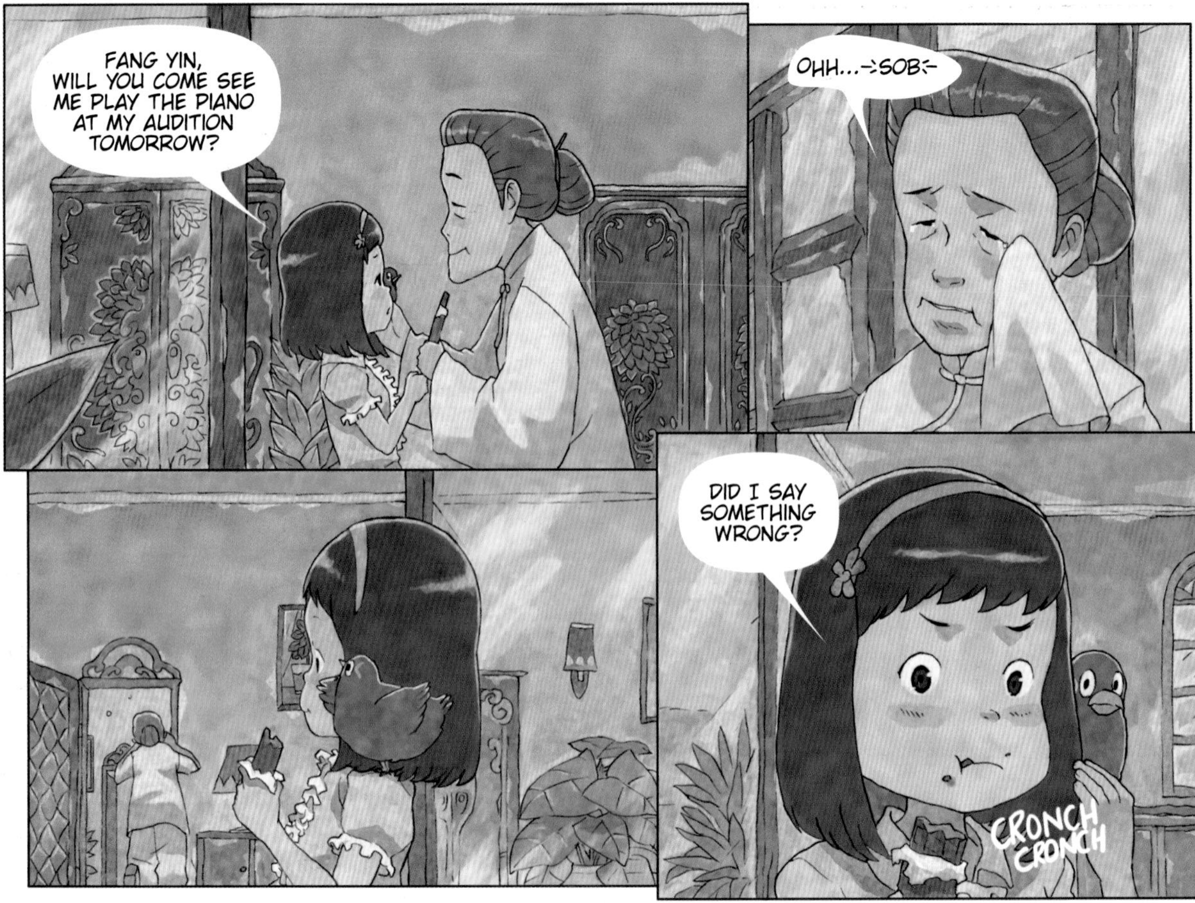
FANG YIN, WILL YOU COME SEE ME PLAY THE PIANO AT MY AUDITION TOMORROW?
OHH... -SOB-
DID I SAY SOMETHING WRONG?
CRONCH CRONCH

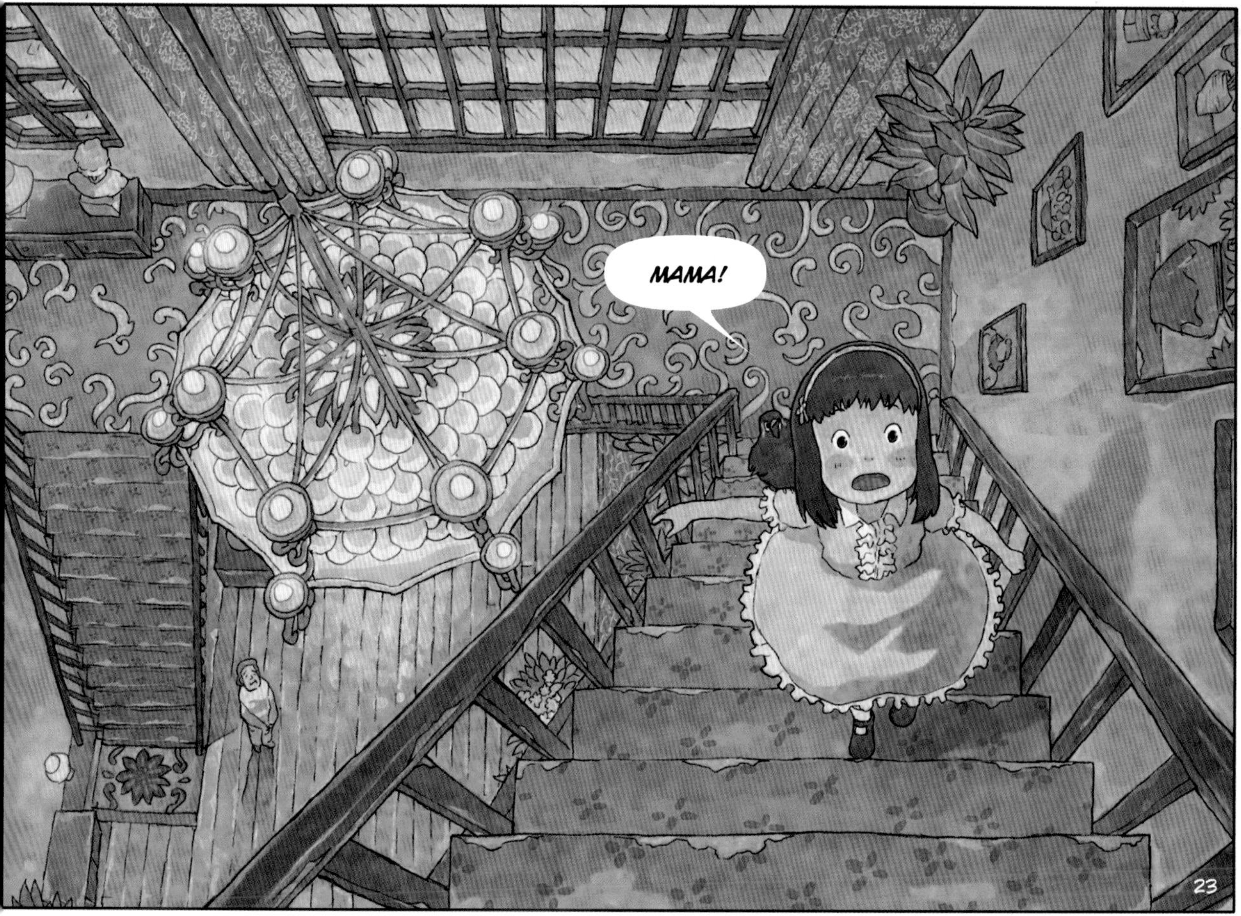
MAMA!

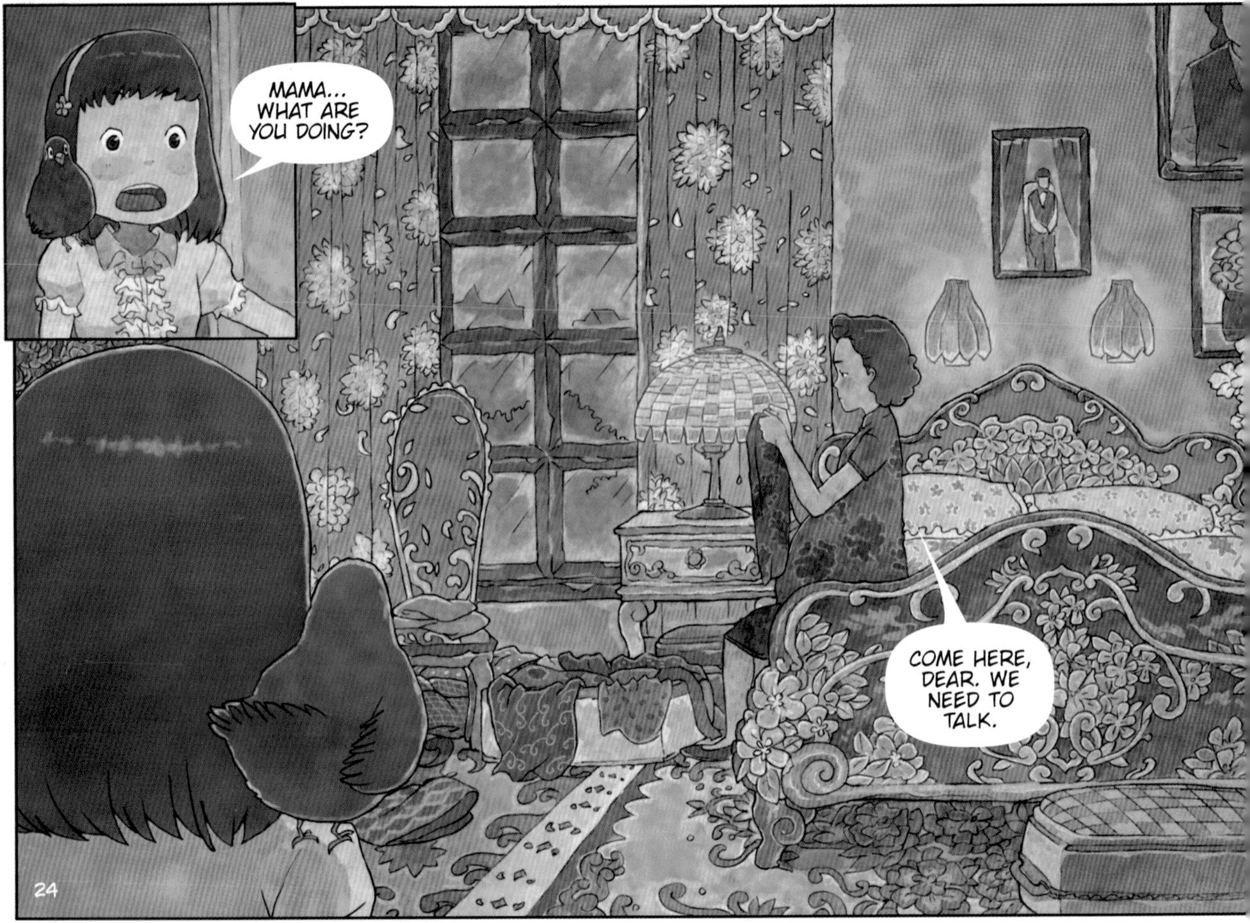
MAMA... WHAT ARE YOU DOING?
COME HERE, DEAR. WE NEED TO TALK.

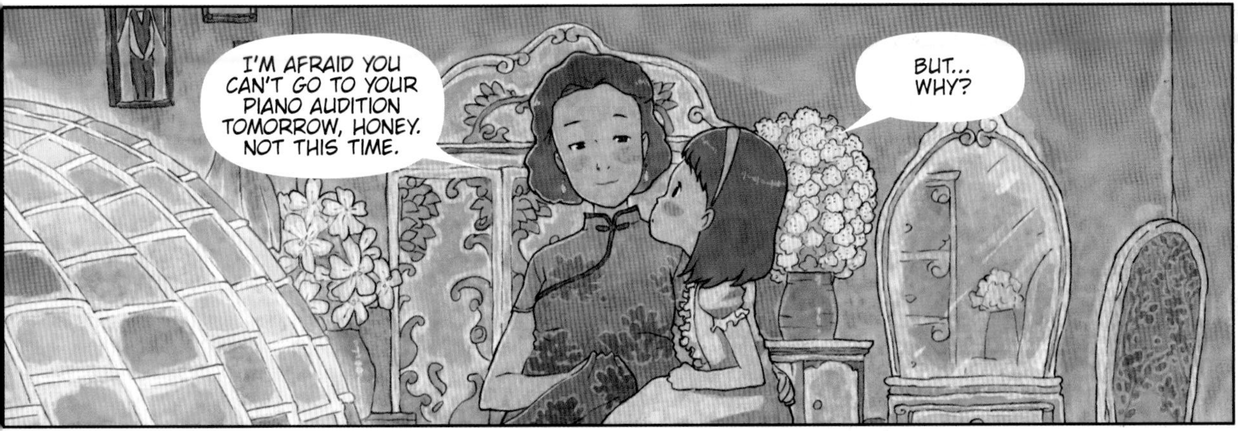
I'M AFRAID YOU CAN'T GO TO YOUR PIANO AUDITION TOMORROW, HONEY. NOT THIS TIME.
BUT... WHY?

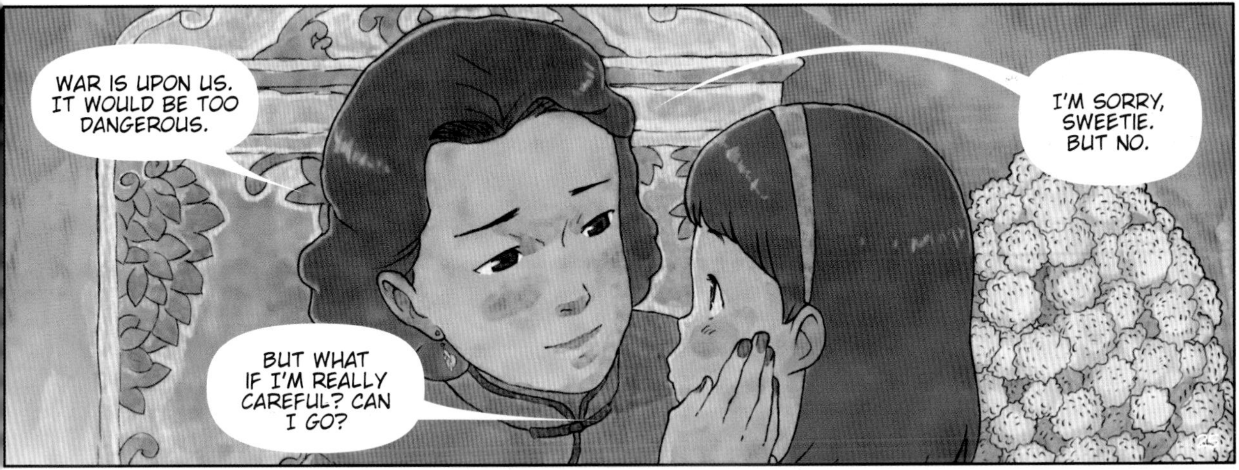
WAR IS UPON US. IT WOULD BE TOO DANGEROUS.
BUT WHAT IF I'M REALLY CAREFUL? CAN I GO?
I'M SORRY, SWEETIE. BUT NO.

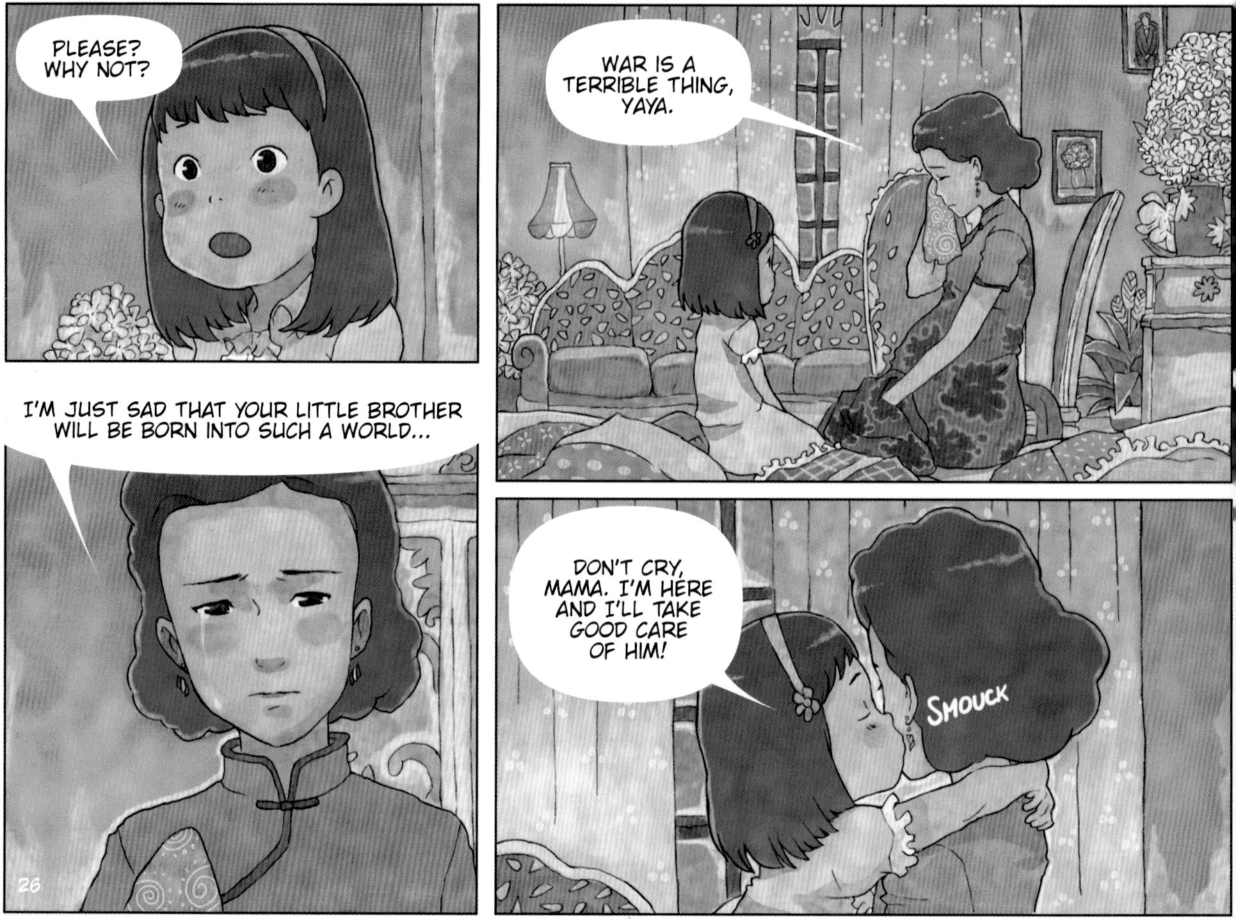
PLEASE? WHY NOT?
I'M JUST SAD THAT YOUR LITTLE BROTHER WILL BE BORN INTO SUCH A WORLD...
WAR IS A TERRIBLE THING, YAYA.
DON'T CRY, MAMA. I'M HERE AND I'LL TAKE GOOD CARE OF HIM!
SMOUCK

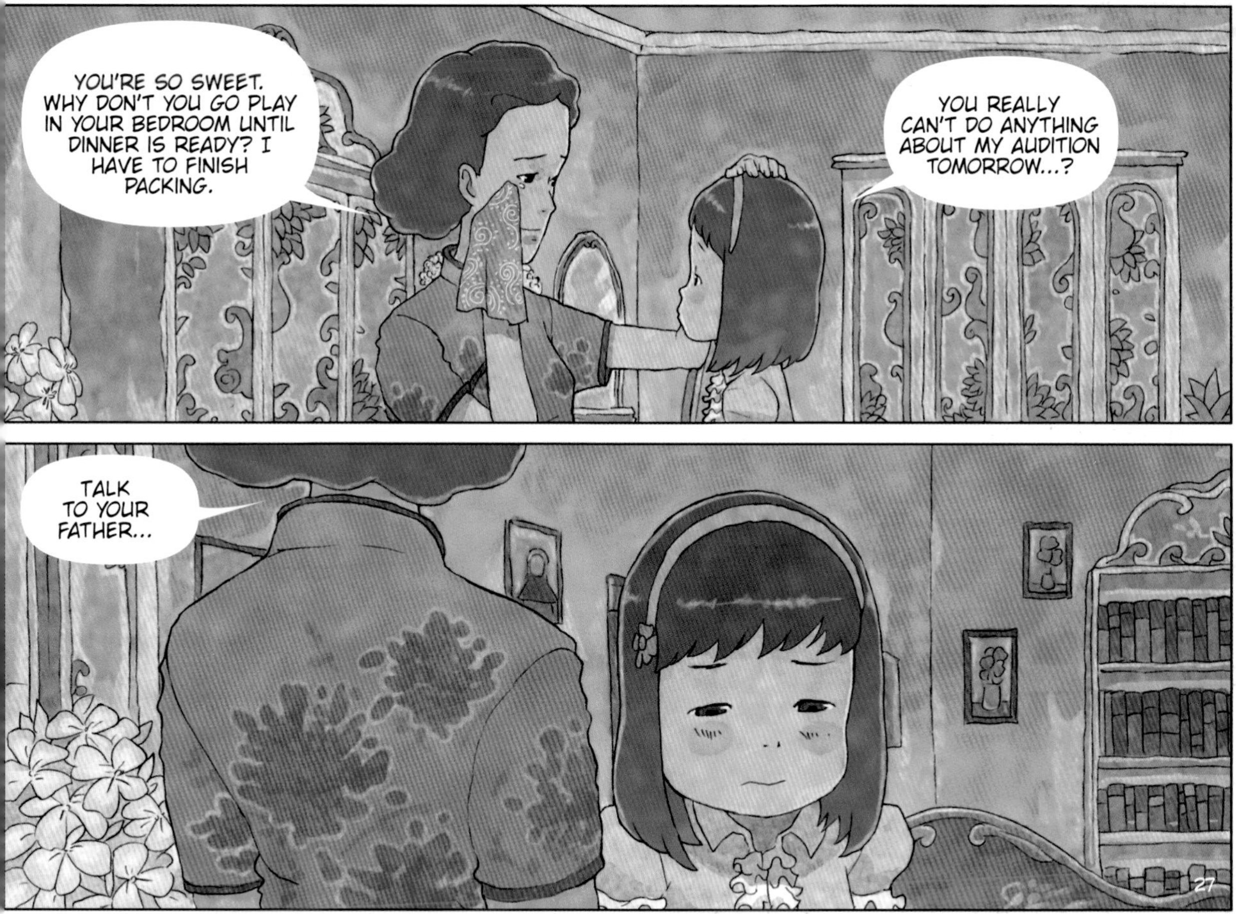
YOU'RE SO SWEET. WHY DON'T YOU GO PLAY IN YOUR BEDROOM UNTIL DINNER IS READY? I HAVE TO FINISH PACKING.
YOU REALLY CAN'T DO ANYTHING ABOUT MY AUDITION TOMORROW...?
TALK TO YOUR FATHER...

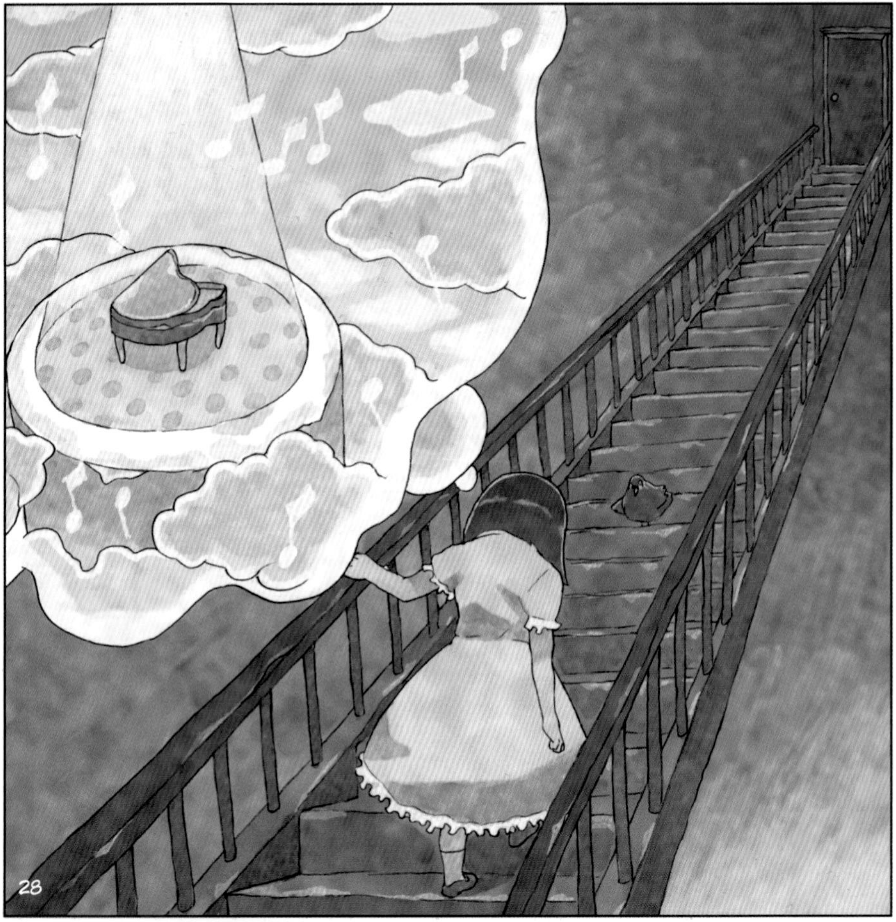

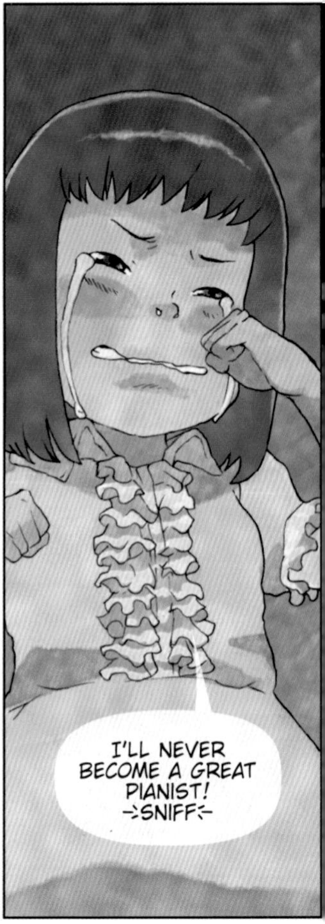
I'LL NEVER BECOME A GREAT PIANIST! -SNIFF-

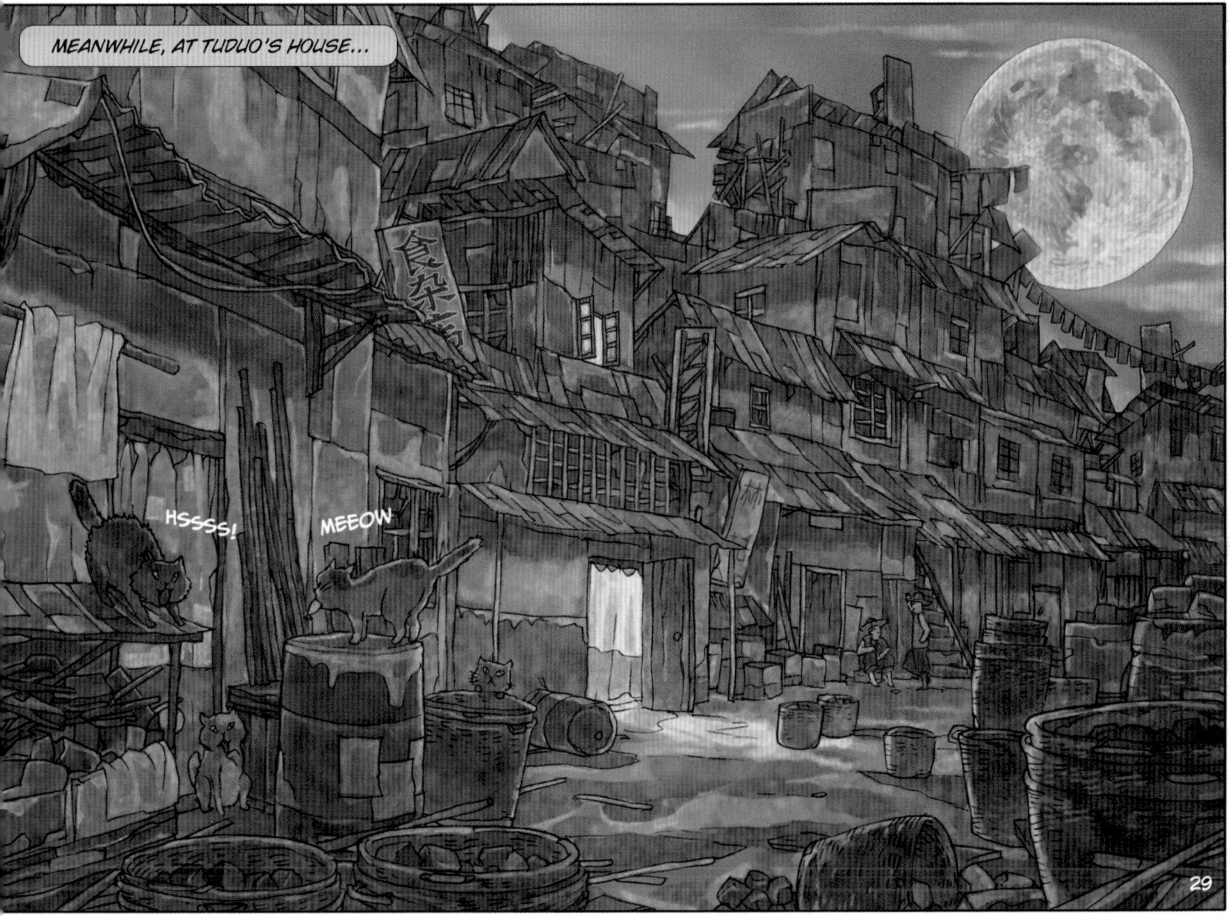
MEANWHILE, AT TUDUO'S HOUSE...
HSSSS!
MEEOW

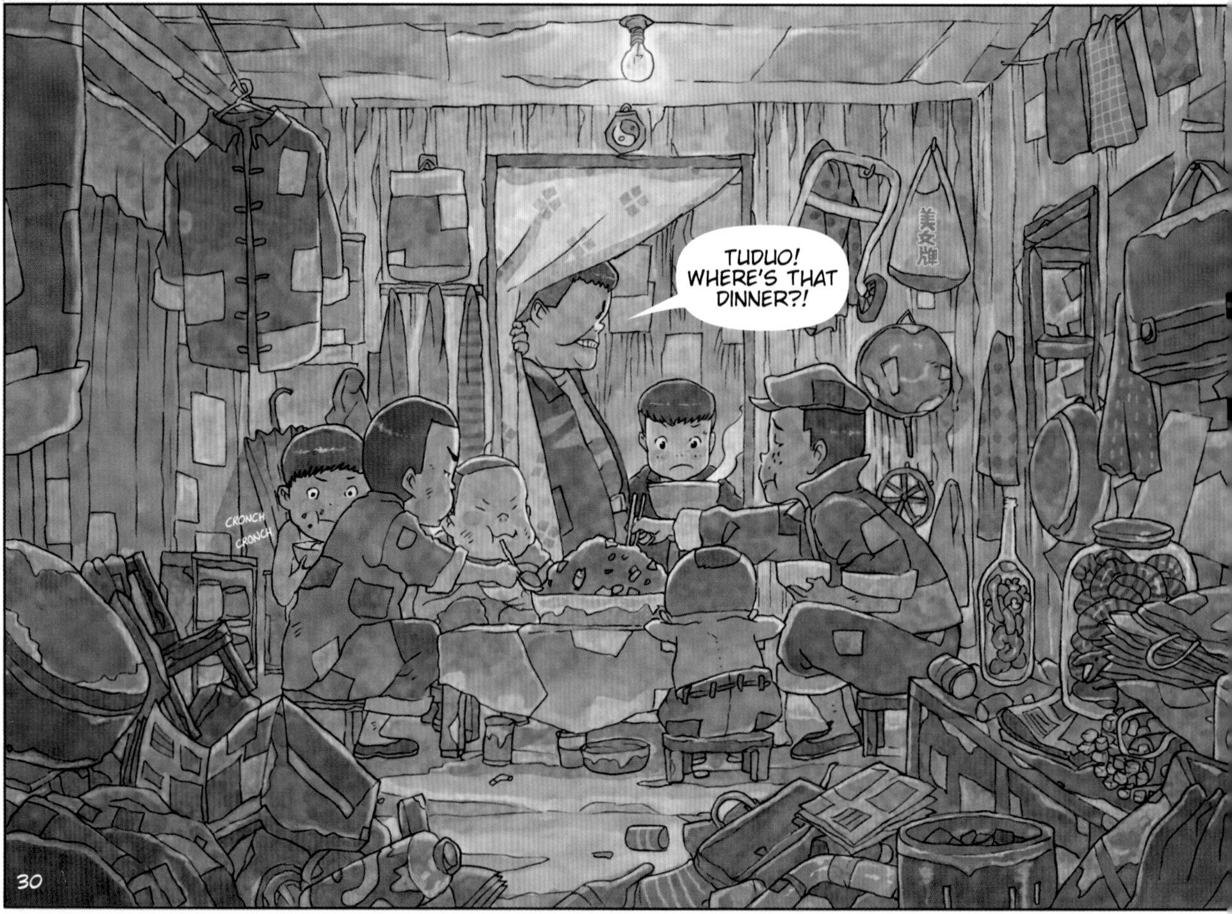
美女牌
TUDUO! WHERE'S THAT DINNER?!
CRONCH
CRONCH

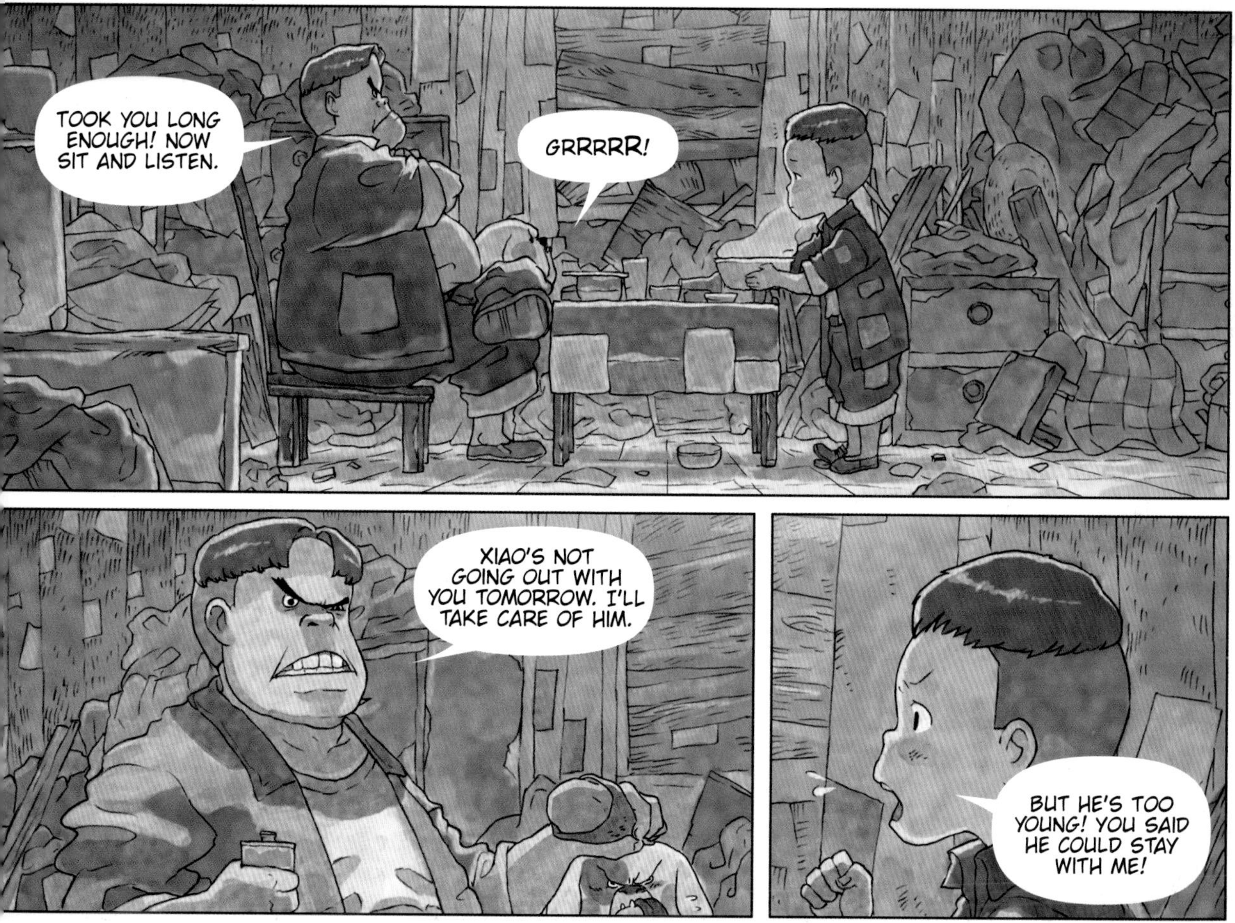
TOOK YOU LONG ENOUGH! NOW SIT AND LISTEN.
GRRRRR!
XIAO'S NOT GOING OUT WITH YOU TOMORROW. I'LL TAKE CARE OF HIM.
BUT HE'S TOO YOUNG! YOU SAID HE COULD STAY WITH ME!

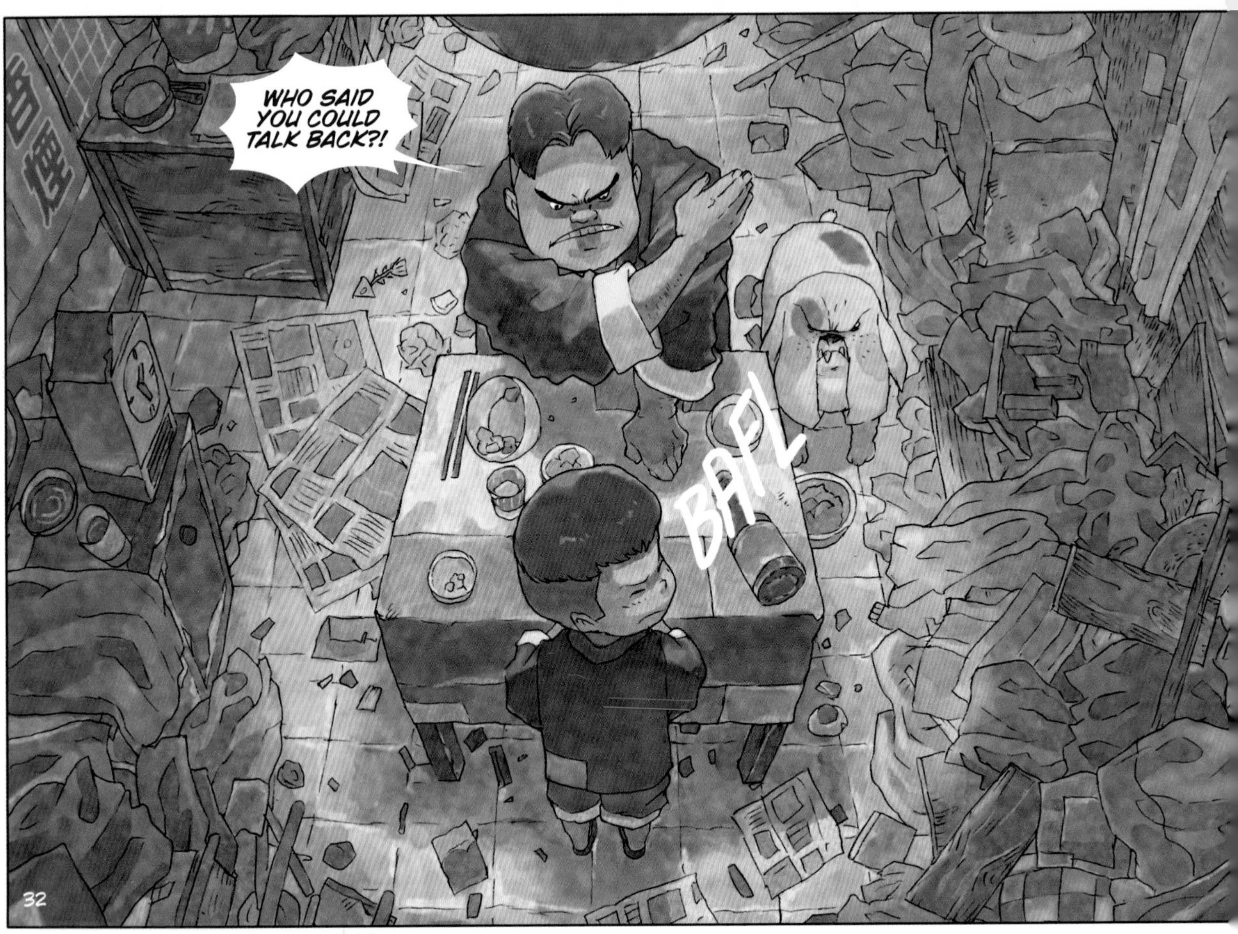
WHO SAID YOU COULD TALK BACK?!
BAF!

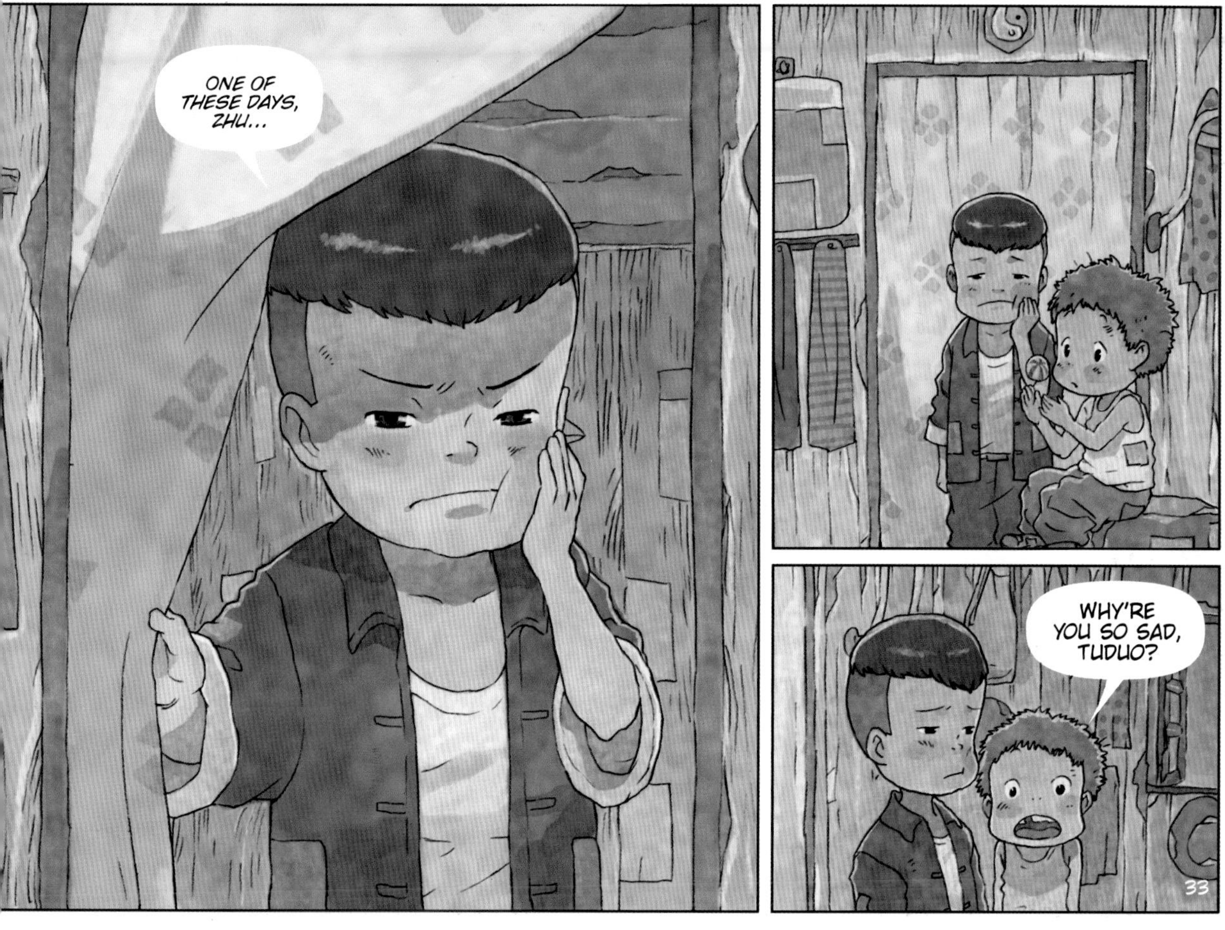
ONE OF THESE DAYS, ZHU...
WHY'RE YOU SO SAD, TUDUO?

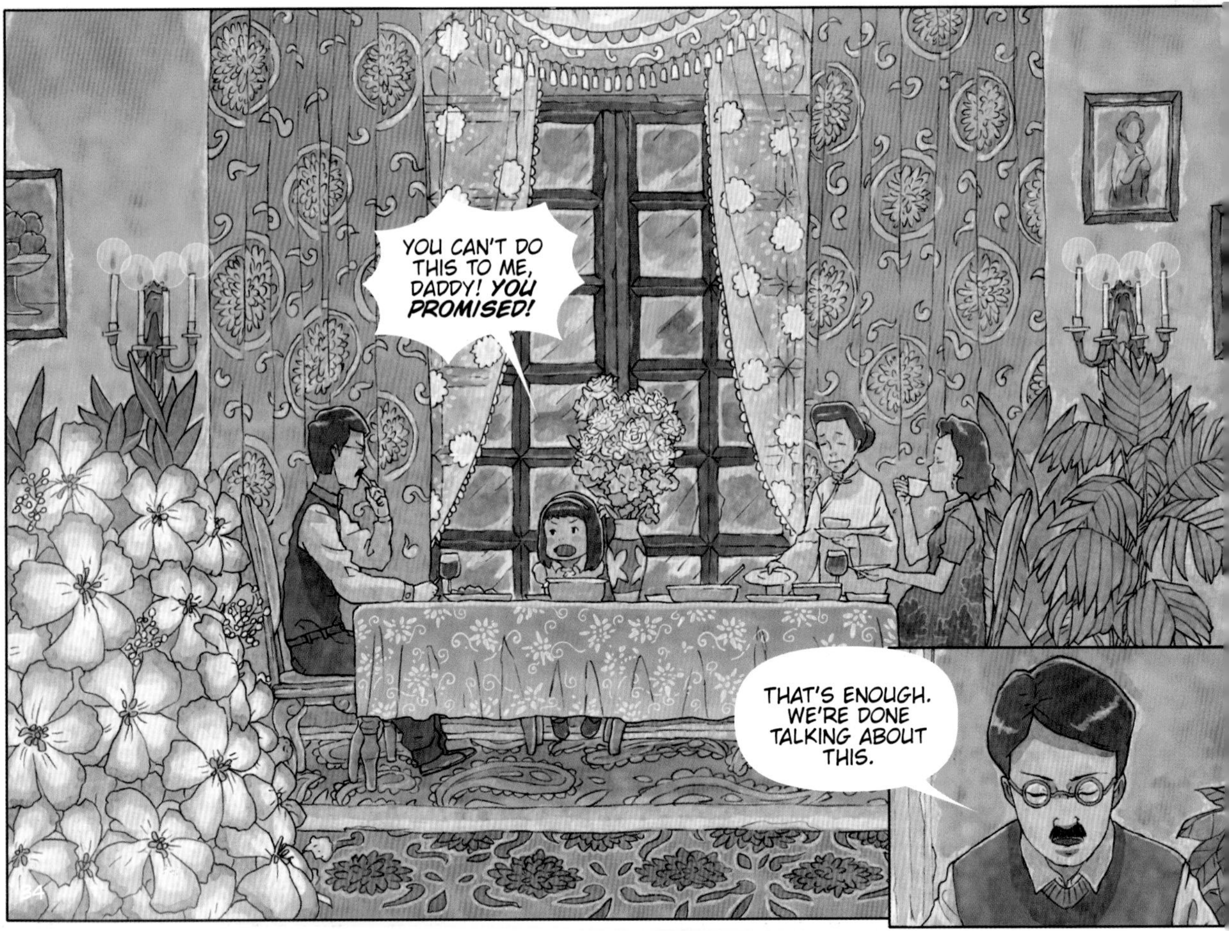
YOU CAN'T DO THIS TO ME, DADDY! *YOU PROMISED!*
THAT'S ENOUGH. WE'RE DONE TALKING ABOUT THIS.

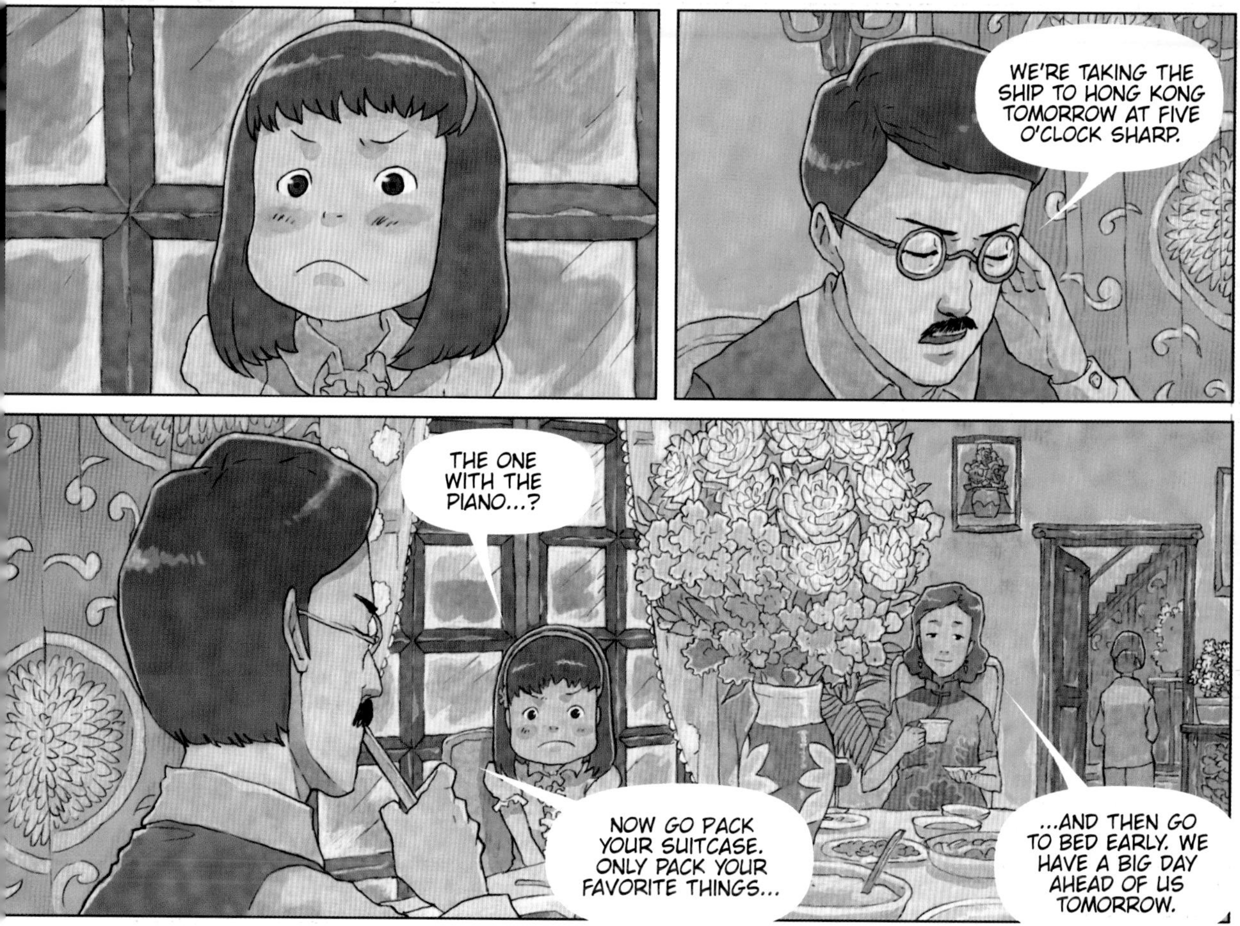

WE'RE TAKING THE SHIP TO HONG KONG TOMORROW AT FIVE O'CLOCK SHARP.
THE ONE WITH THE PIANO...?
NOW GO PACK YOUR SUITCASE. ONLY PACK YOUR FAVORITE THINGS...
...AND THEN GO TO BED EARLY. WE HAVE A BIG DAY AHEAD OF US TOMORROW.

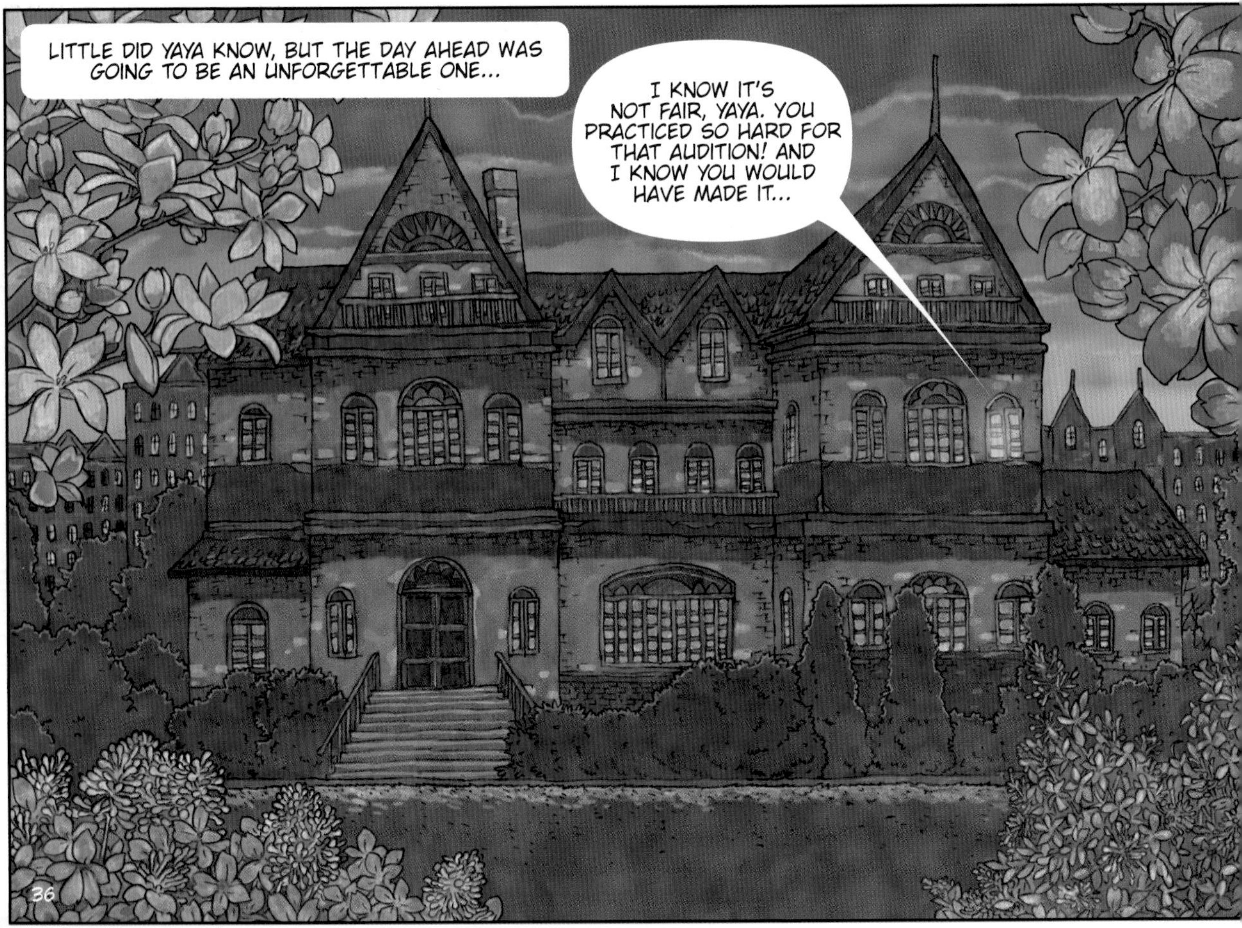
LITTLE DID YAYA KNOW, BUT THE DAY AHEAD WAS GOING TO BE AN UNFORGETTABLE ONE...
I KNOW IT'S NOT FAIR, YAYA. YOU PRACTICED SO HARD FOR THAT AUDITION! AND I KNOW YOU WOULD HAVE MADE IT...

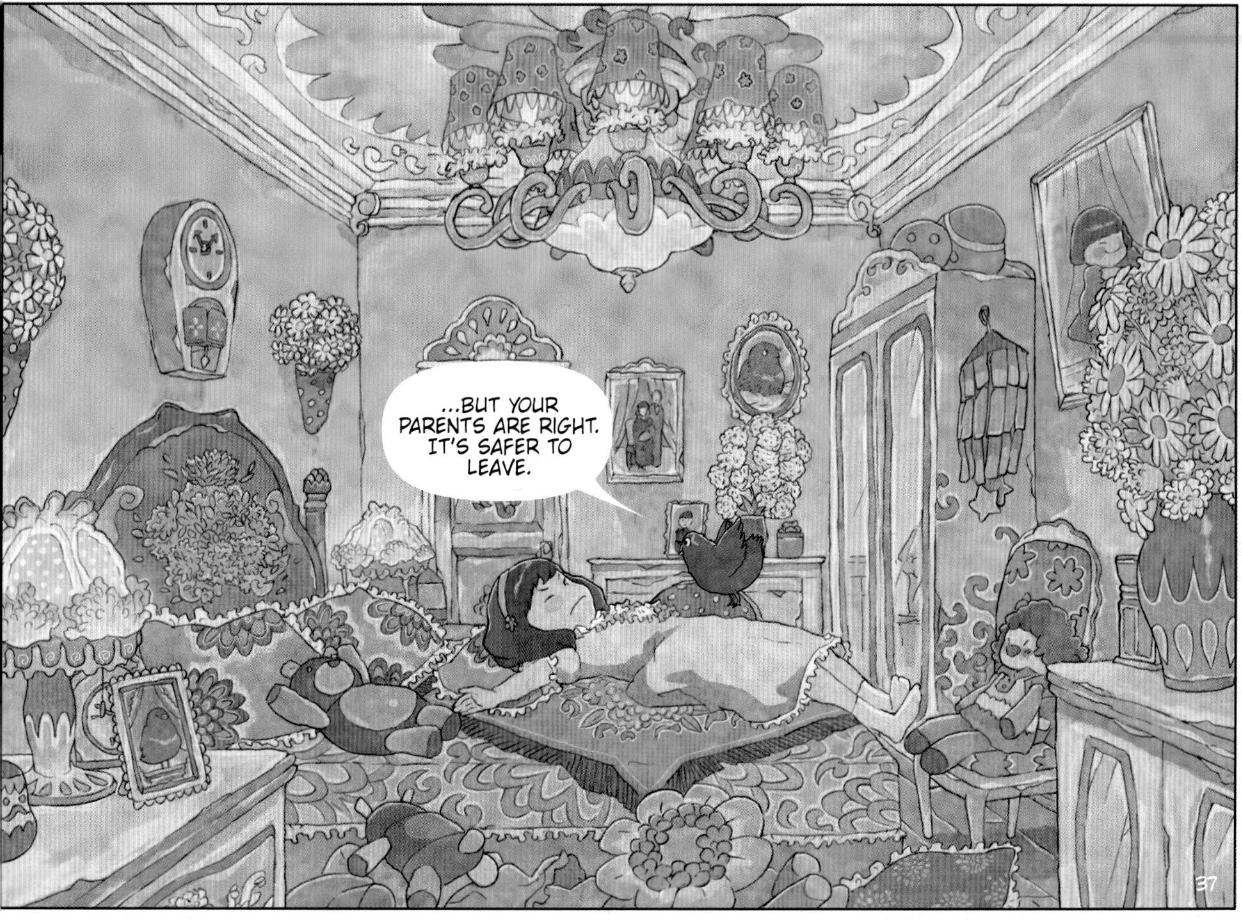
...BUT YOUR PARENTS ARE RIGHT. IT'S SAFER TO LEAVE.

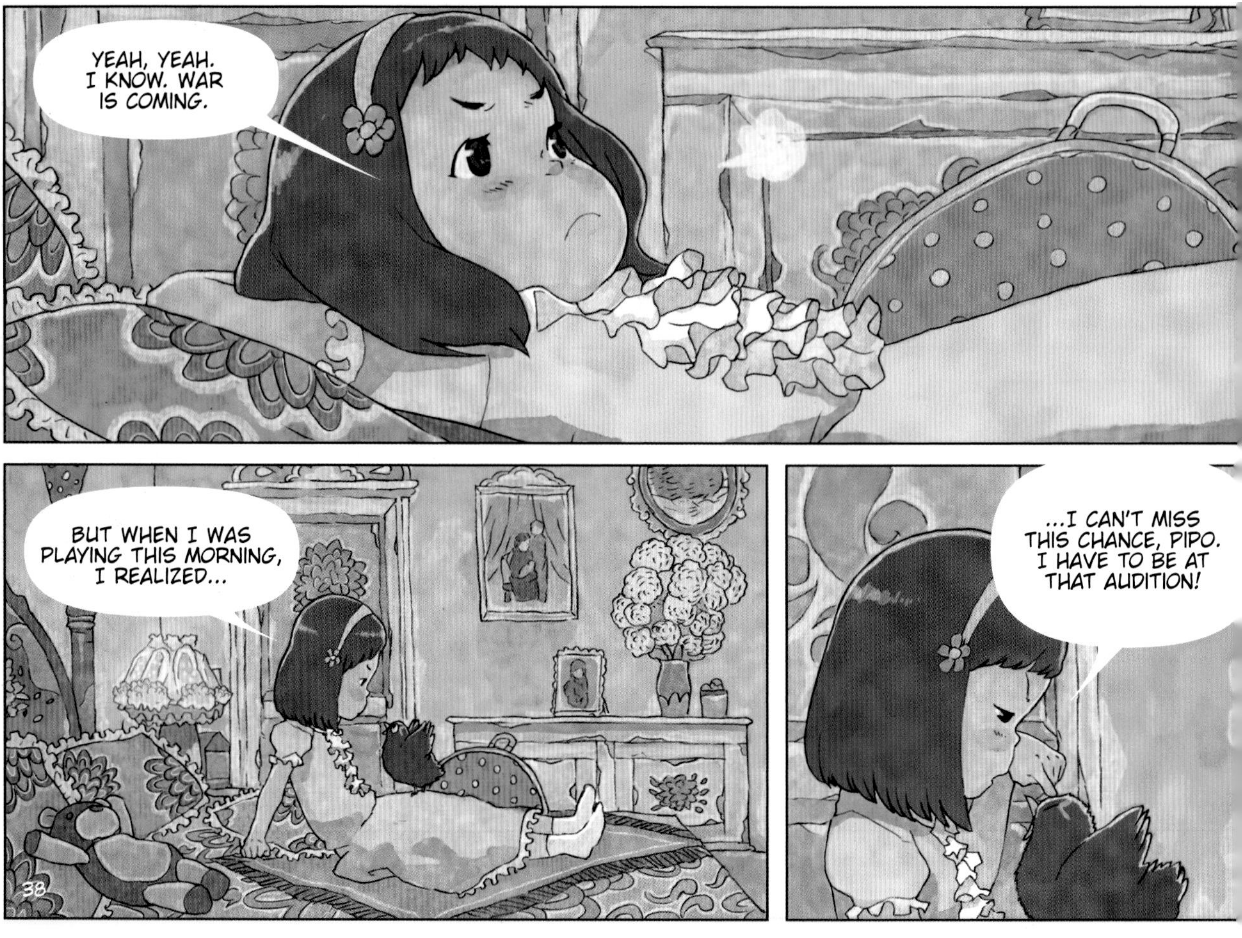
YEAH, YEAH. I KNOW. WAR IS COMING.
BUT WHEN I WAS PLAYING THIS MORNING, I REALIZED...
...I CAN'T MISS THIS CHANCE, PIPO. I HAVE TO BE AT THAT AUDITION!

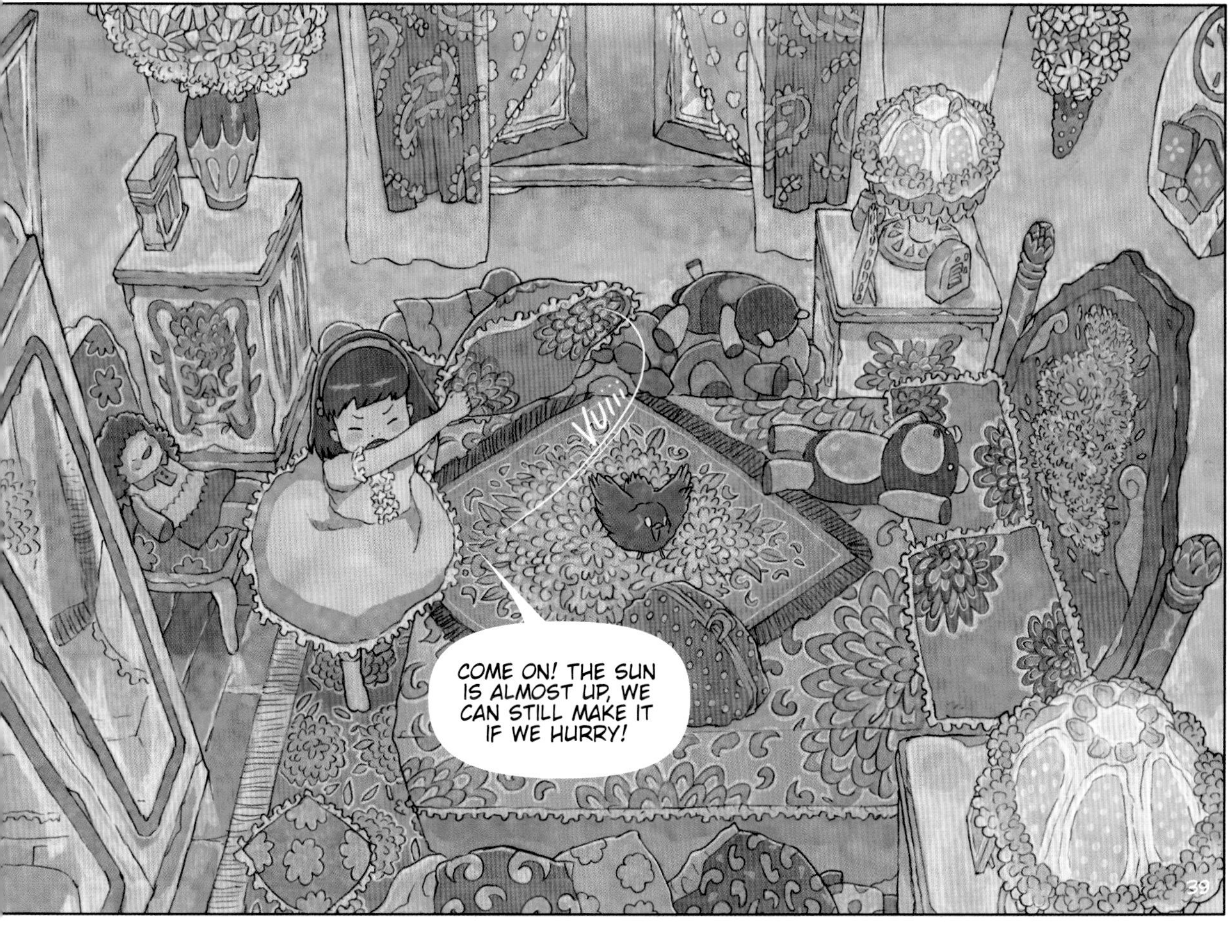
Vuiii
COME ON! THE SUN IS ALMOST UP, WE CAN STILL MAKE IT IF WE HURRY!

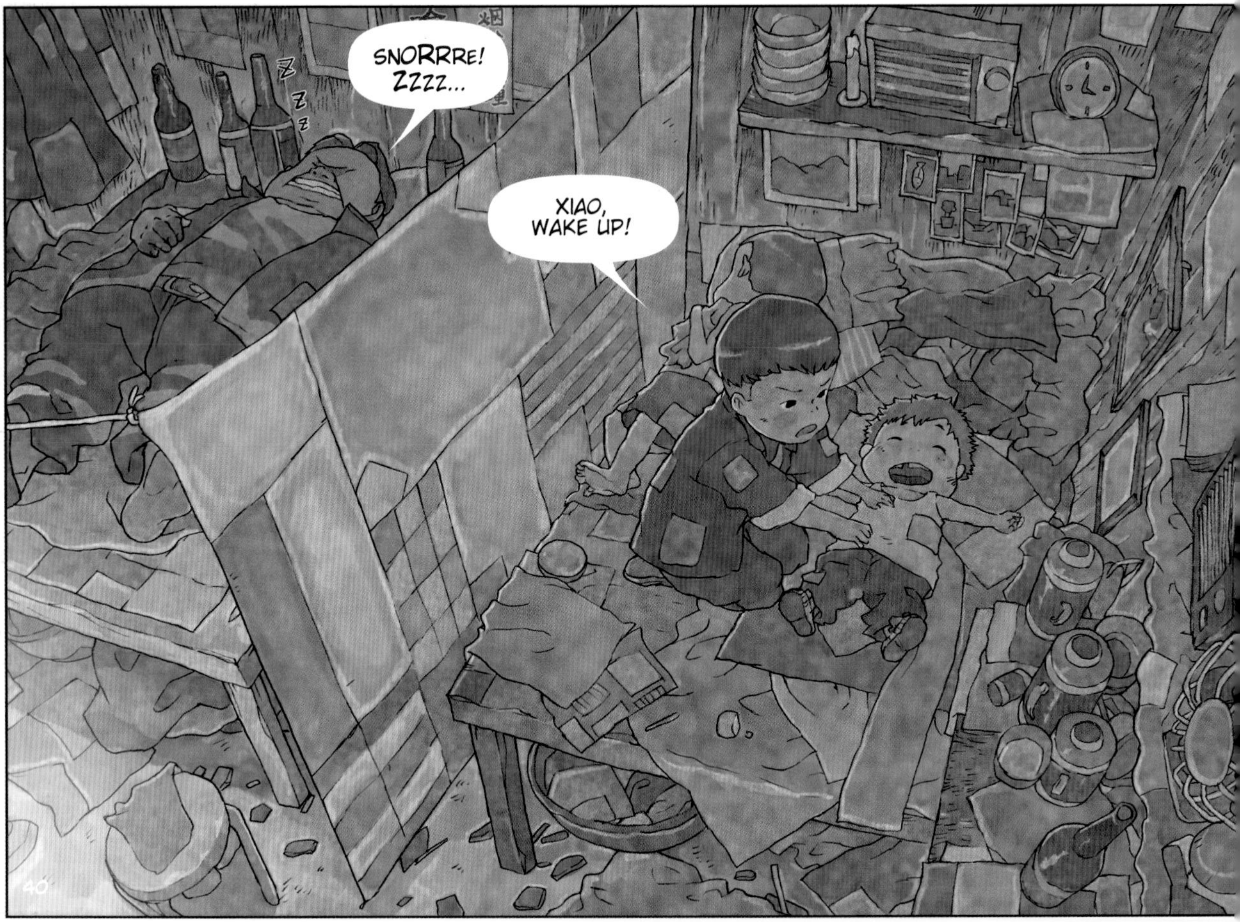
SNORRRE! ZZZZ...
Z Z Z Z
XIAO, WAKE UP!

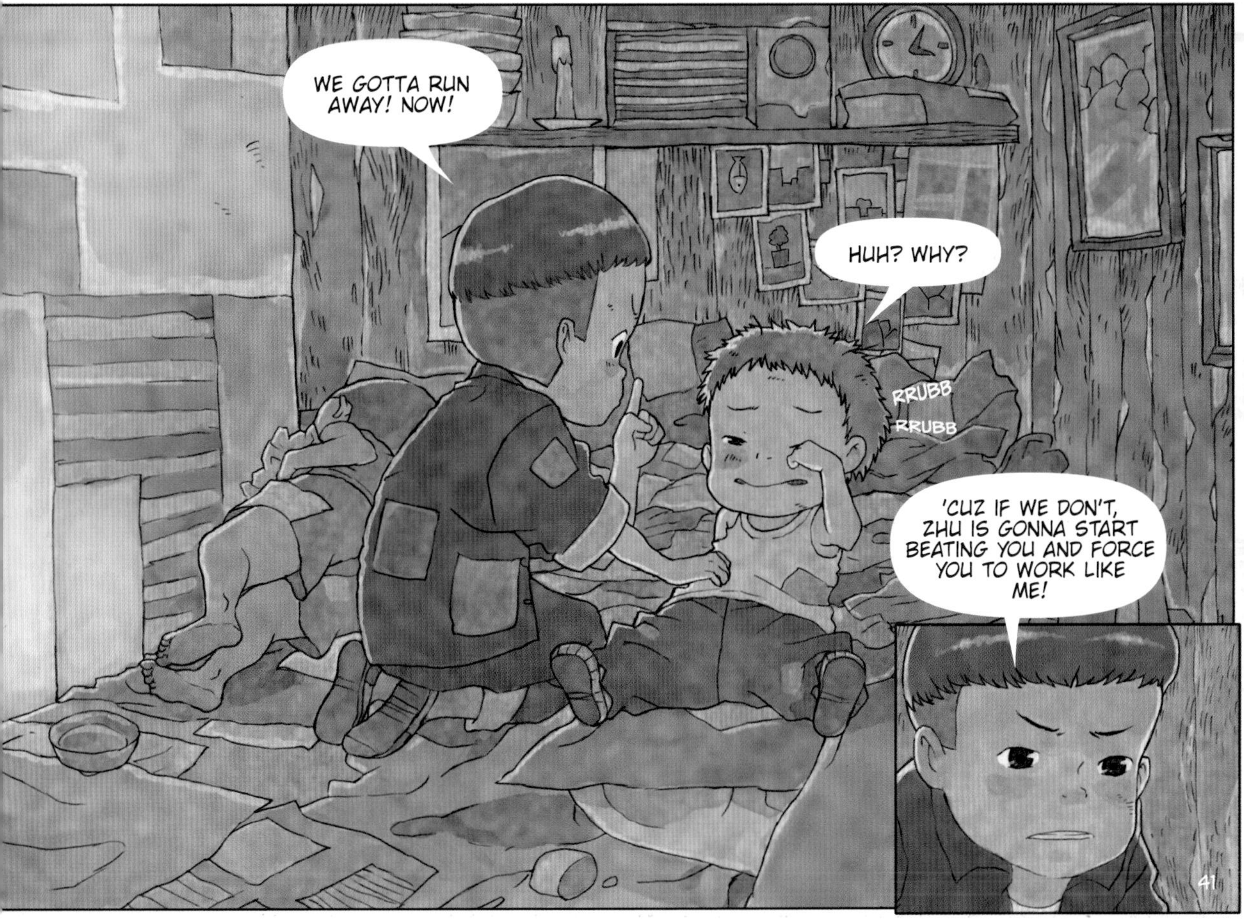

WE GOTTA RUN AWAY! NOW!
HUH? WHY?
RRUBB
RRUBB
'CUZ IF WE DON'T, ZHU IS GONNA START BEATING YOU AND FORCE YOU TO WORK LIKE ME!

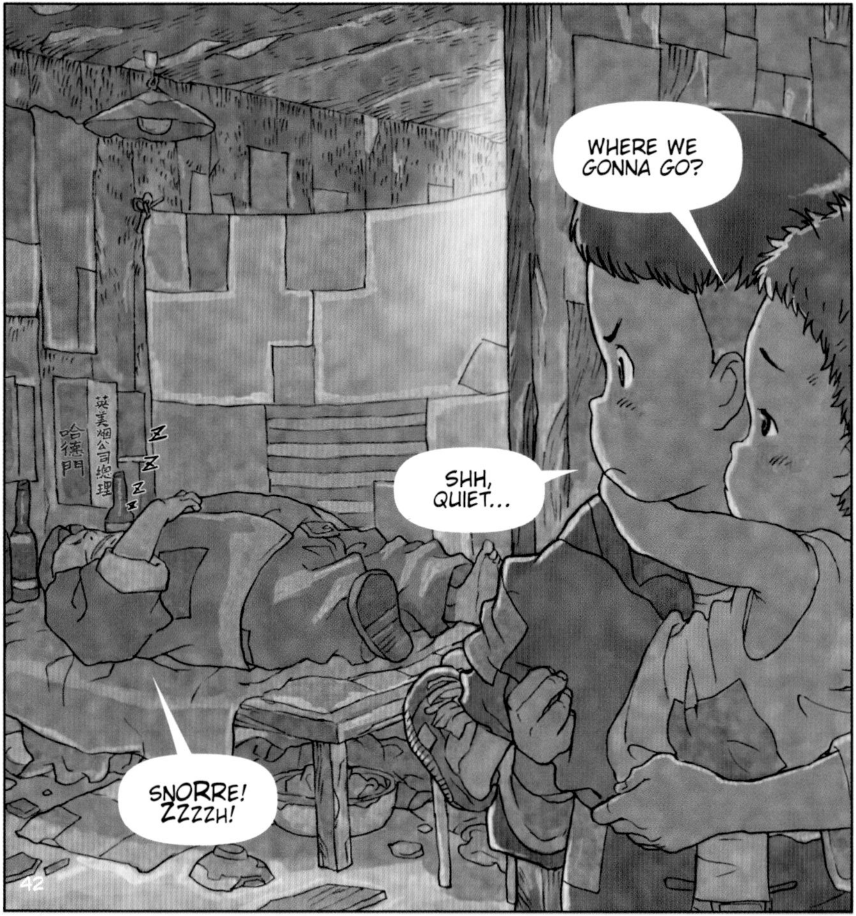
英美烟公司總理
哈德門
Z Z Z Z
WHERE WE GONNA GO?
SHH, QUIET...
SNORRE! ZZZZH!

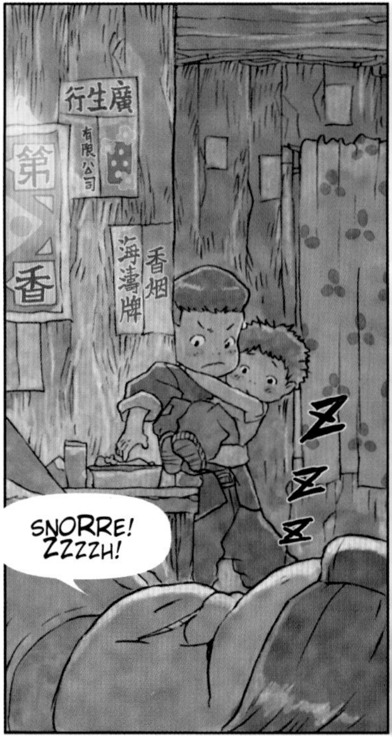
廣生行
有限公司
海濤牌
香烟
Z Z Z
SNORRE! ZZZZH!

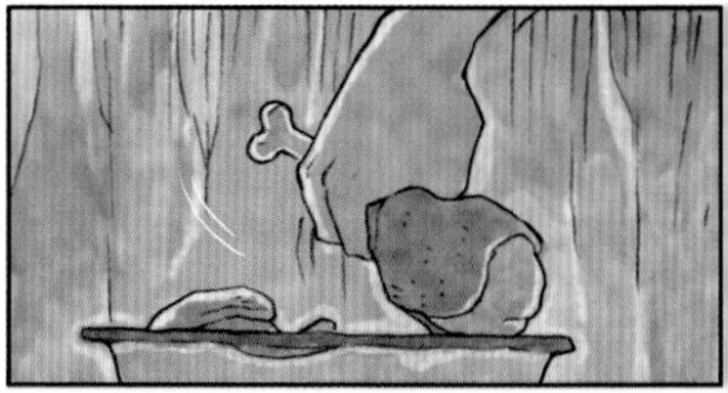

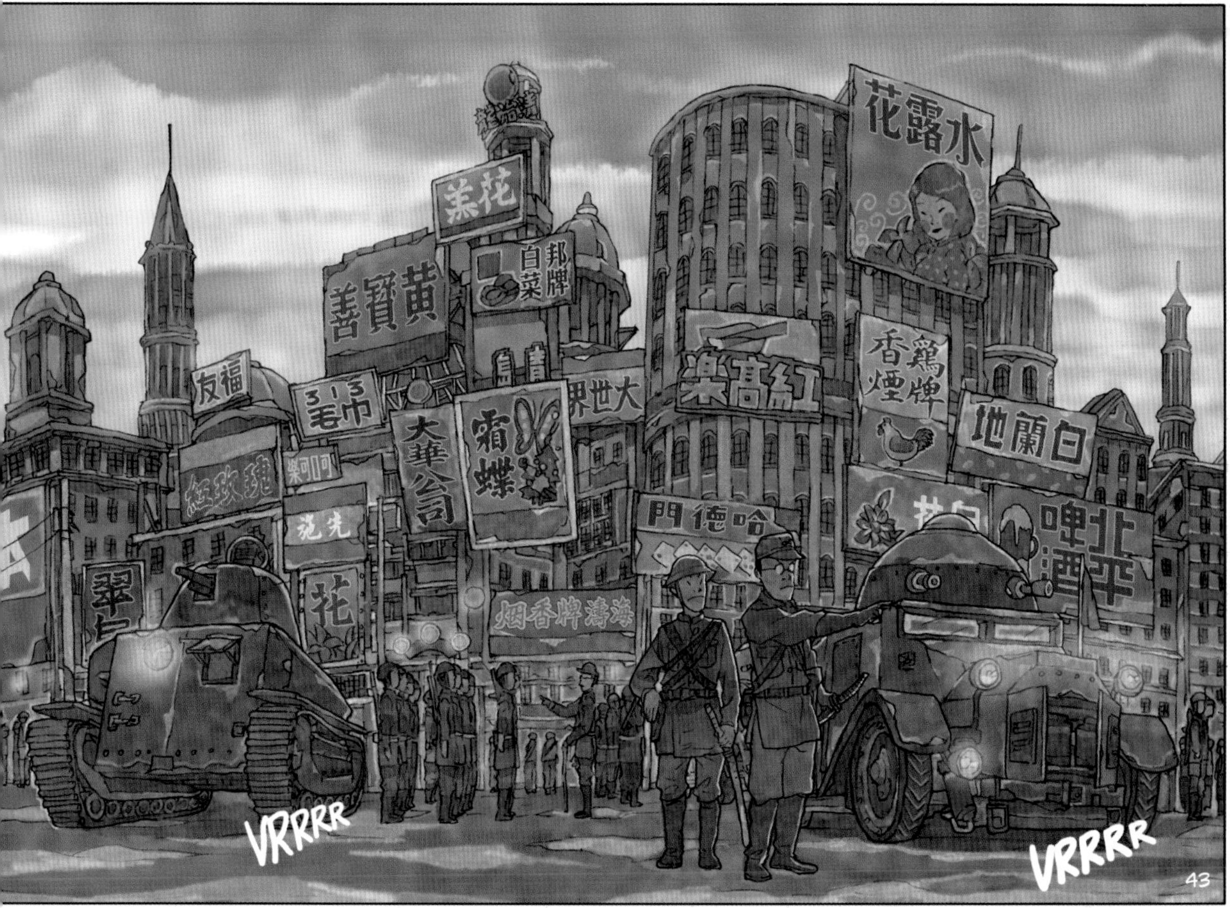
花露水
善寶黃
友福
313
毛巾
大華公司
霜蝶
界世大
楽高紅
鷄牌
香煙
地蘭白
門德哈
烟香牌濤海
VRRRR
VRRRR

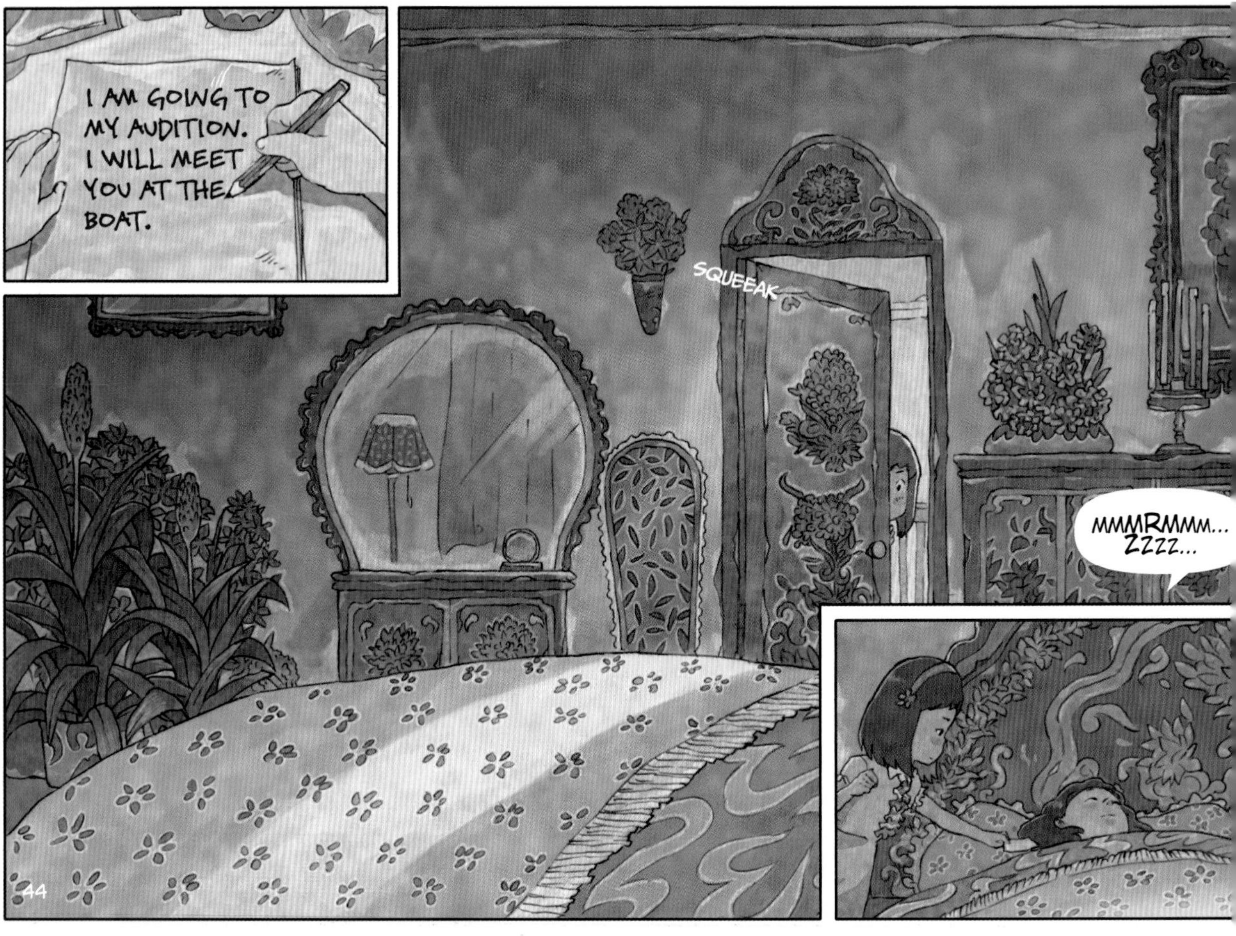
I AM GOING TO MY AUDITION. I WILL MEET YOU AT THE BOAT.
SQUEEEAK
MMMRMMM... ZZZZ...

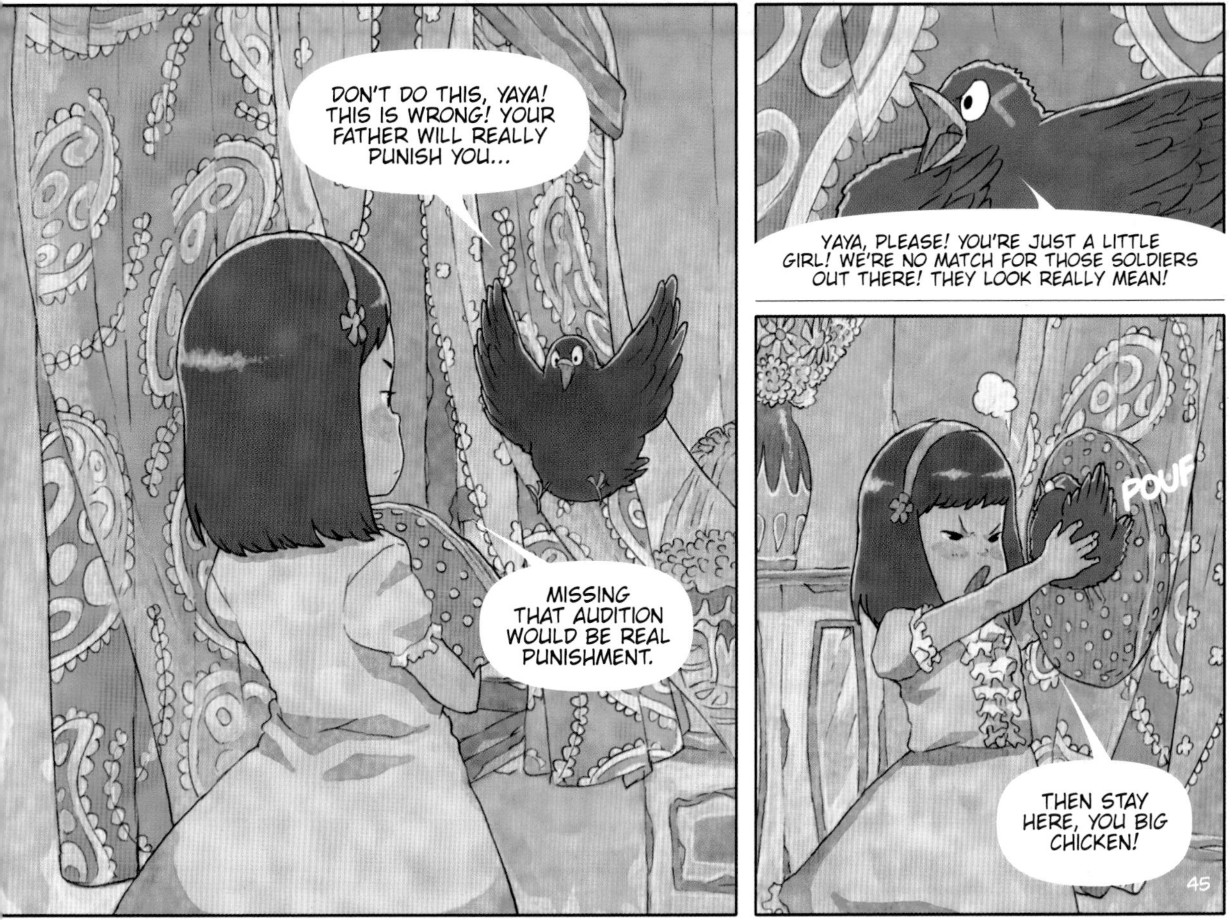
DON'T DO THIS, YAYA! THIS IS WRONG! YOUR FATHER WILL REALLY PUNISH YOU...
MISSING THAT AUDITION WOULD BE REAL PUNISHMENT.
YAYA, PLEASE! YOU'RE JUST A LITTLE GIRL! WE'RE NO MATCH FOR THOSE SOLDIERS OUT THERE! THEY LOOK REALLY MEAN!
POUF
THEN STAY HERE, YOU BIG CHICKEN!

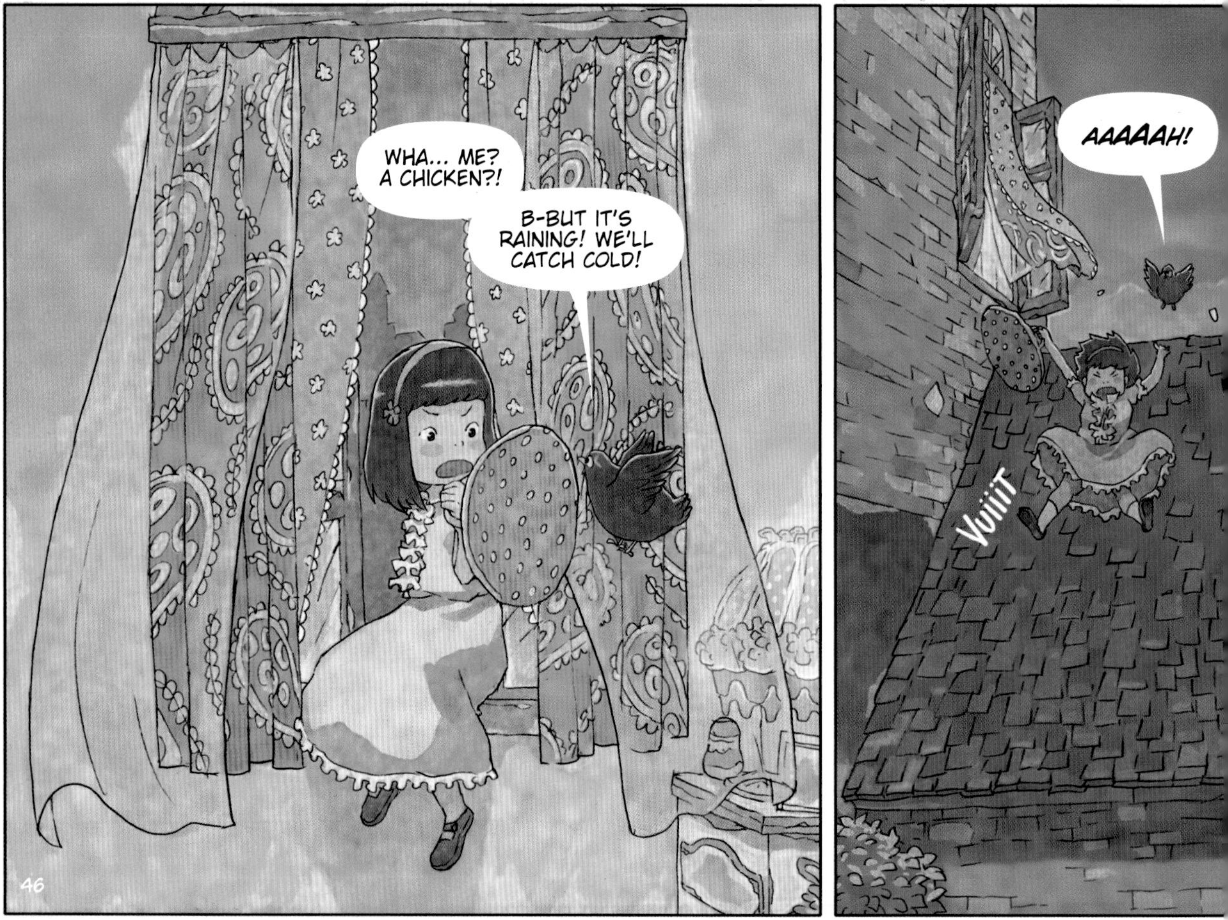
WHA... ME? A CHICKEN?!
B-BUT IT'S RAINING! WE'LL CATCH COLD!
AAAAAH!
VUIIIT

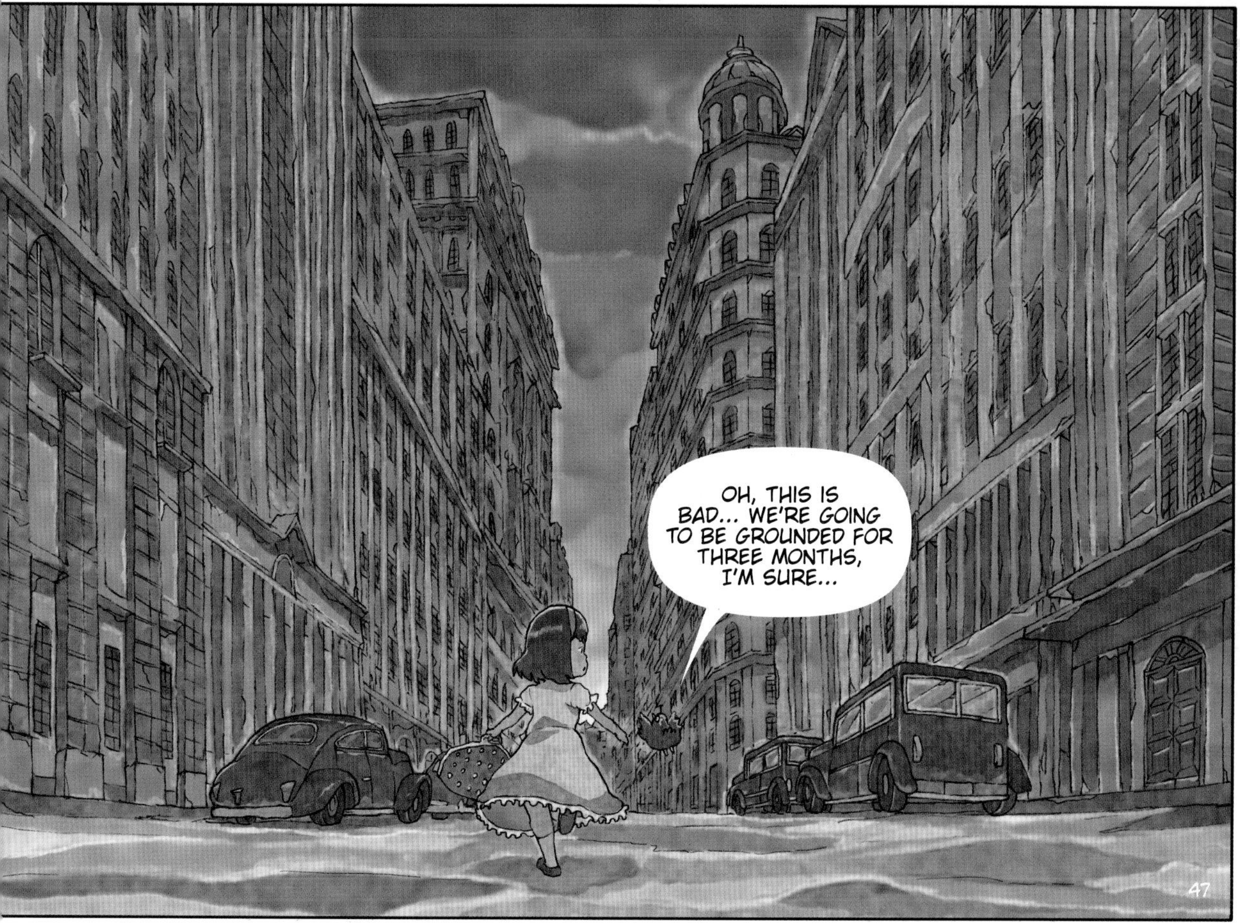
OH, THIS IS BAD... WE'RE GOING TO BE GROUNDED FOR THREE MONTHS, I'M SURE...

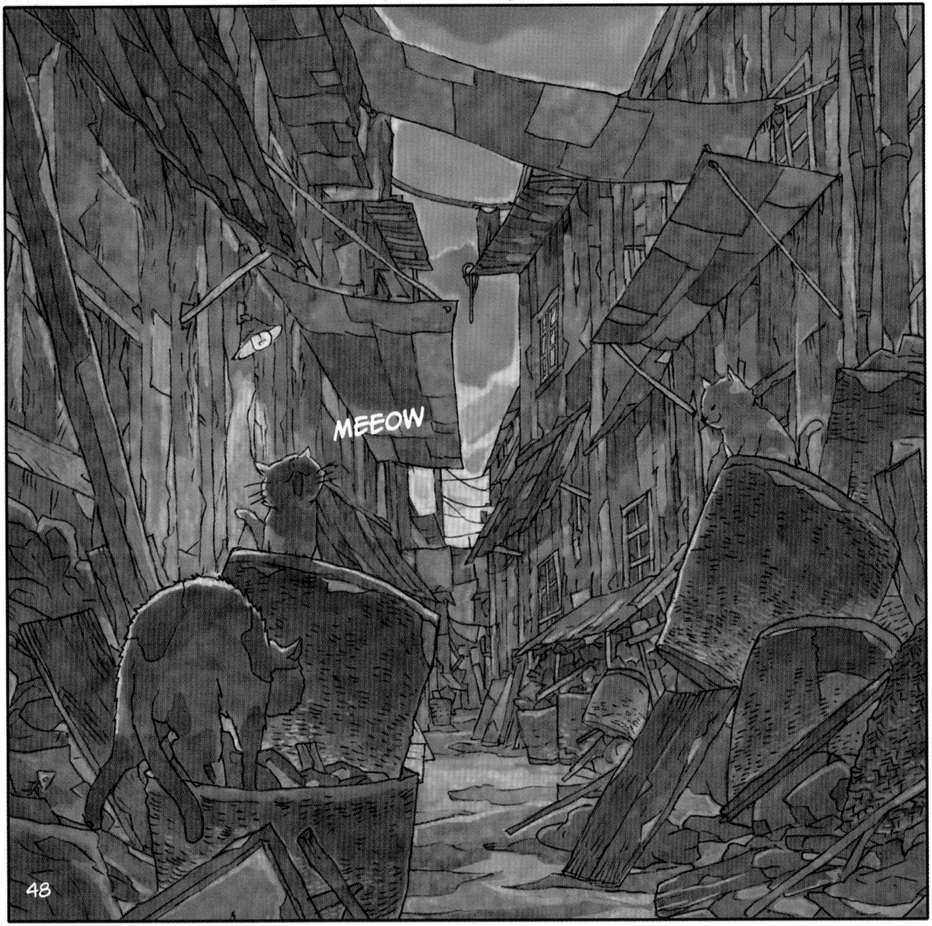
MEEOW
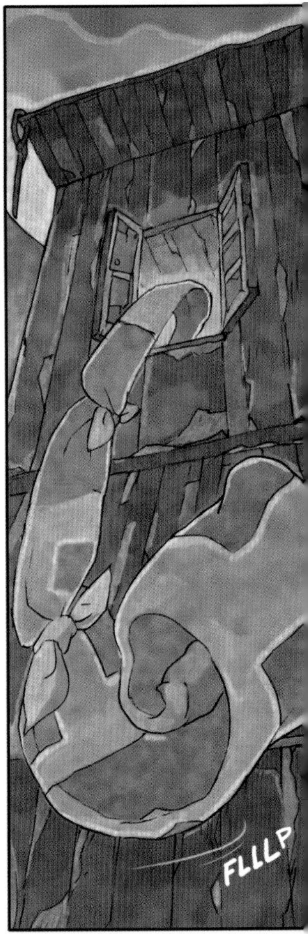
FLLLP

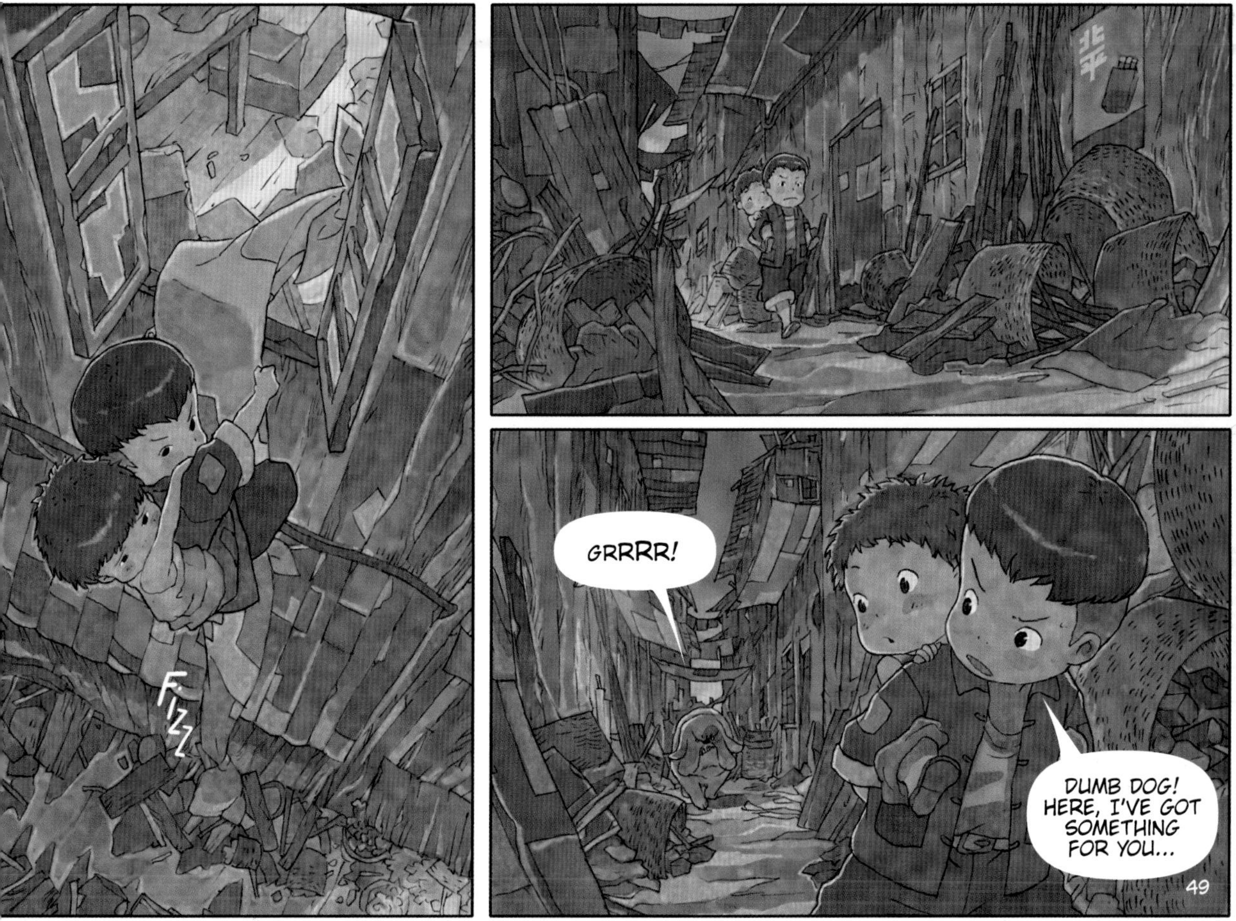
FIZZ
GRRRR!
DUMB DOG! HERE, I'VE GOT SOMETHING FOR YOU...

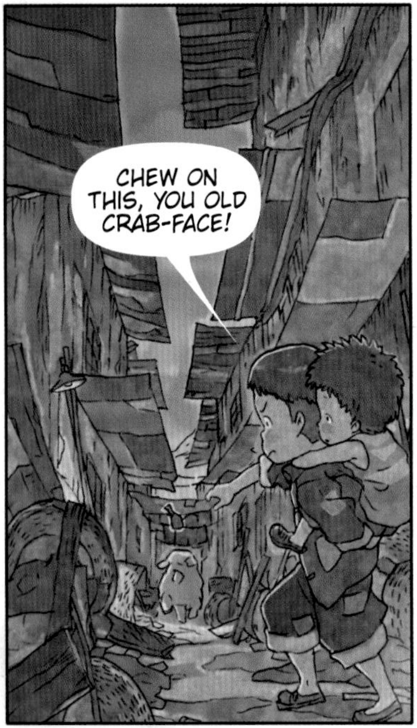
CHEW ON THIS, YOU OLD CRAB-FACE!

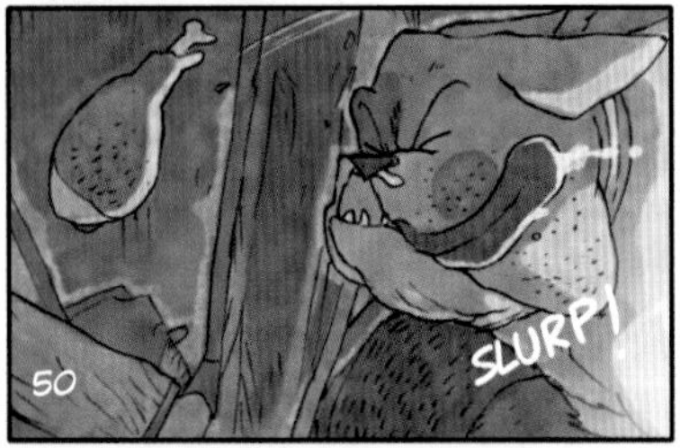
SLURP!

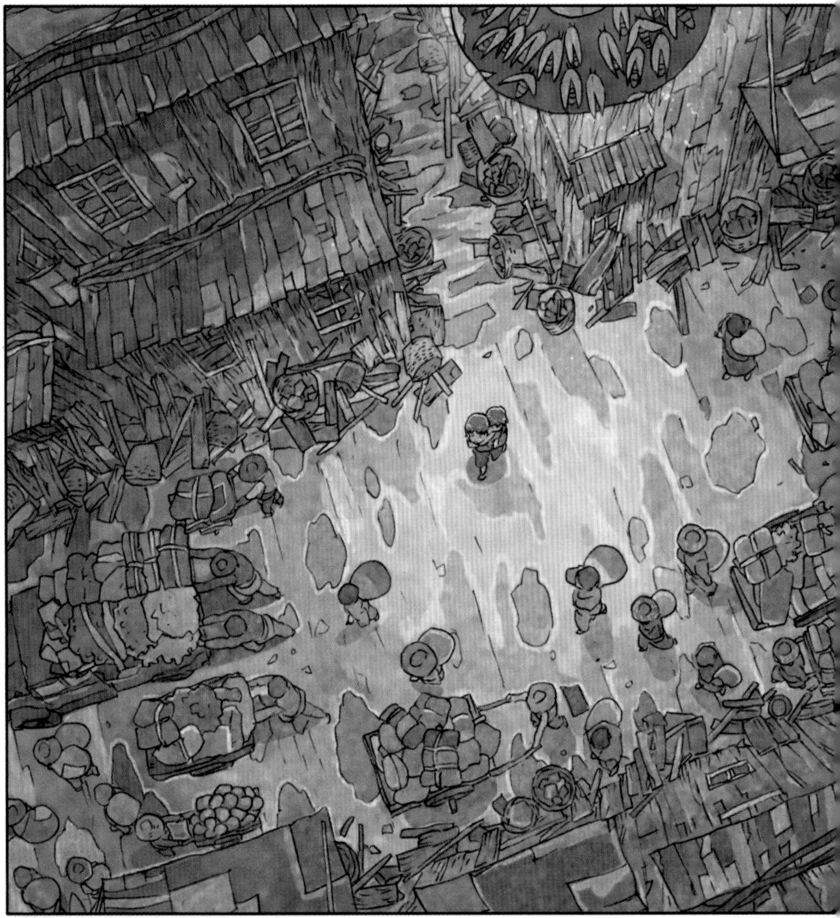

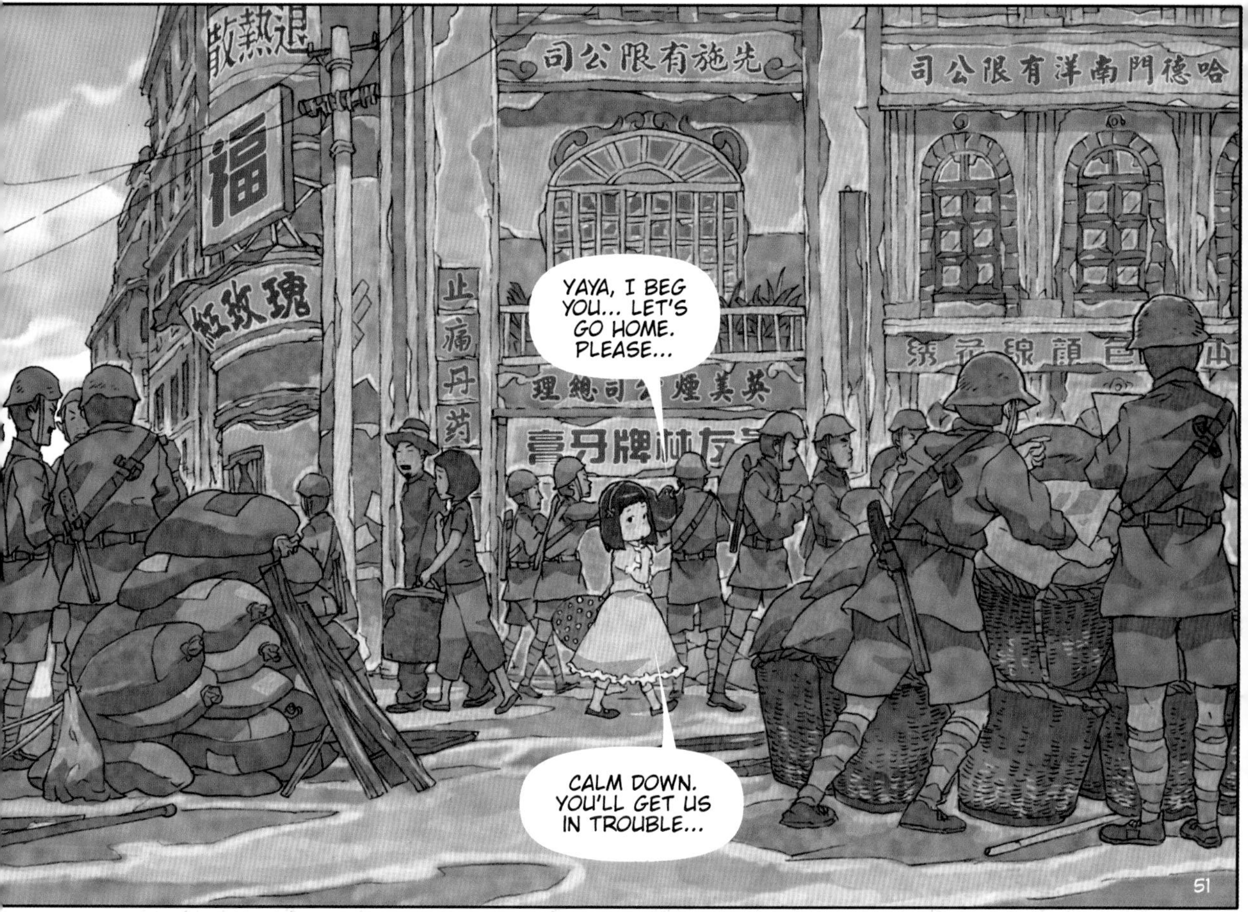
退熱散
福
先施有限公司
哈德門南洋有限公司
YAYA, I BEG YOU... LET'S GO HOME. PLEASE...
CALM DOWN. YOU'LL GET US IN TROUBLE...

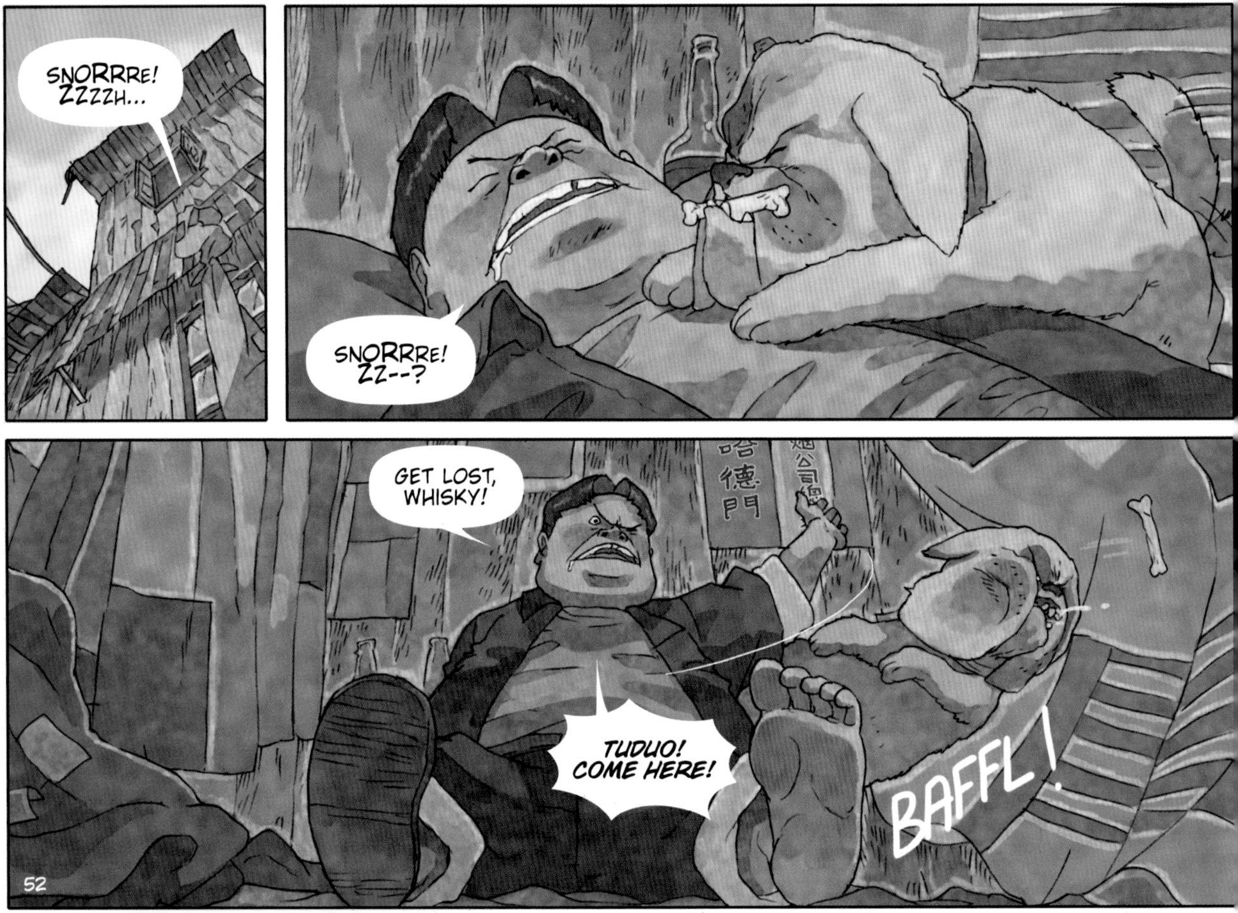
SNORRRE! ZZZZH...
SNORRRE! ZZ--?
GET LOST, WHISKY!
TUDUO! COME HERE!
BAFFL!

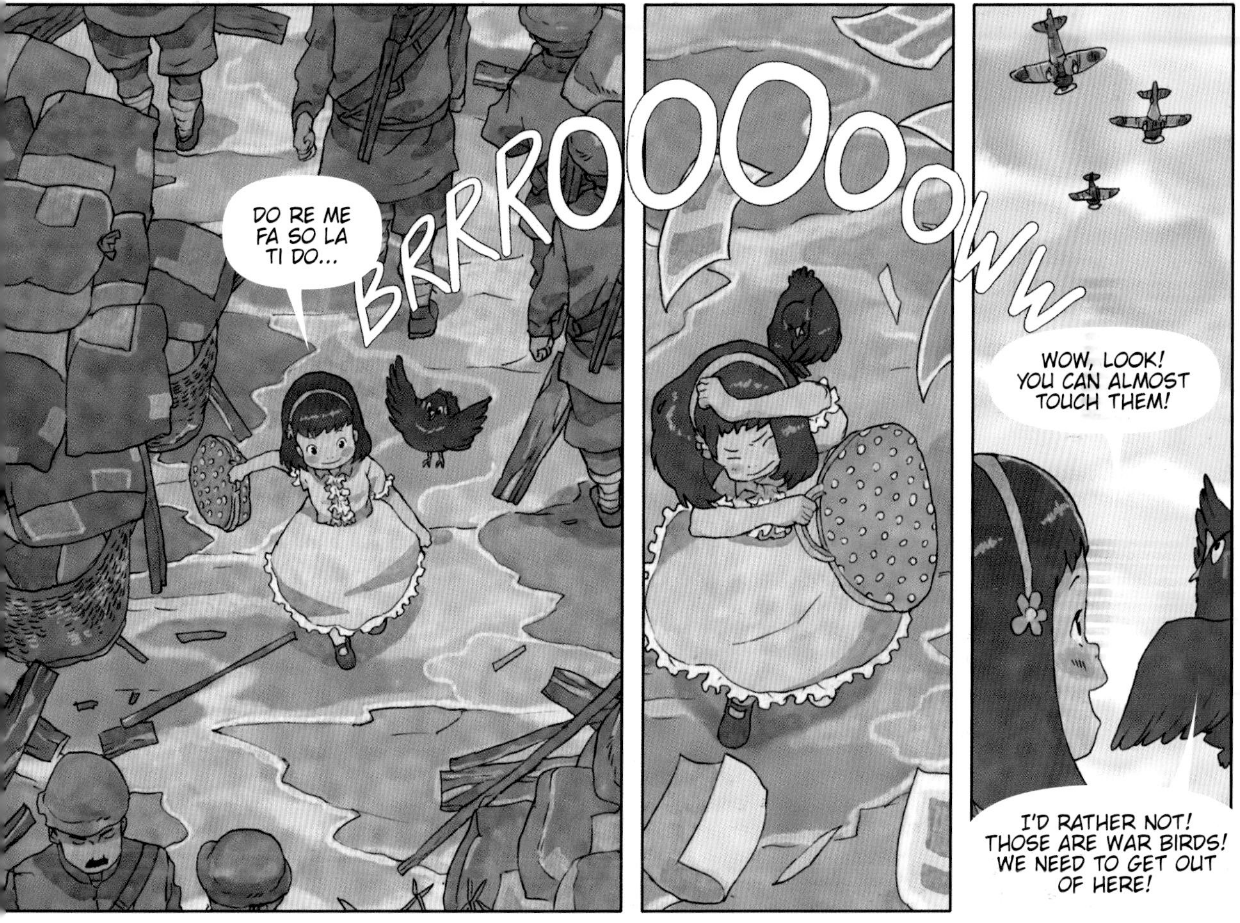
DO RE ME FA SO LA TI DO...
BRRROOOOOOWW
WOW, LOOK! YOU CAN ALMOST TOUCH THEM!
I'D RATHER NOT! THOSE ARE WAR BIRDS! WE NEED TO GET OUT OF HERE!

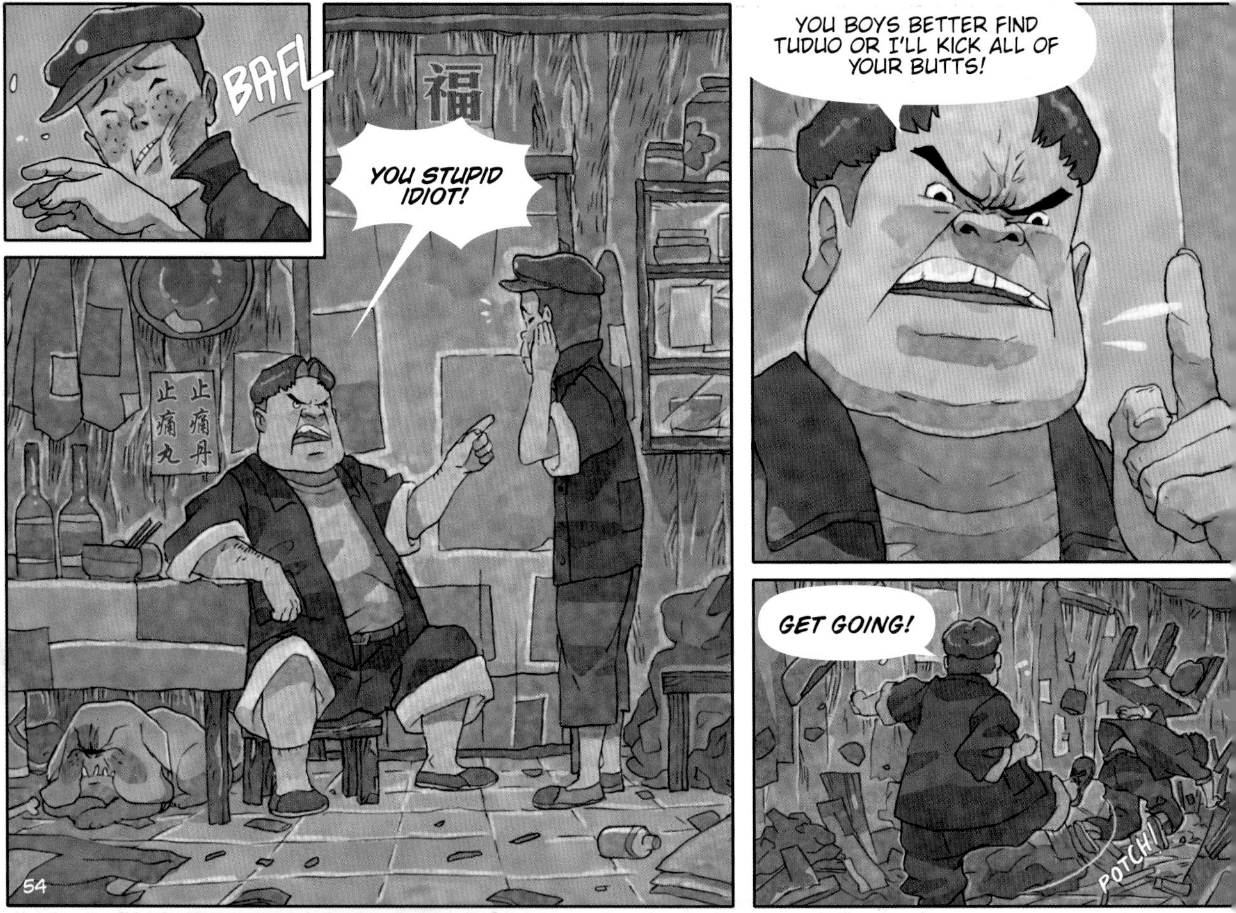
BAFL
福
YOU STUPID IDIOT!
止痛丹
止痛丸
YOU BOYS BETTER FIND TUDUO OR I'LL KICK ALL OF YOUR BUTTS!
GET GOING!
POTCH!

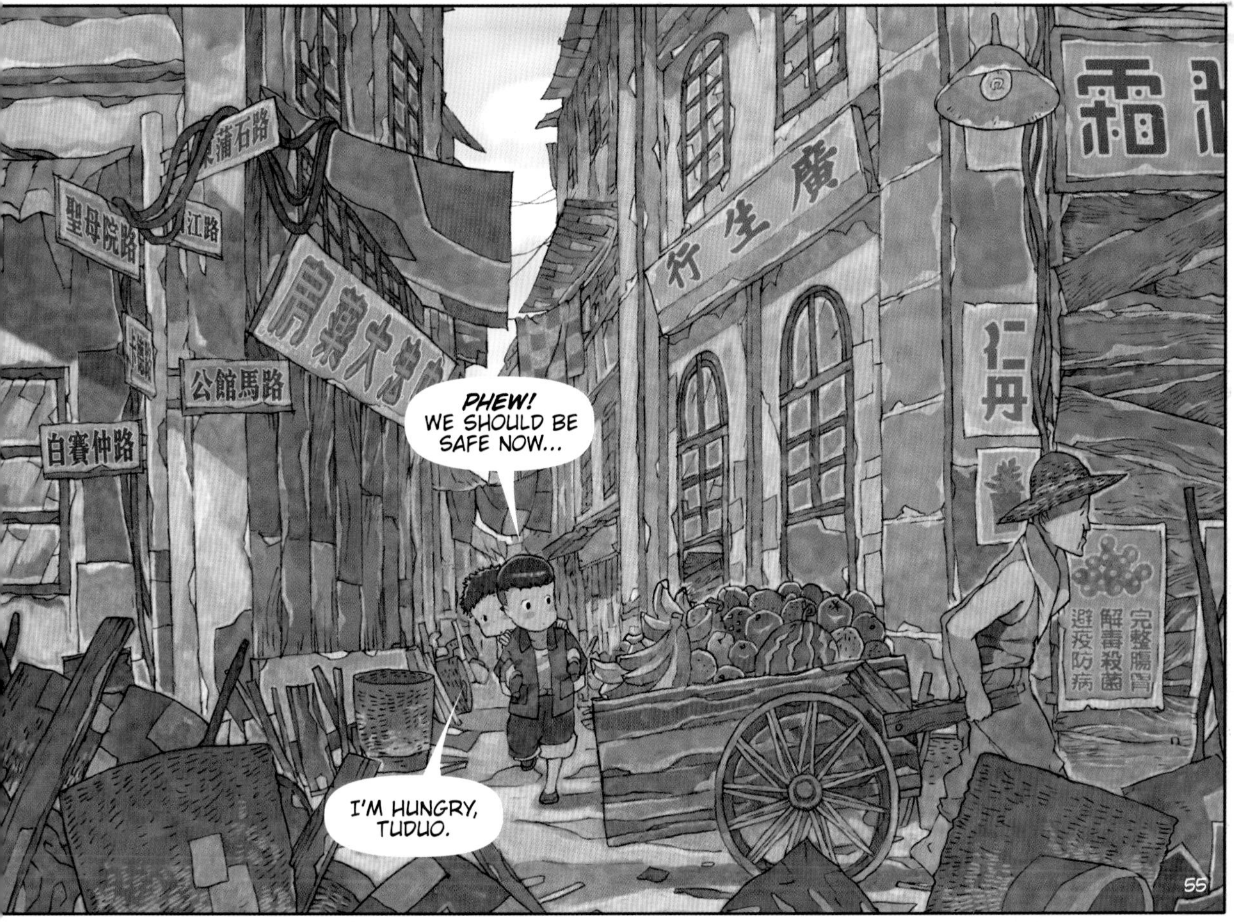
PHEW!
WE SHOULD BE SAFE NOW...
I'M HUNGRY, TUDUO.
聖母院路
公館馬路
白賽仲路
廣生行
完整腸胃
解毒殺菌
避疫防病

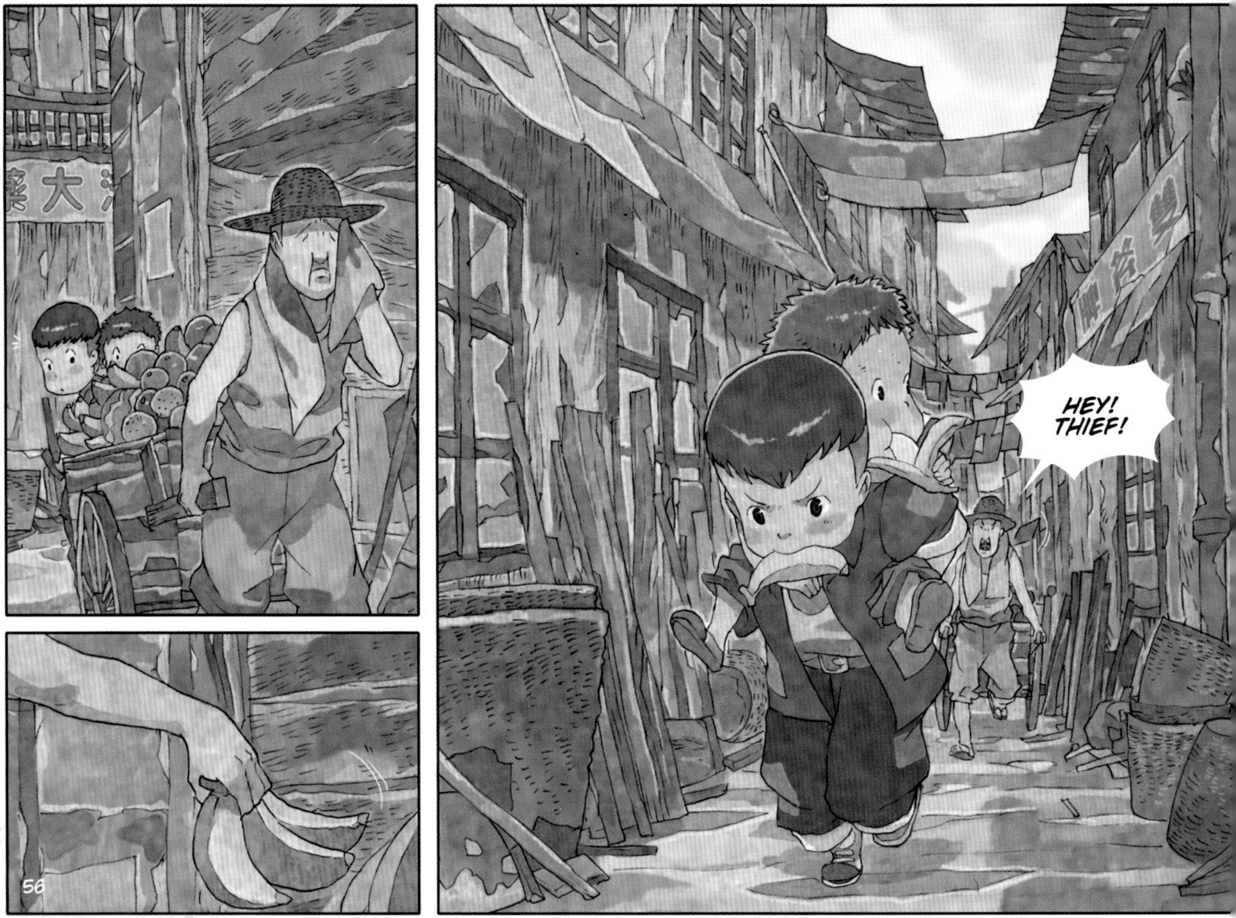
HEY! THIEF!

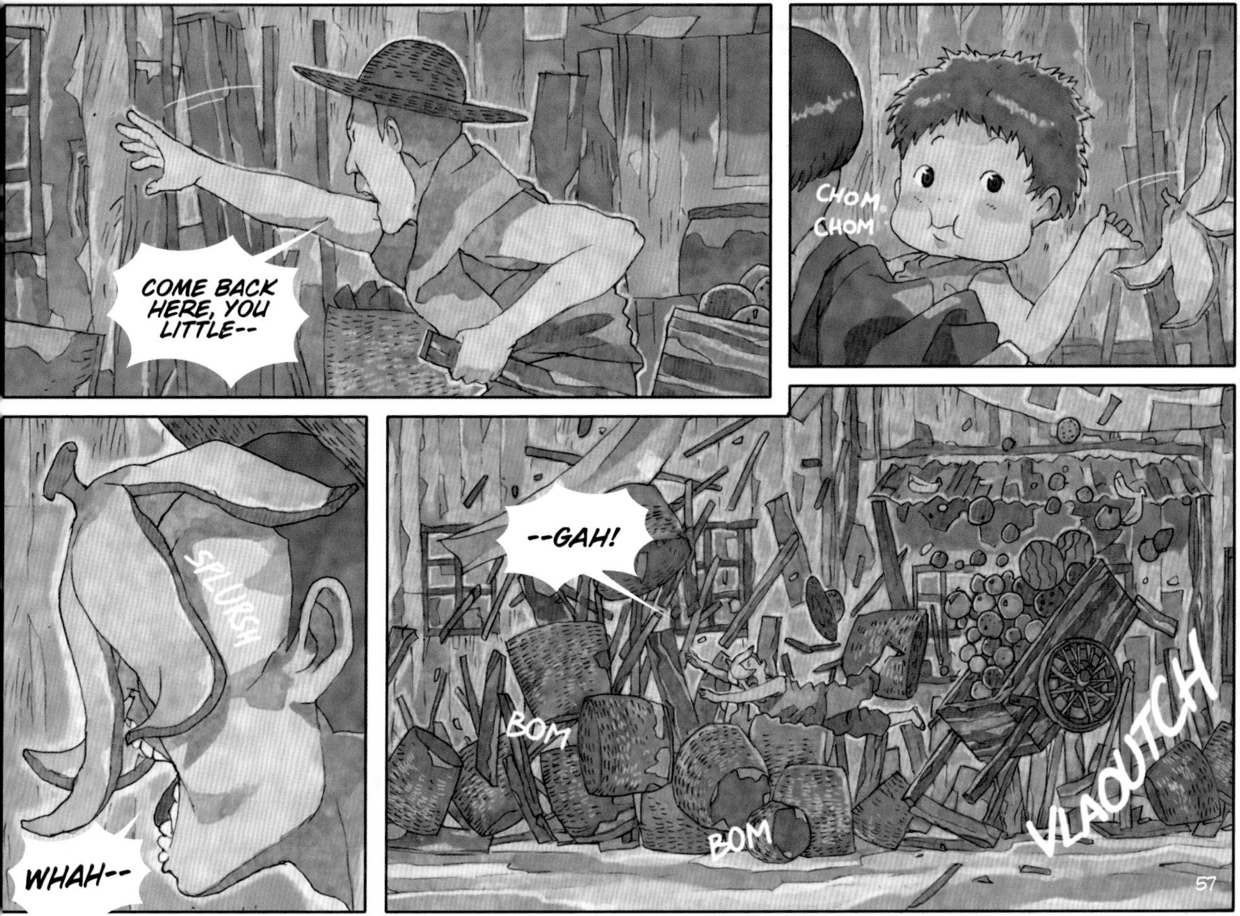
COME BACK HERE, YOU LITTLE--
CHOM CHOM
SPLURSH
WHAH--
--GAH!
BOM
BOM
VLAOUTCH

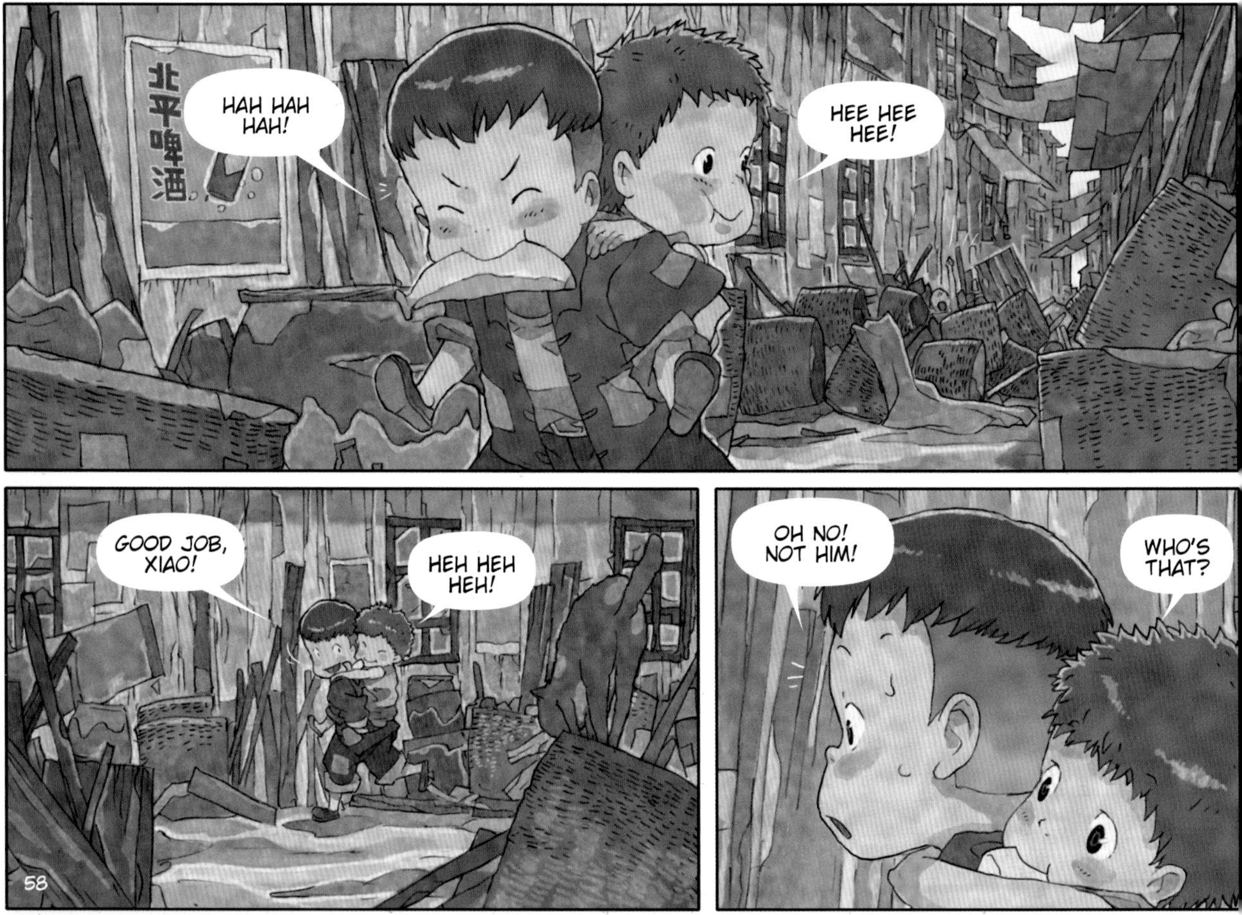
北平啤酒
HAH HAH HAH!
HEE HEE HEE!
GOOD JOB, XIAO!
HEH HEH HEH!
OH NO! NOT HIM!
WHO'S THAT?

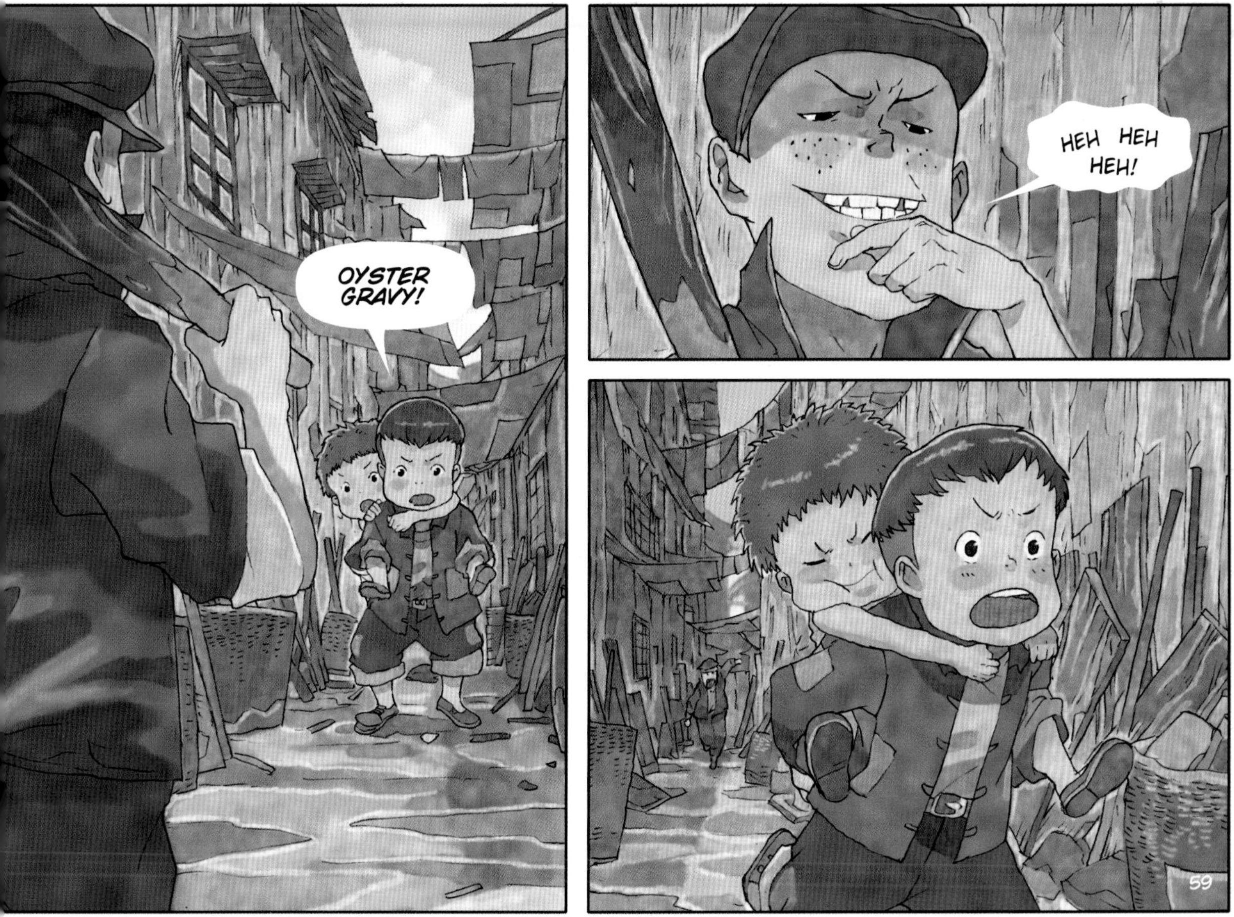
OYSTER GRAVY!
HEH HEH HEH!

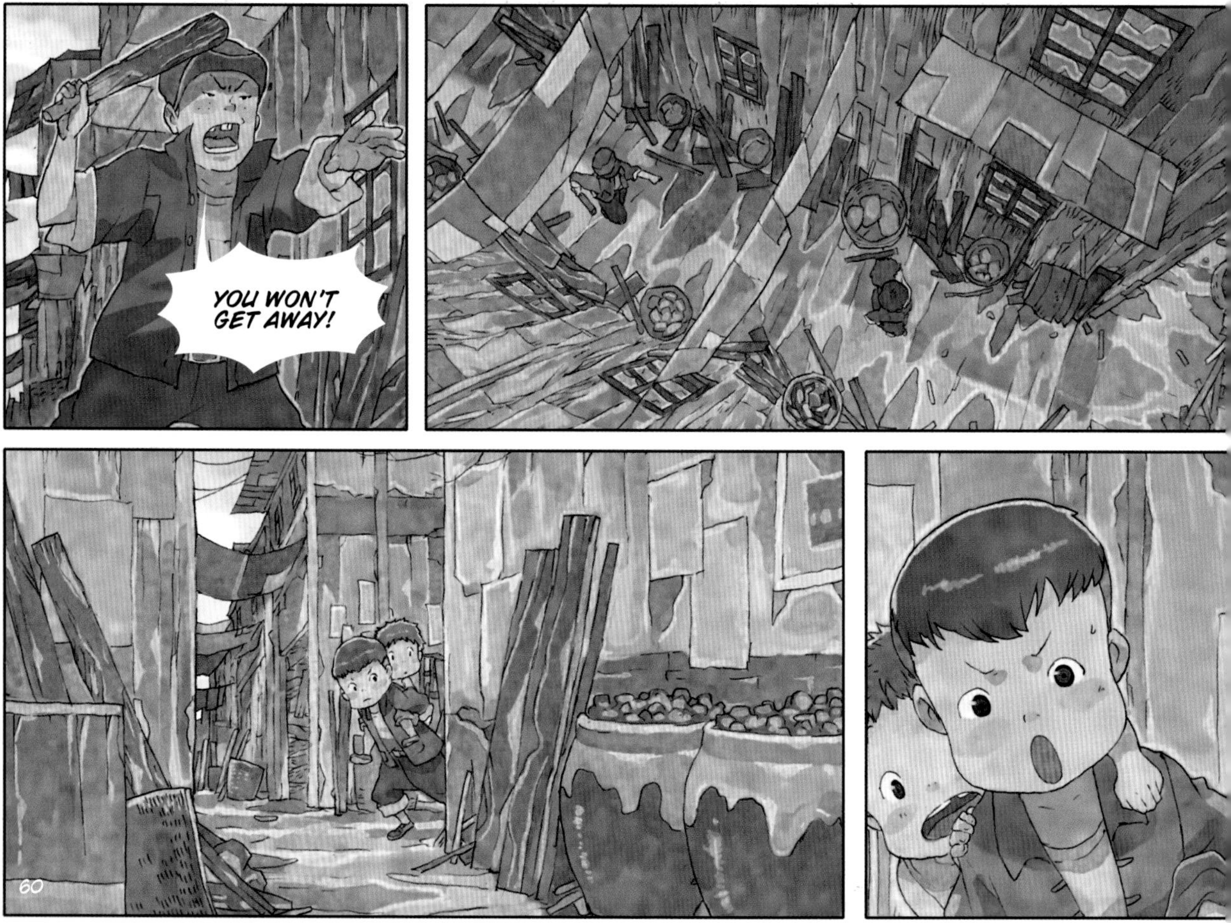
YOU WON'T GET AWAY!

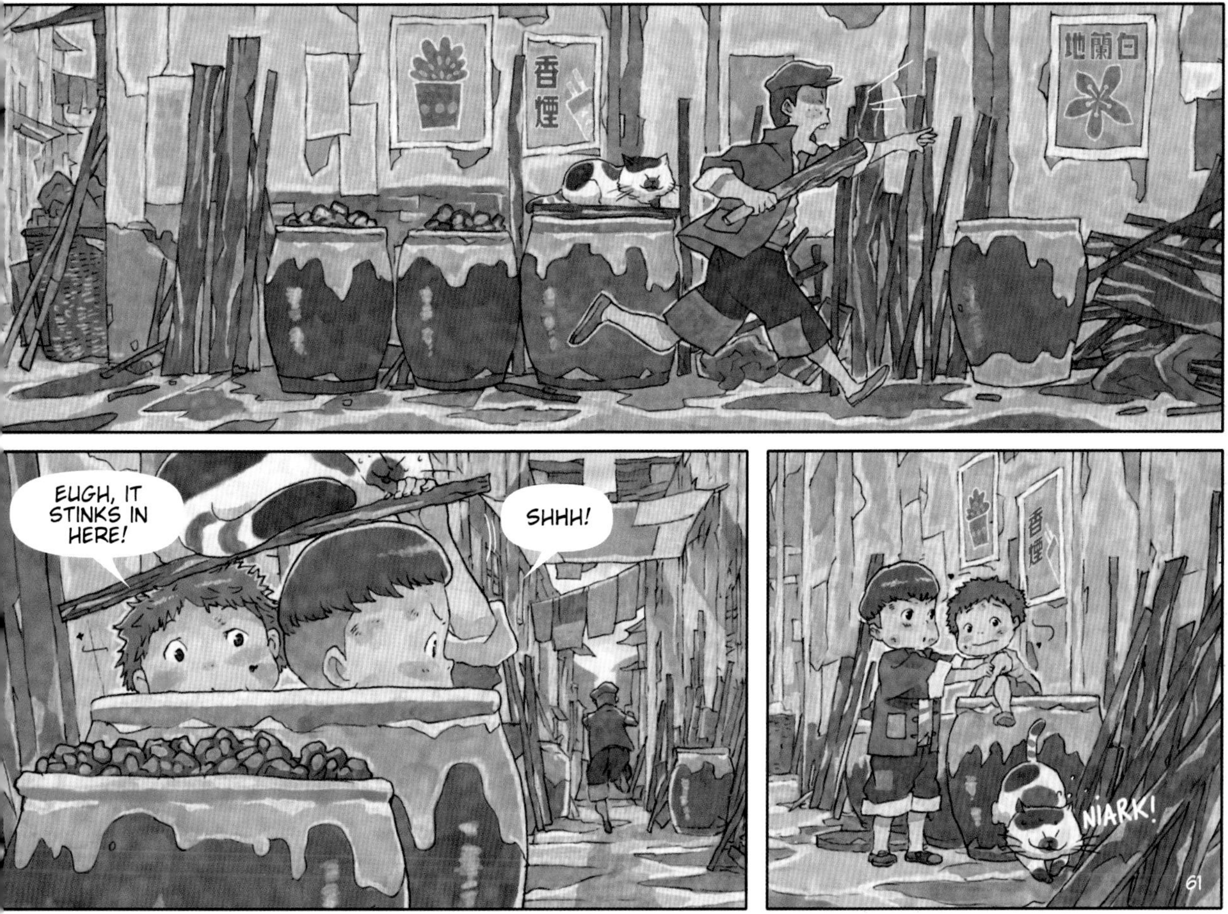
香煙
白蘭地
EUGH, IT STINKS IN HERE!
SHHH!
香煙
NIARK!

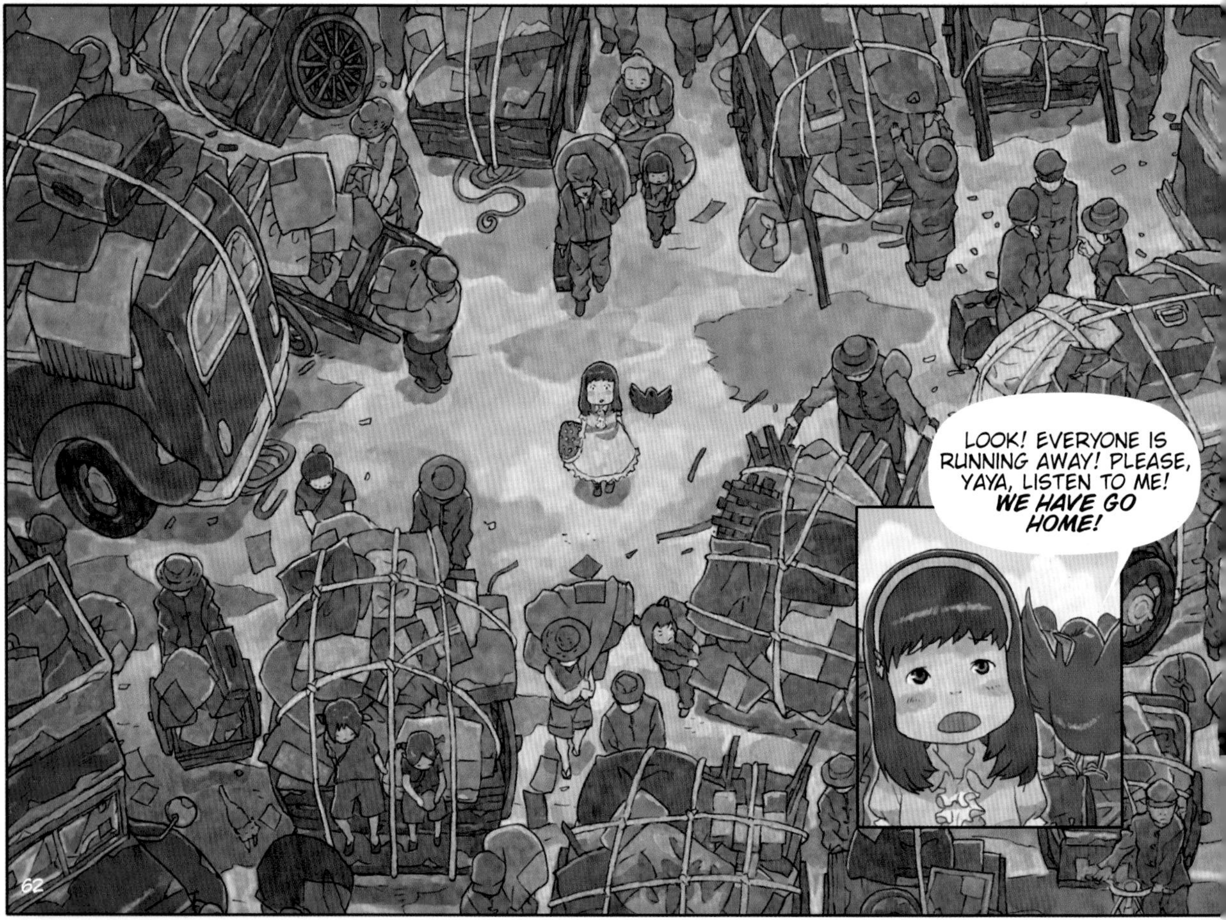
LOOK! EVERYONE IS RUNNING AWAY! PLEASE, YAYA, LISTEN TO ME! **WE HAVE GO HOME!**

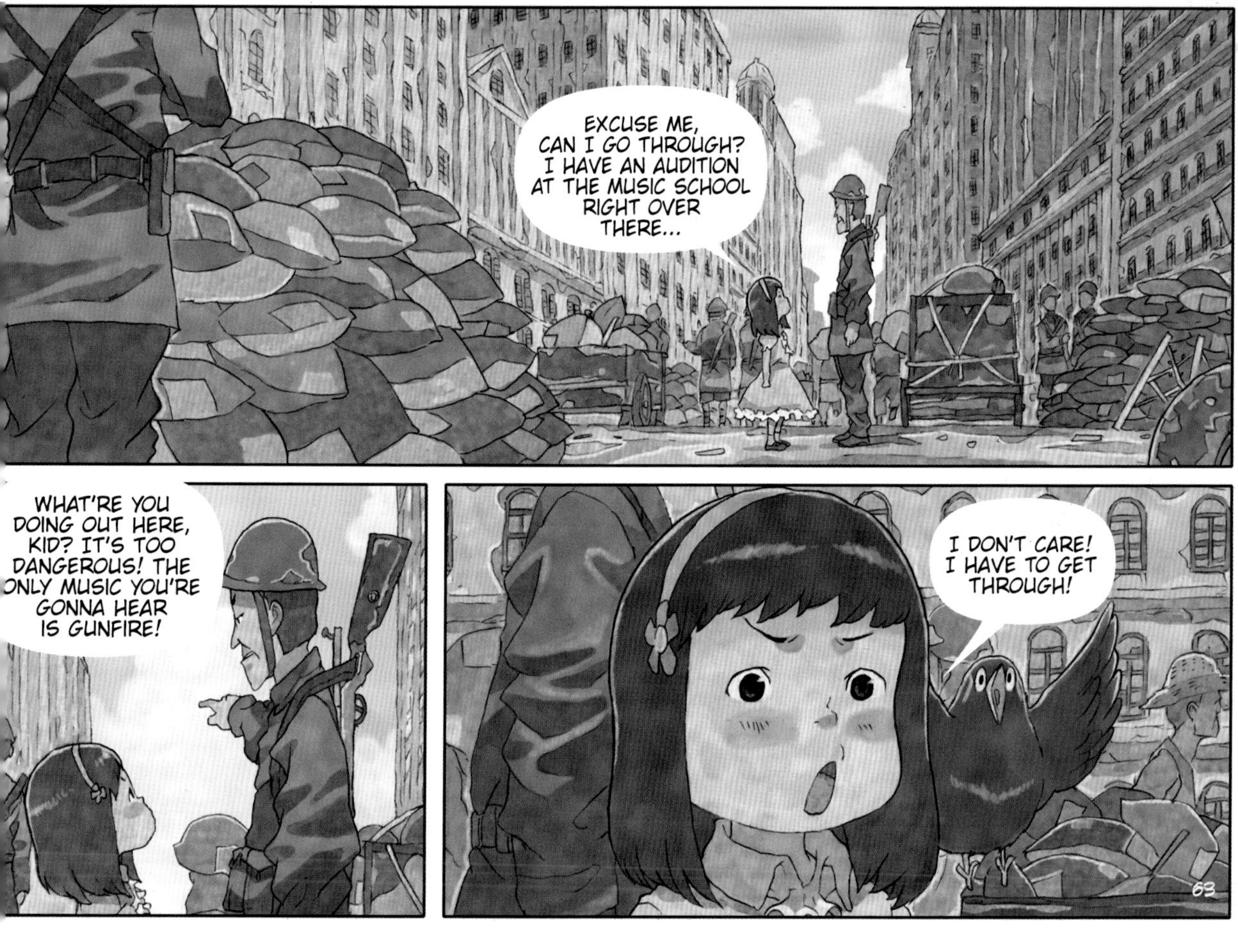

EXCUSE ME, CAN I GO THROUGH? I HAVE AN AUDITION AT THE MUSIC SCHOOL RIGHT OVER THERE...
WHAT'RE YOU DOING OUT HERE, KID? IT'S TOO DANGEROUS! THE ONLY MUSIC YOU'RE GONNA HEAR IS GUNFIRE!
I DON'T CARE! I HAVE TO GET THROUGH!

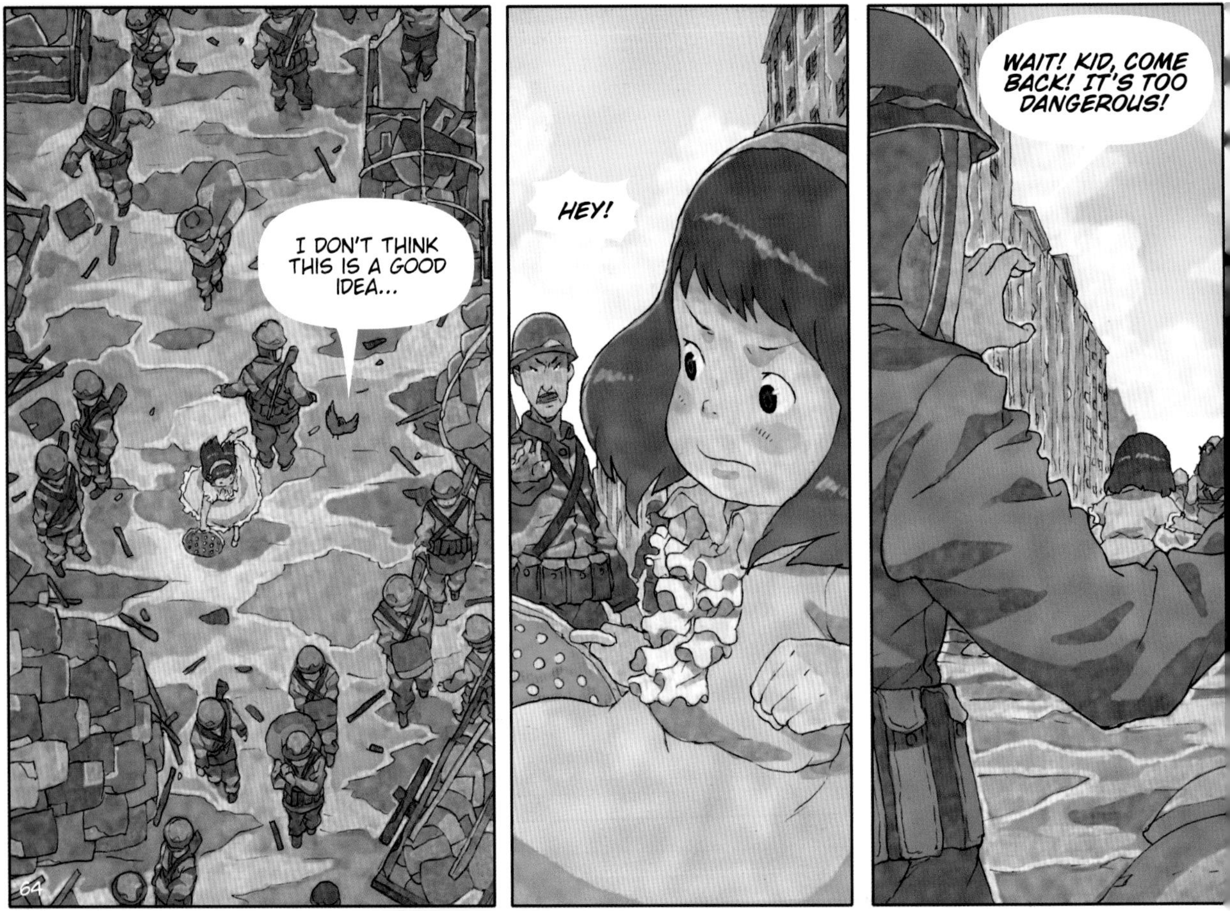
I DON'T THINK THIS IS A GOOD IDEA...
HEY!
WAIT! KID, COME BACK! IT'S TOO DANGEROUS!

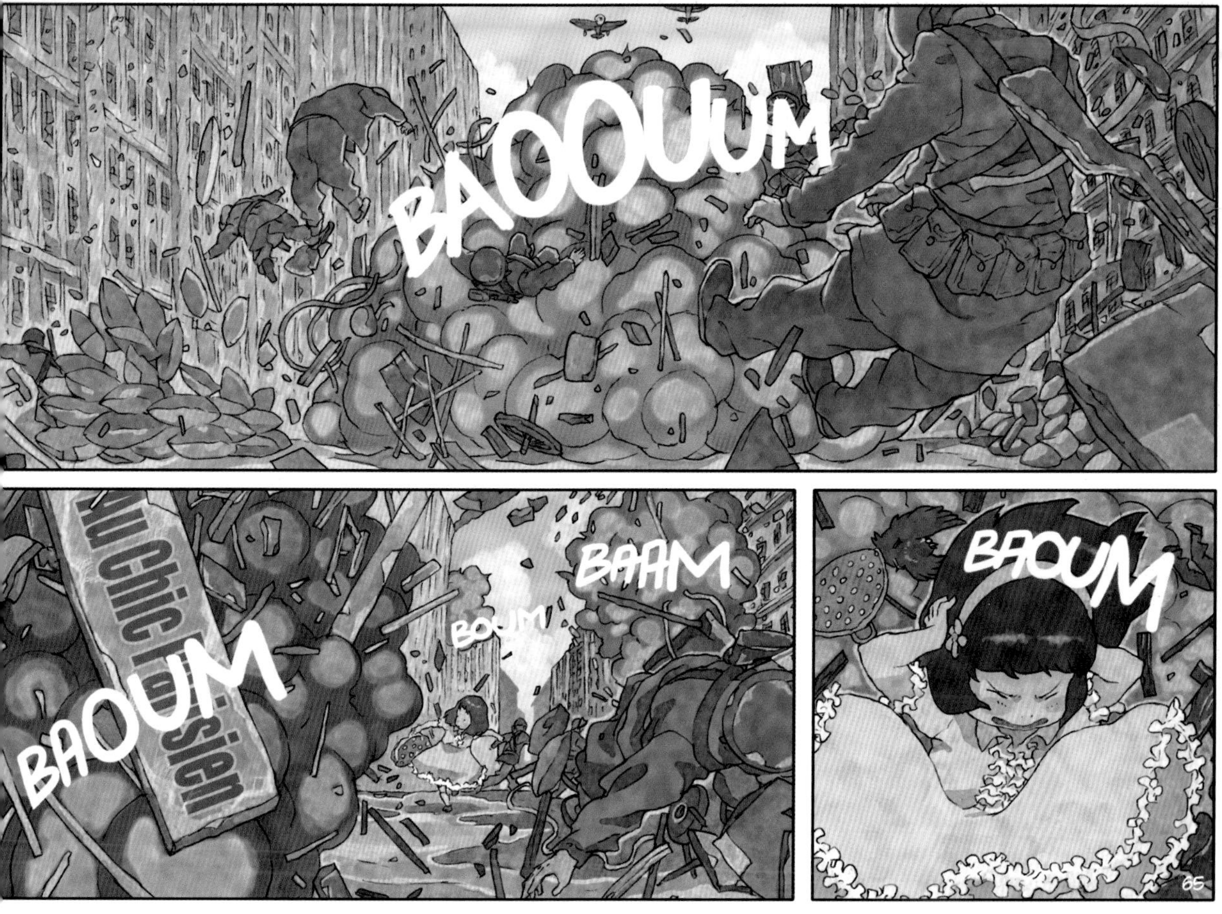
BAOOUUUM
BAOUM
BOUM
BAAAM
BAOUM

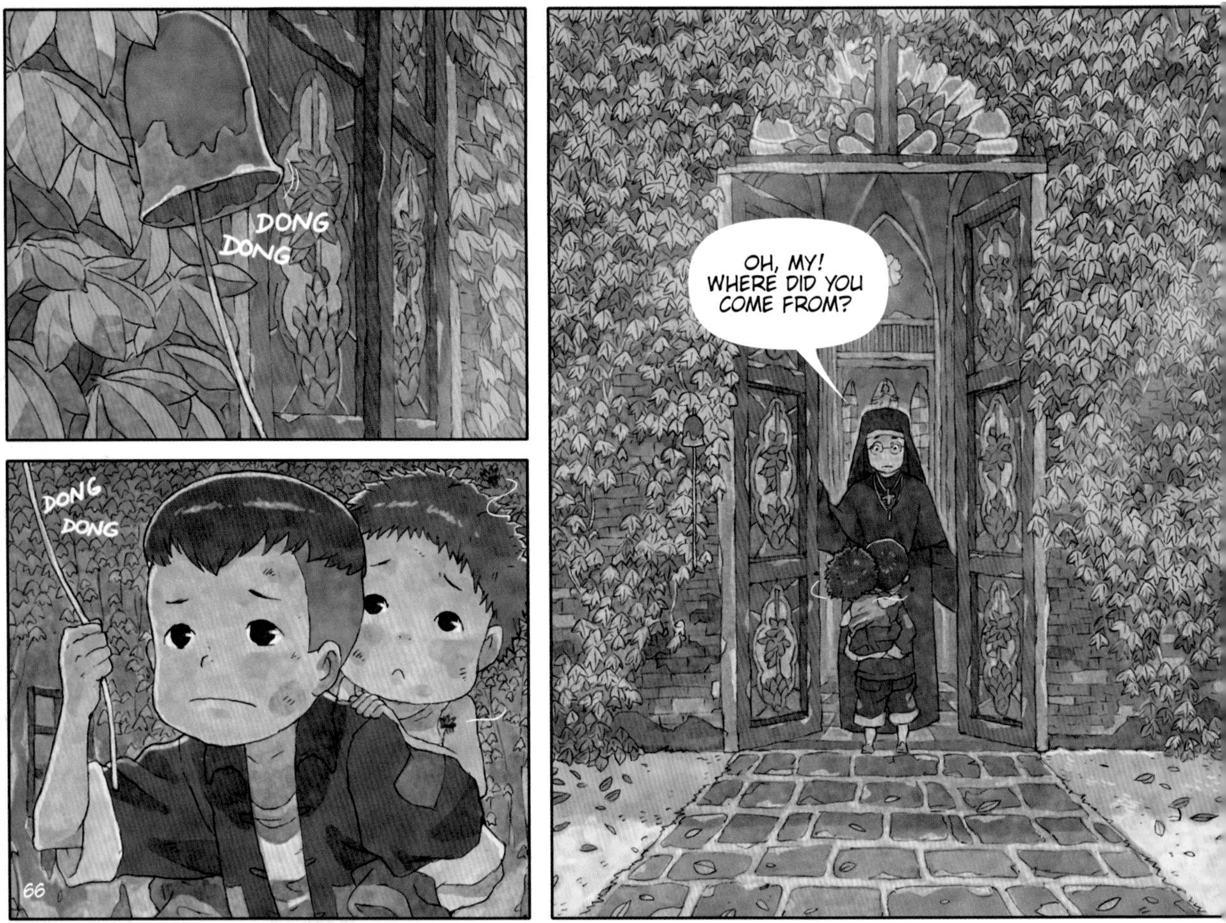
DONG
DONG
DONG
DONG
OH, MY! WHERE DID YOU COME FROM?

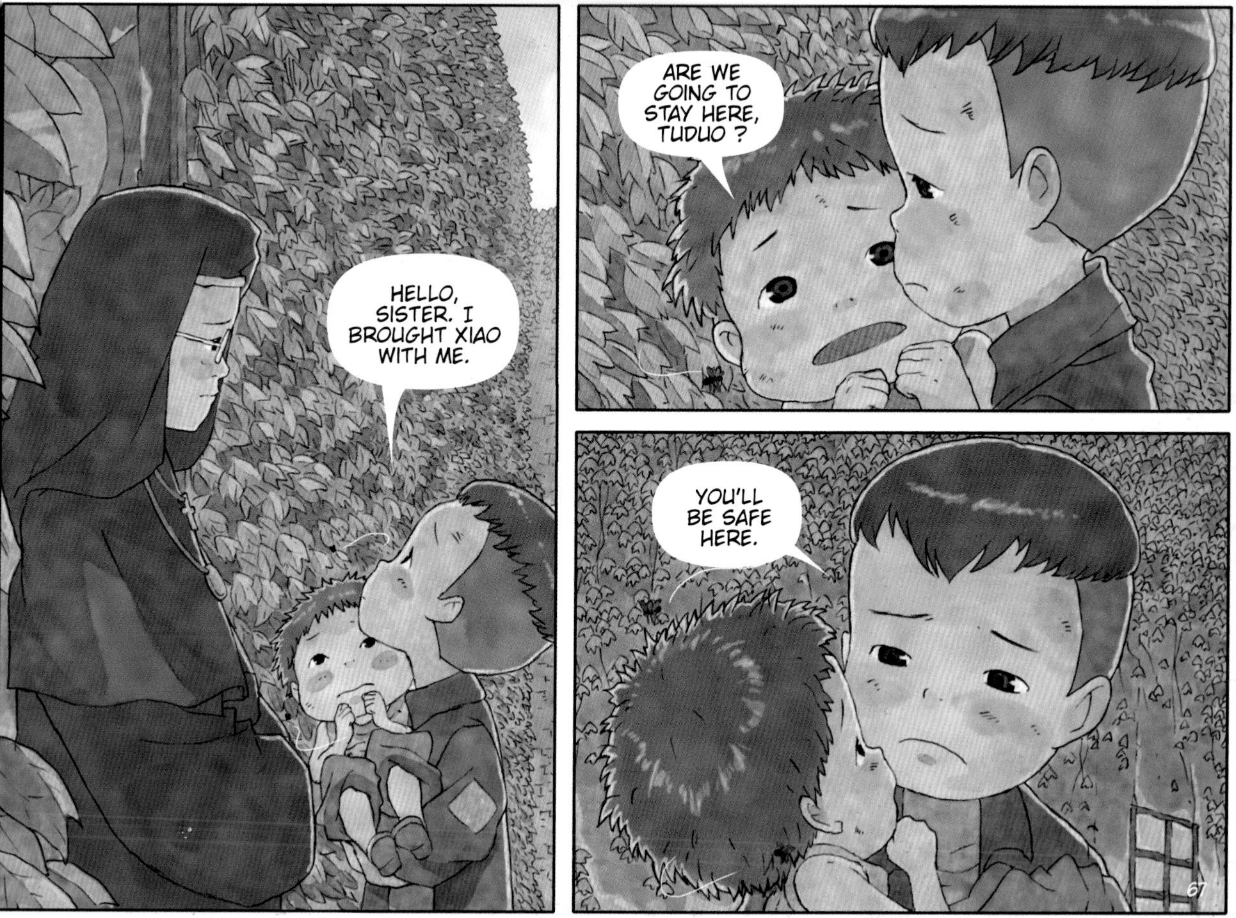
HELLO, SISTER. I BROUGHT XIAO WITH ME.
ARE WE GOING TO STAY HERE, TUDUO ?
YOU'LL BE SAFE HERE.

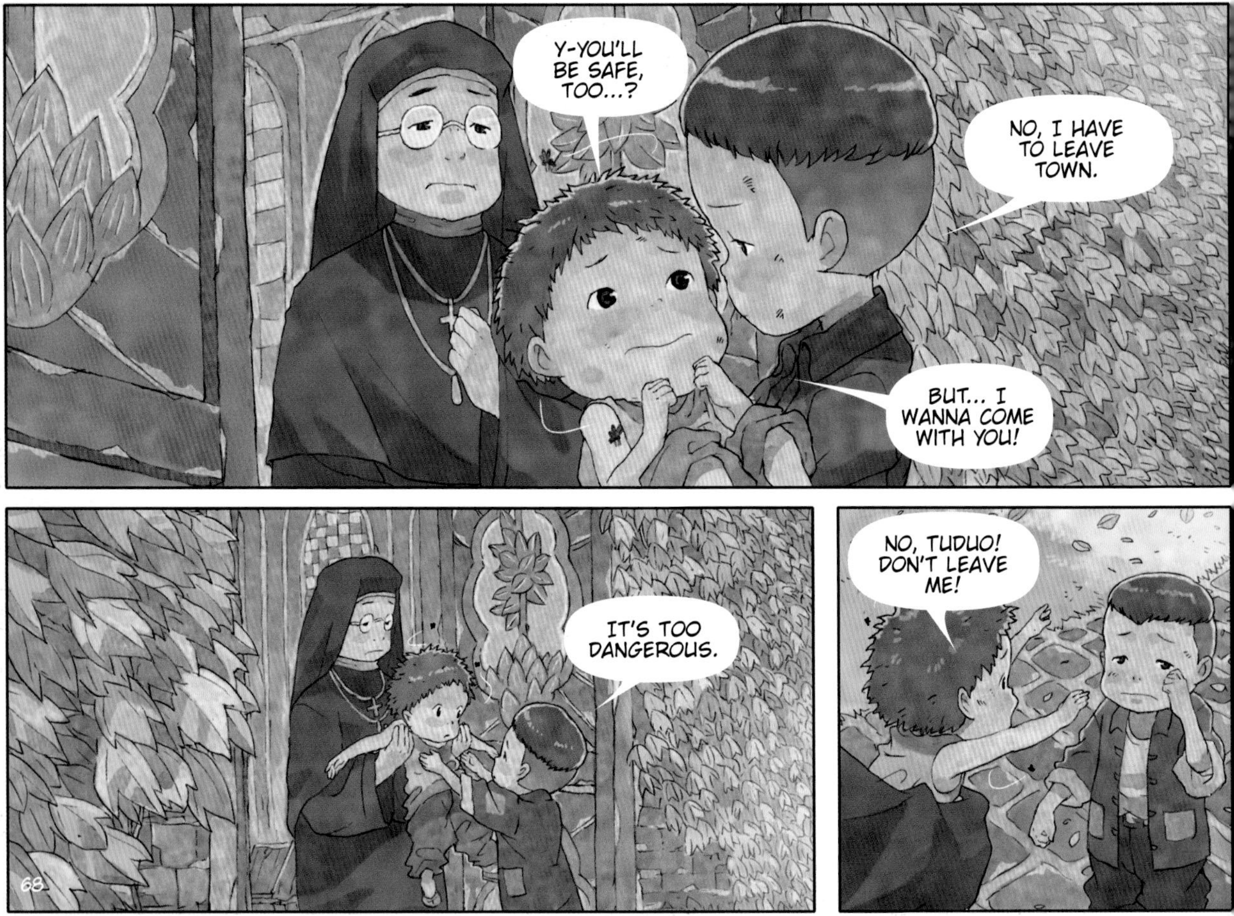
Y-YOU'LL BE SAFE, TOO...?
NO, I HAVE TO LEAVE TOWN.
BUT... I WANNA COME WITH YOU!
IT'S TOO DANGEROUS.
NO, TUDUO! DON'T LEAVE ME!

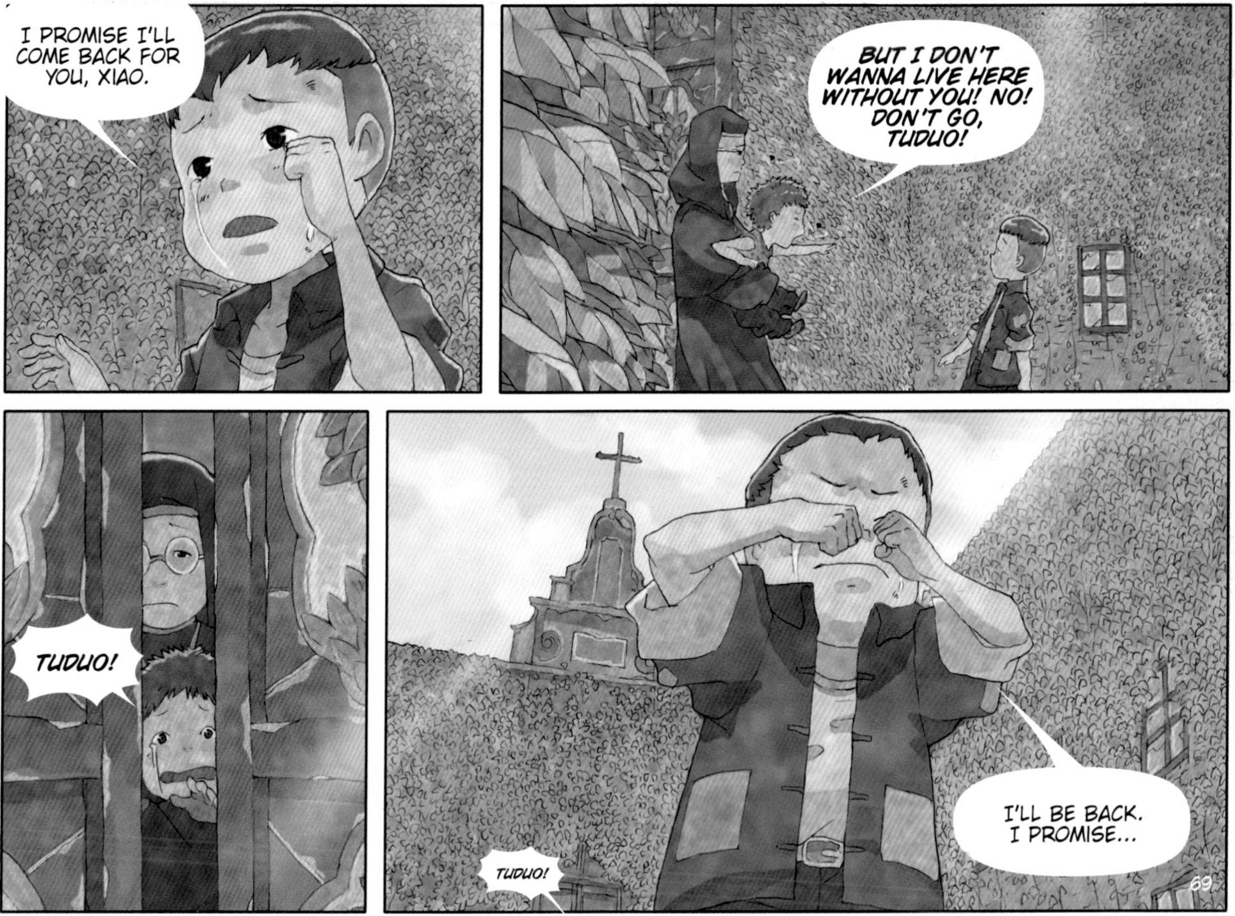
I PROMISE I'LL COME BACK FOR YOU, XIAO.
BUT I DON'T WANNA LIVE HERE WITHOUT YOU! NO! DON'T GO, TUDUO!
TUDUO!
TUDUO!
I'LL BE BACK. I PROMISE...

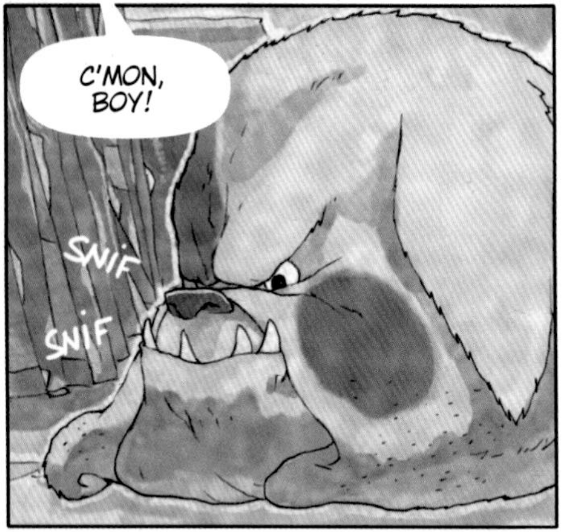
C'MON, BOY!
SNIF
SNIF

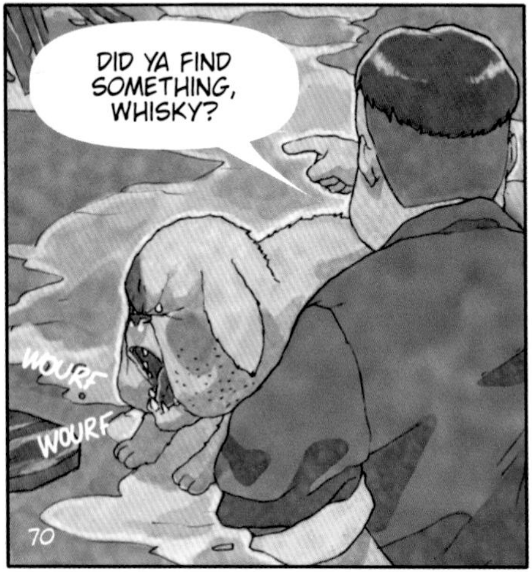
DID YA FIND SOMETHING, WHISKY?
WOURF
WOURF

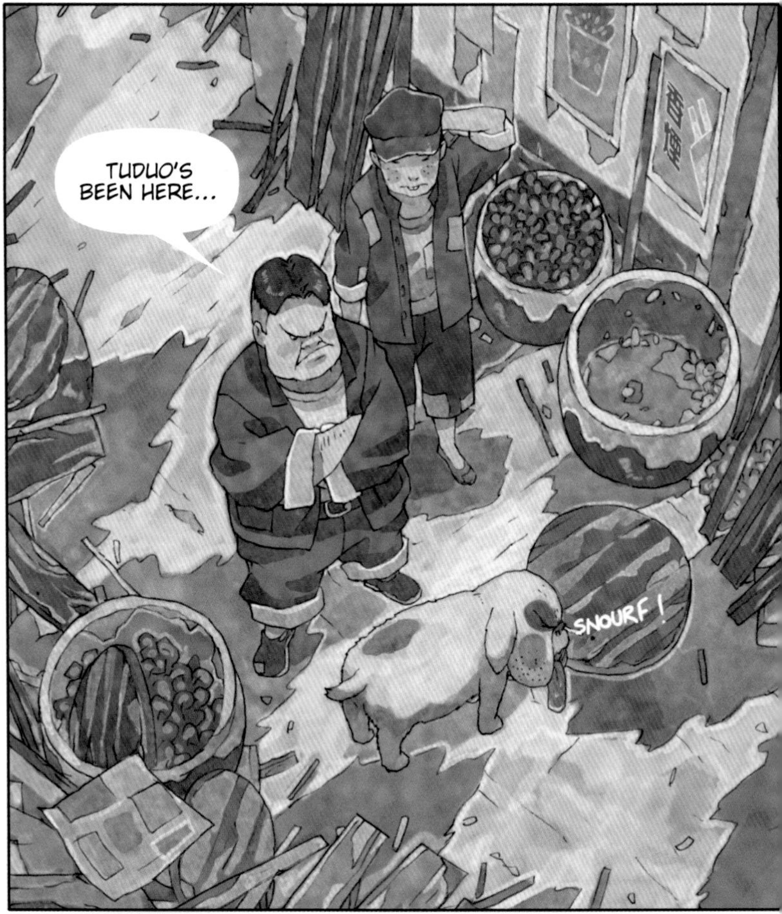
TUDUO'S BEEN HERE...
SNOURF !

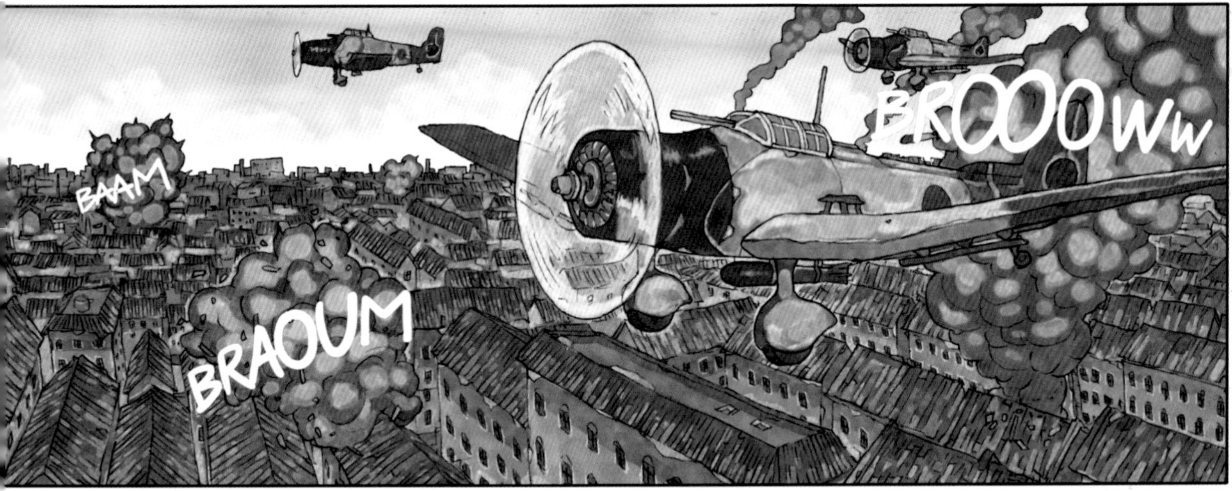
BROOOOWW
BAAM
BRAOUM

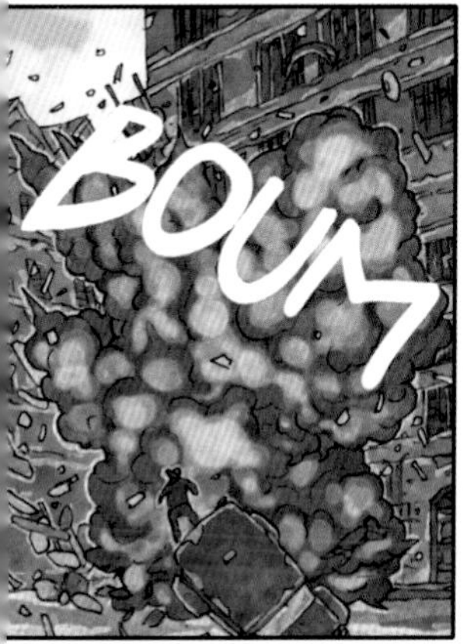
BOUM

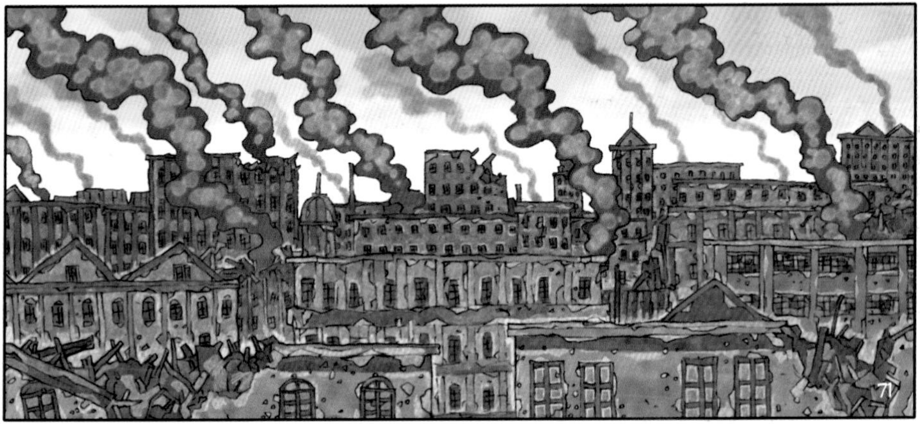

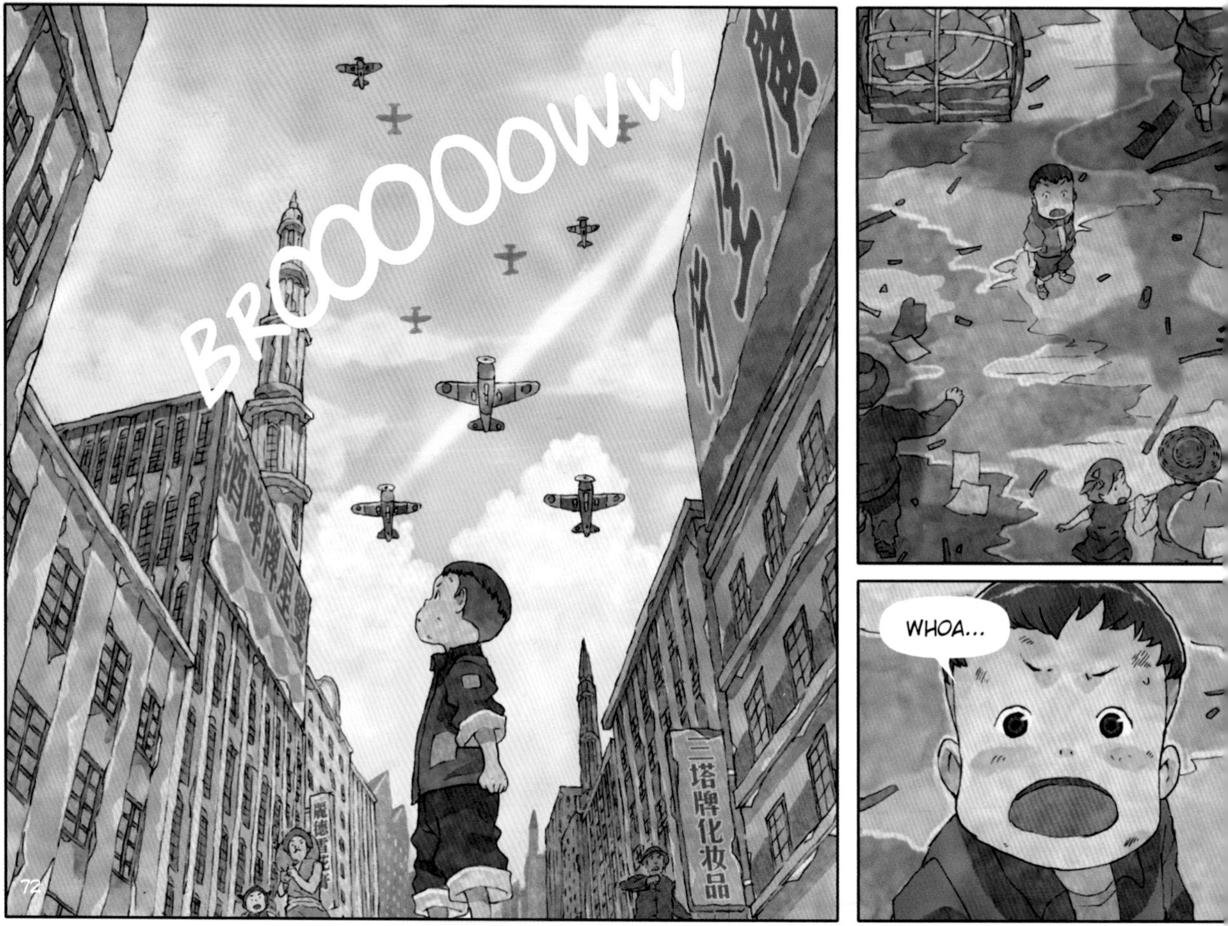
BROOOOOOWW
三塔牌化妝品
WHOA...

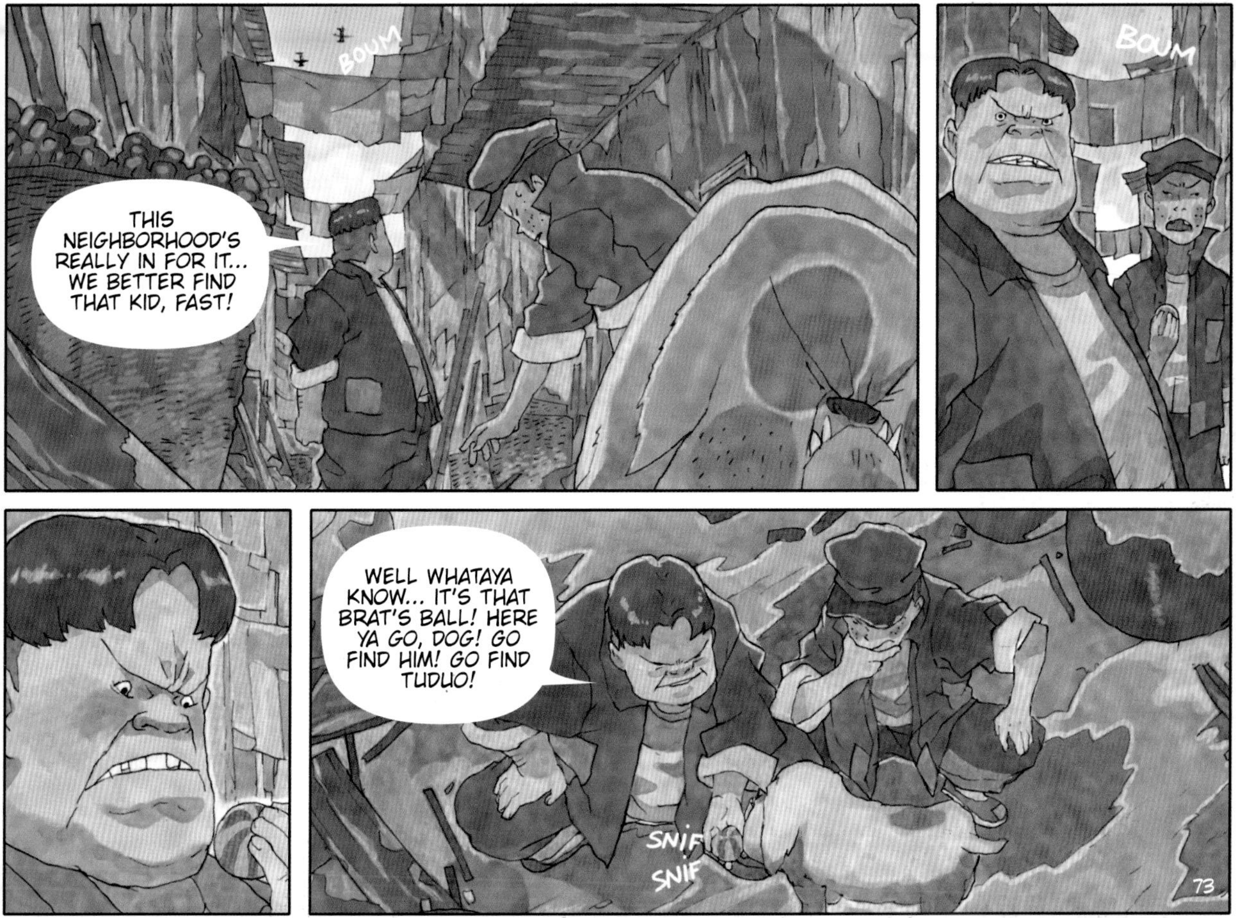
BOUM
THIS NEIGHBORHOOD'S REALLY IN FOR IT... WE BETTER FIND THAT KID, FAST!
BOUM
WELL WHATAYA KNOW... IT'S THAT BRAT'S BALL! HERE YA GO, DOG! GO FIND HIM! GO FIND TUDUO!
SNIF
SNIF

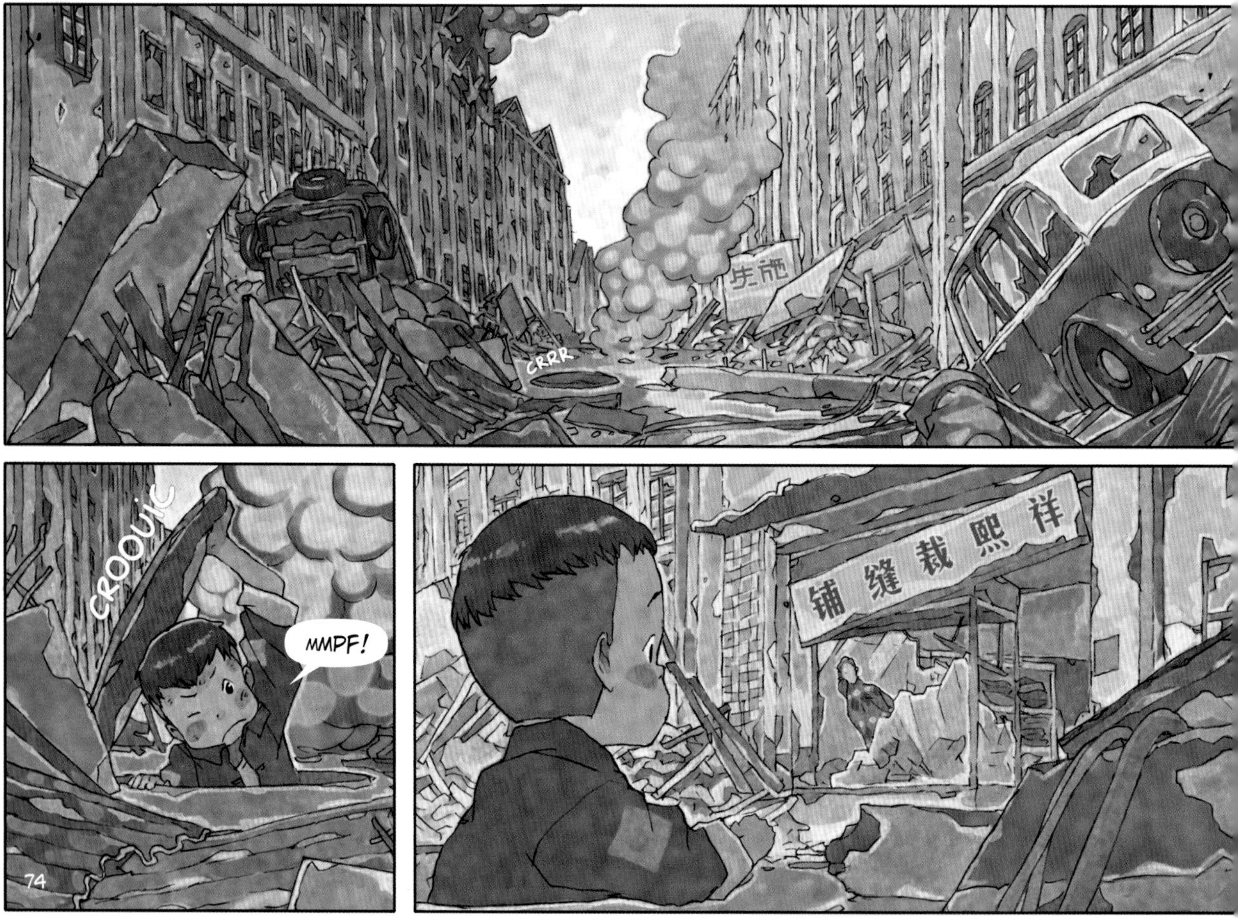
先施
CRRR
CROOUIC
MMPF!
祥熙裁縫铺

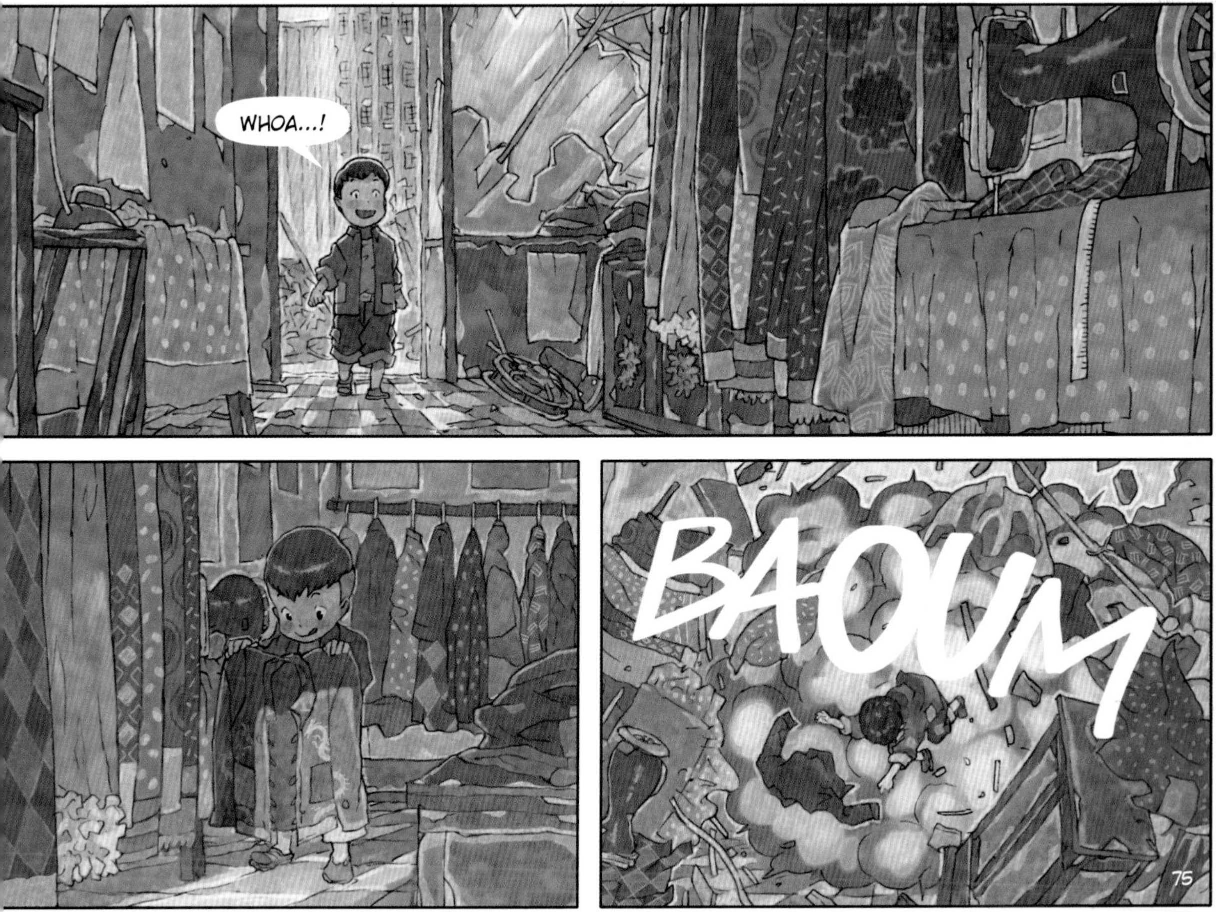
WHOA...!
BAOUM

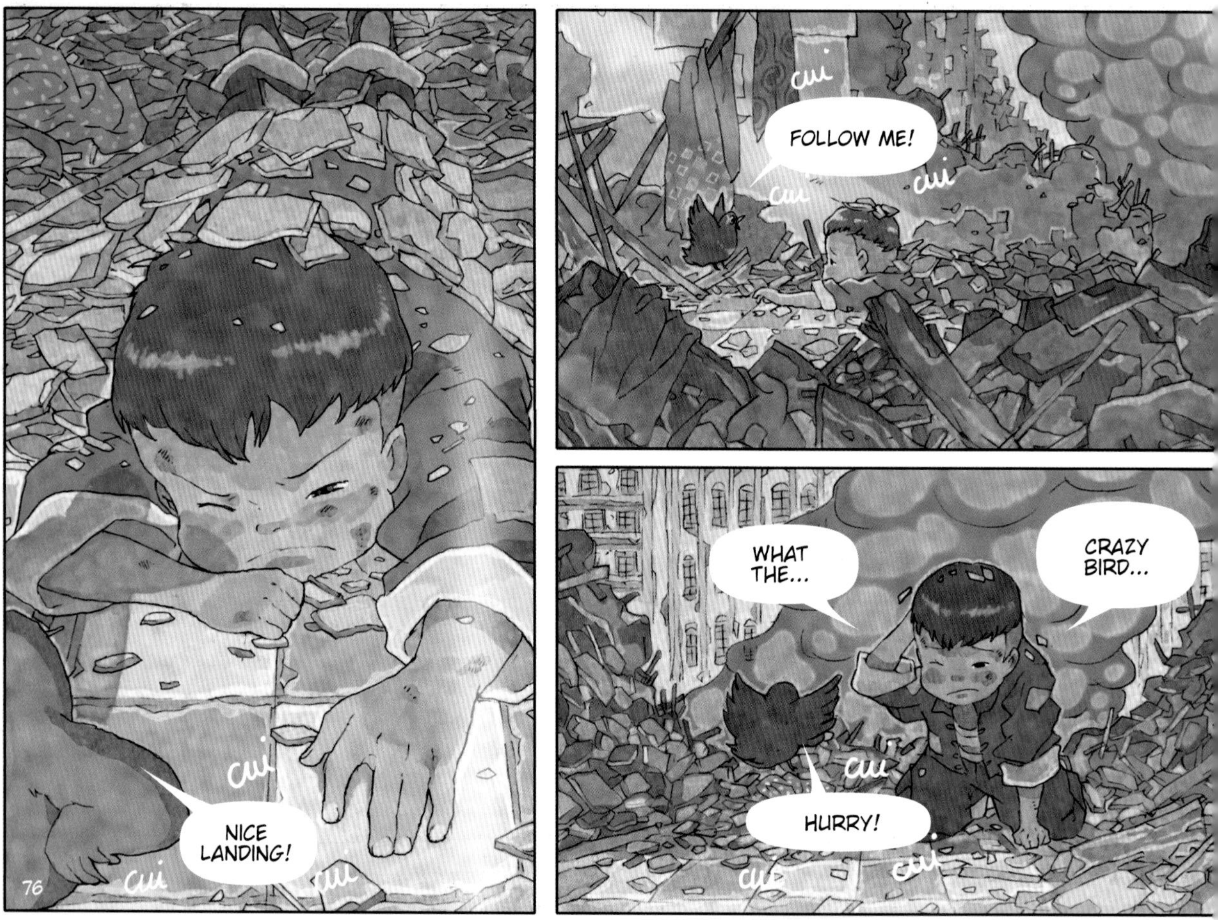
cui
NICE LANDING!
cui
cui
cui
FOLLOW ME!
cui
cui
WHAT THE...
CRAZY BIRD...
cui
HURRY!
cui
cui

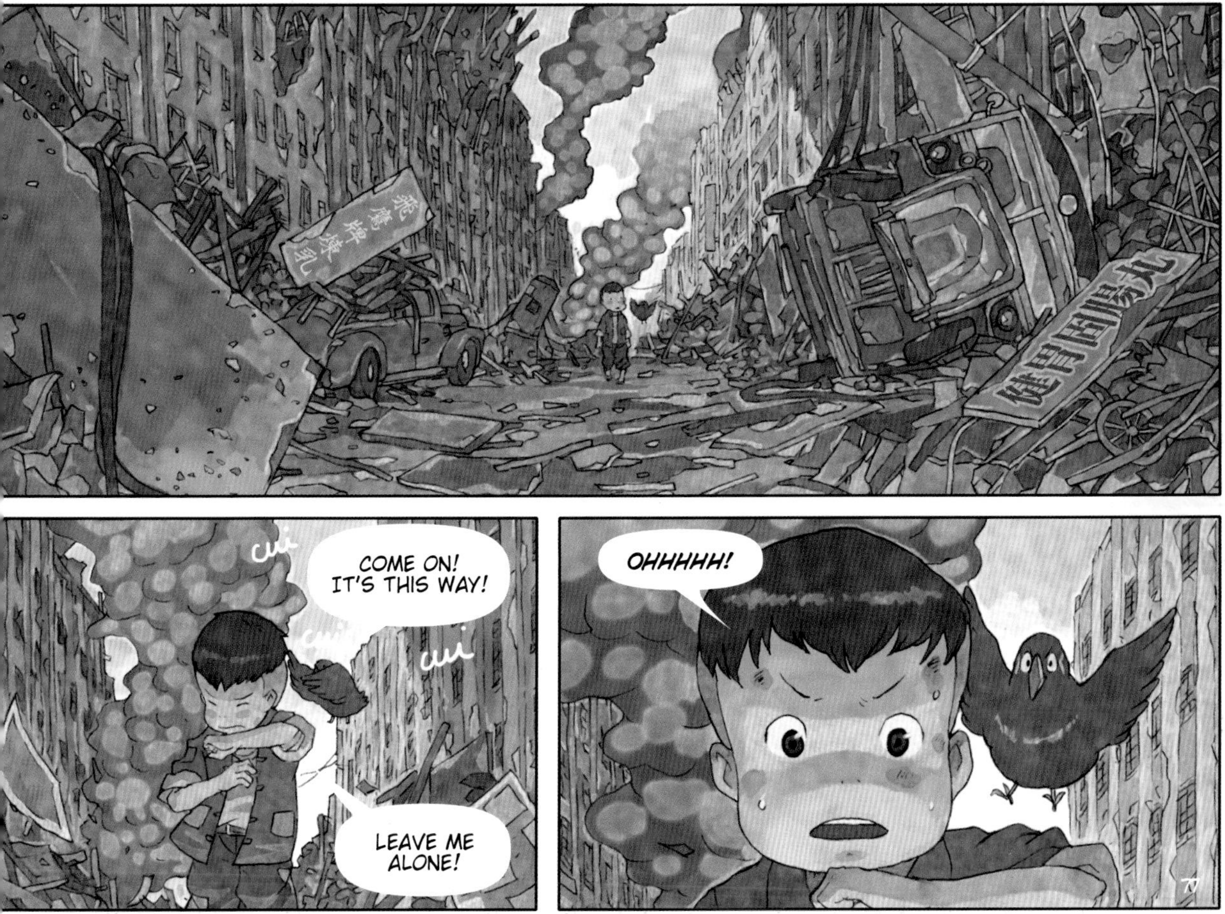
飛鷹牌煉乳
健胃固腸丸
cui
COME ON! IT'S THIS WAY!
cui
cui
LEAVE ME ALONE!
OHHHHH!

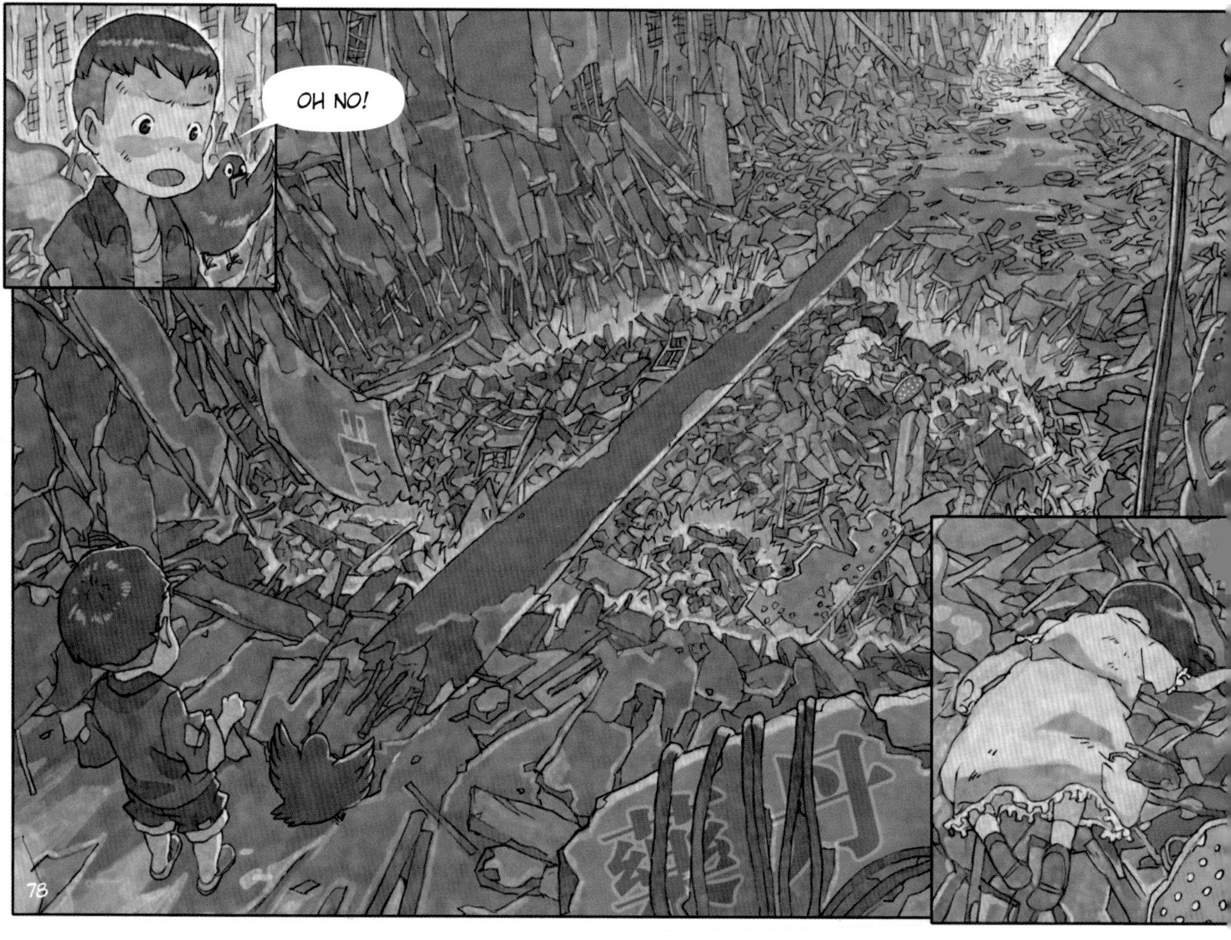
OH NO!

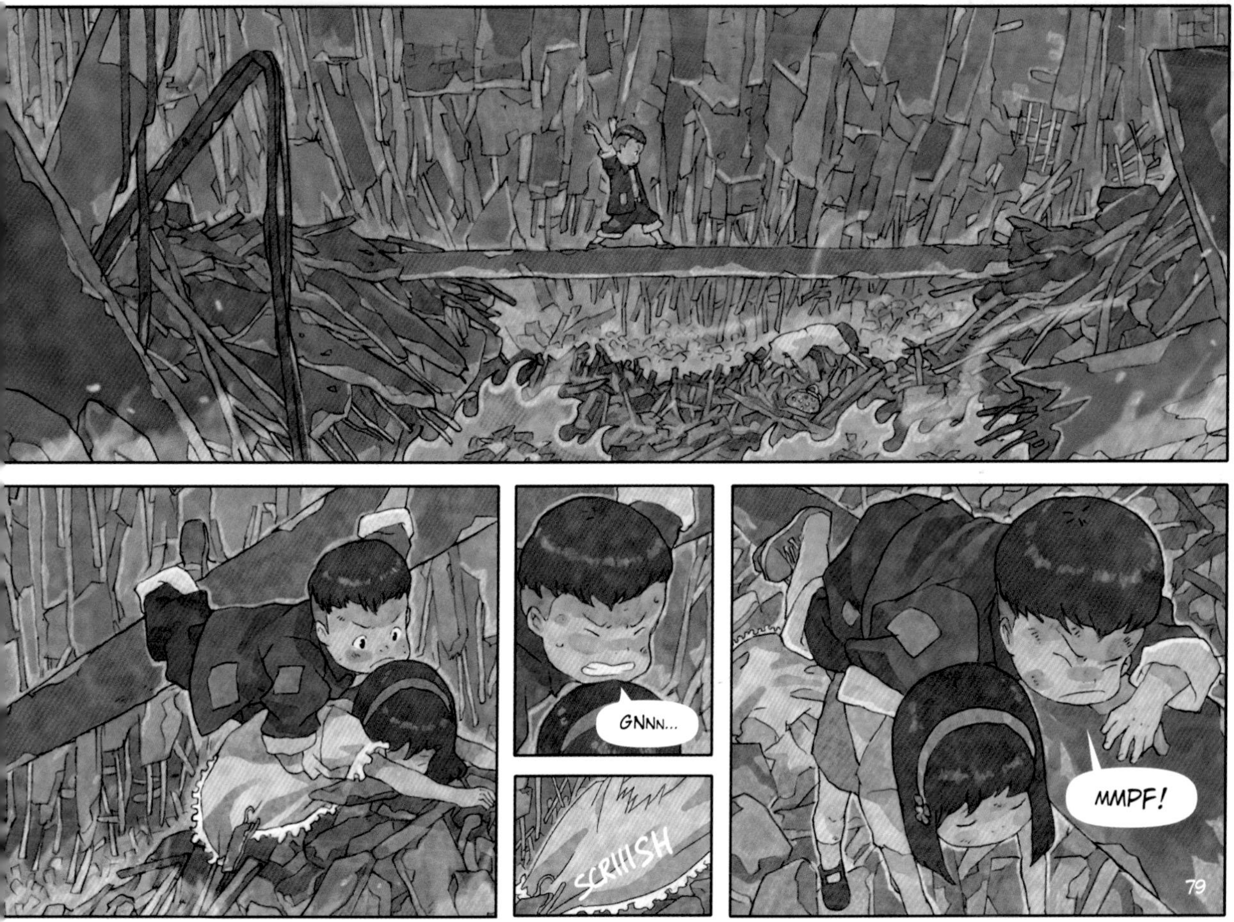
GNNN...
SCRIIISH
MMPF!

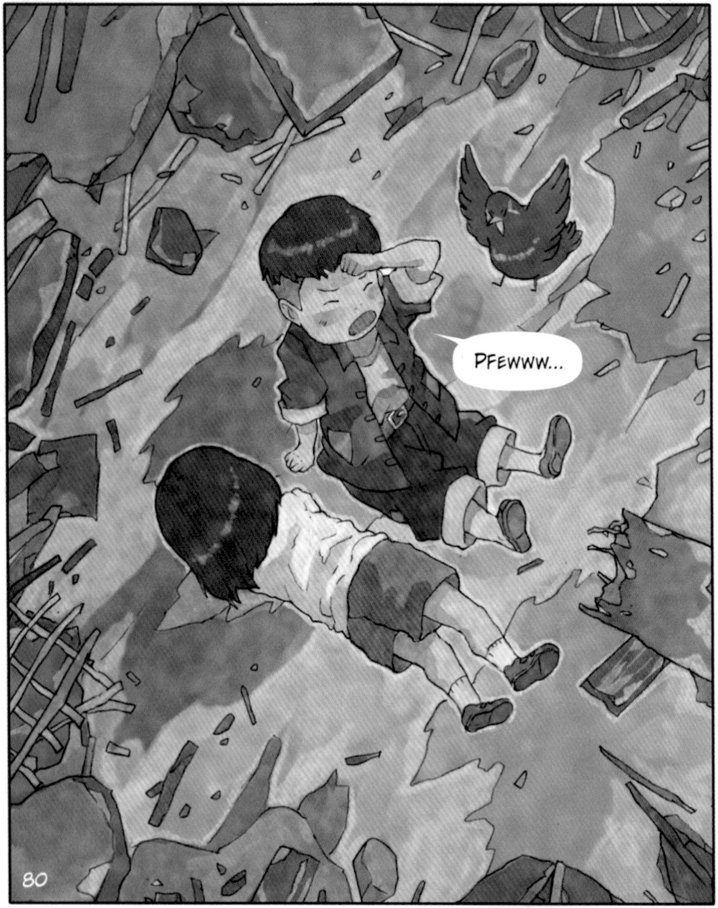
PFEWWW...

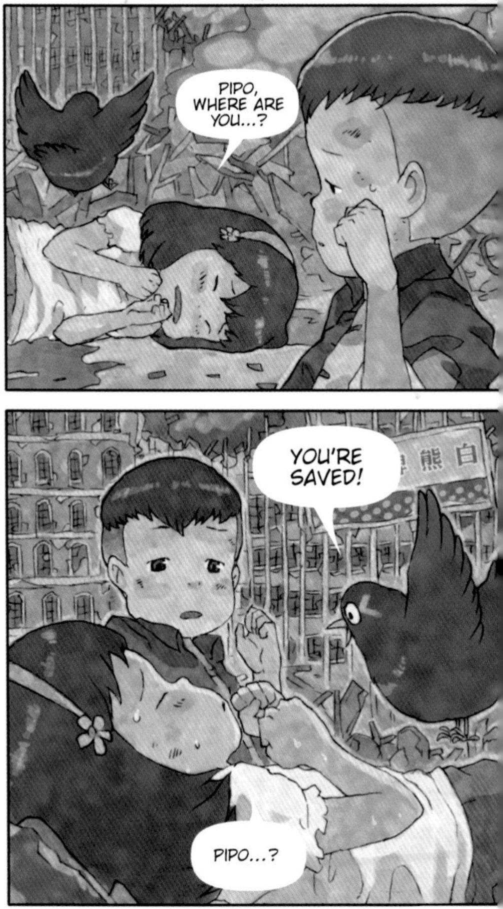
PIPO, WHERE ARE YOU...?
YOU'RE SAVED!
PIPO...?

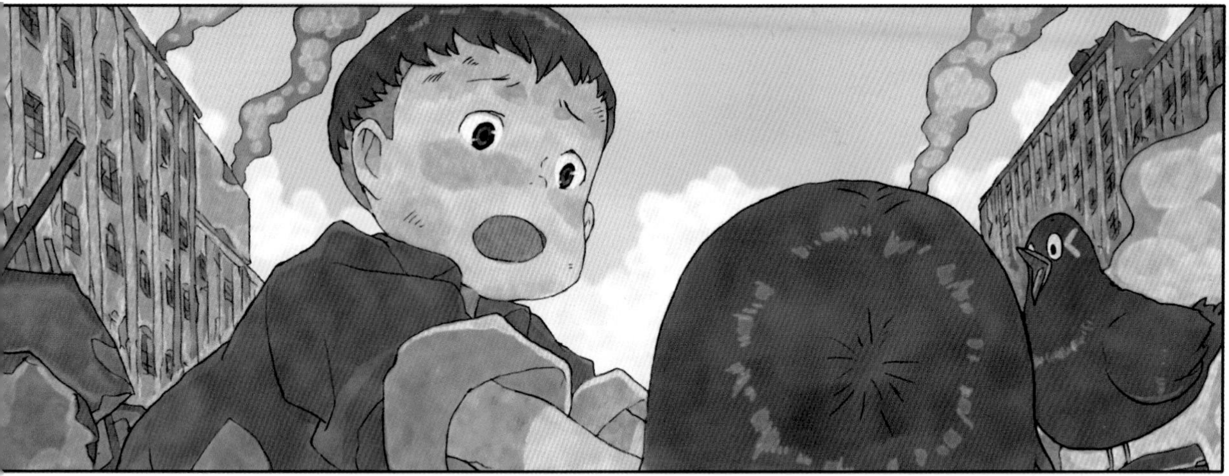

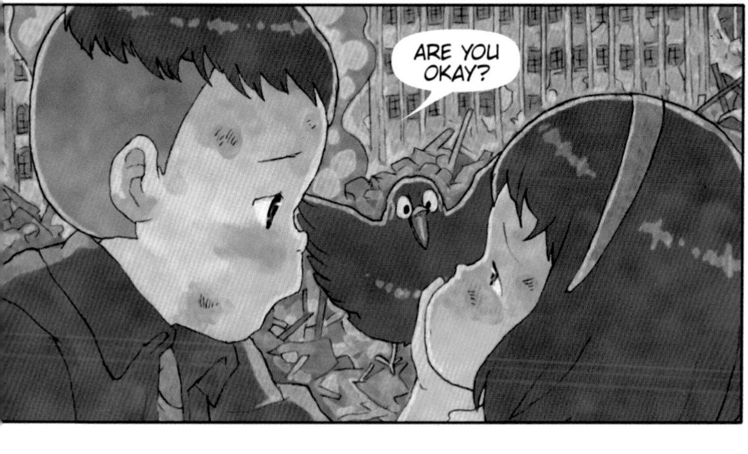
ARE YOU OKAY?

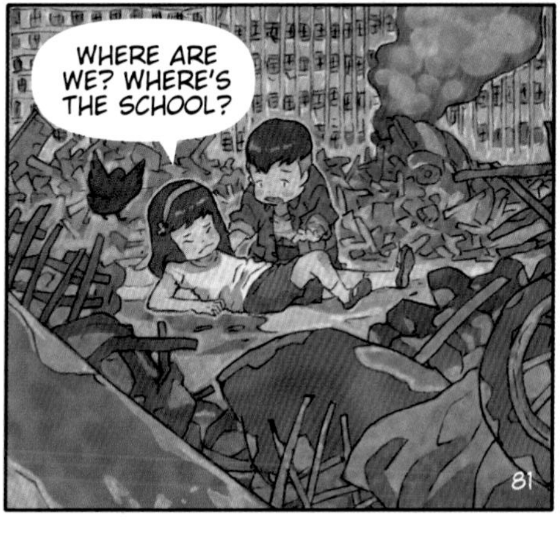
WHERE ARE WE? WHERE'S THE SCHOOL?

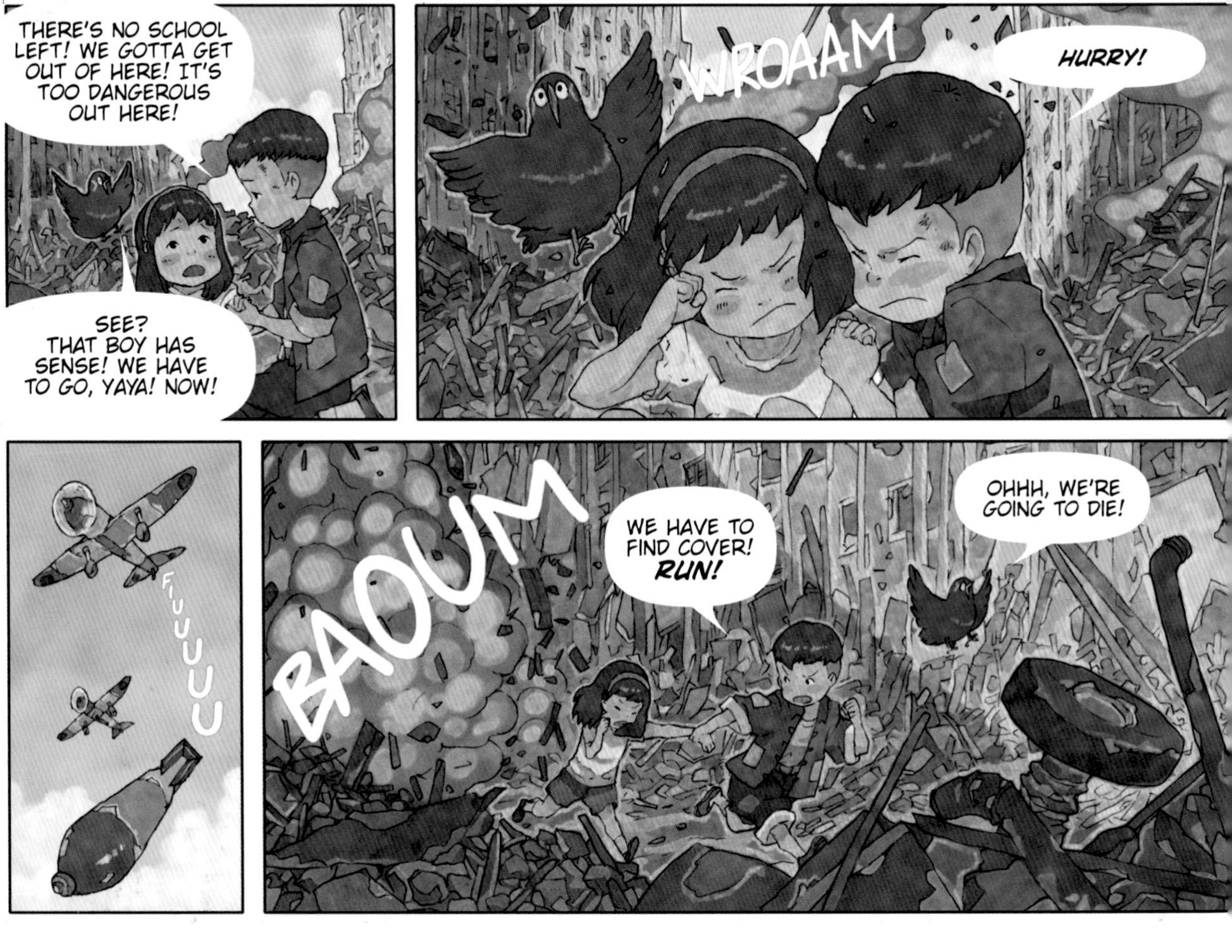
THERE'S NO SCHOOL LEFT! WE GOTTA GET OUT OF HERE! IT'S TOO DANGEROUS OUT HERE!
SEE? THAT BOY HAS SENSE! WE HAVE TO GO, YAYA! NOW!
WROAAM
HURRY!
FIUUUUUU
BAOUM
WE HAVE TO FIND COVER! RUN!
OHHH, WE'RE GOING TO DIE!

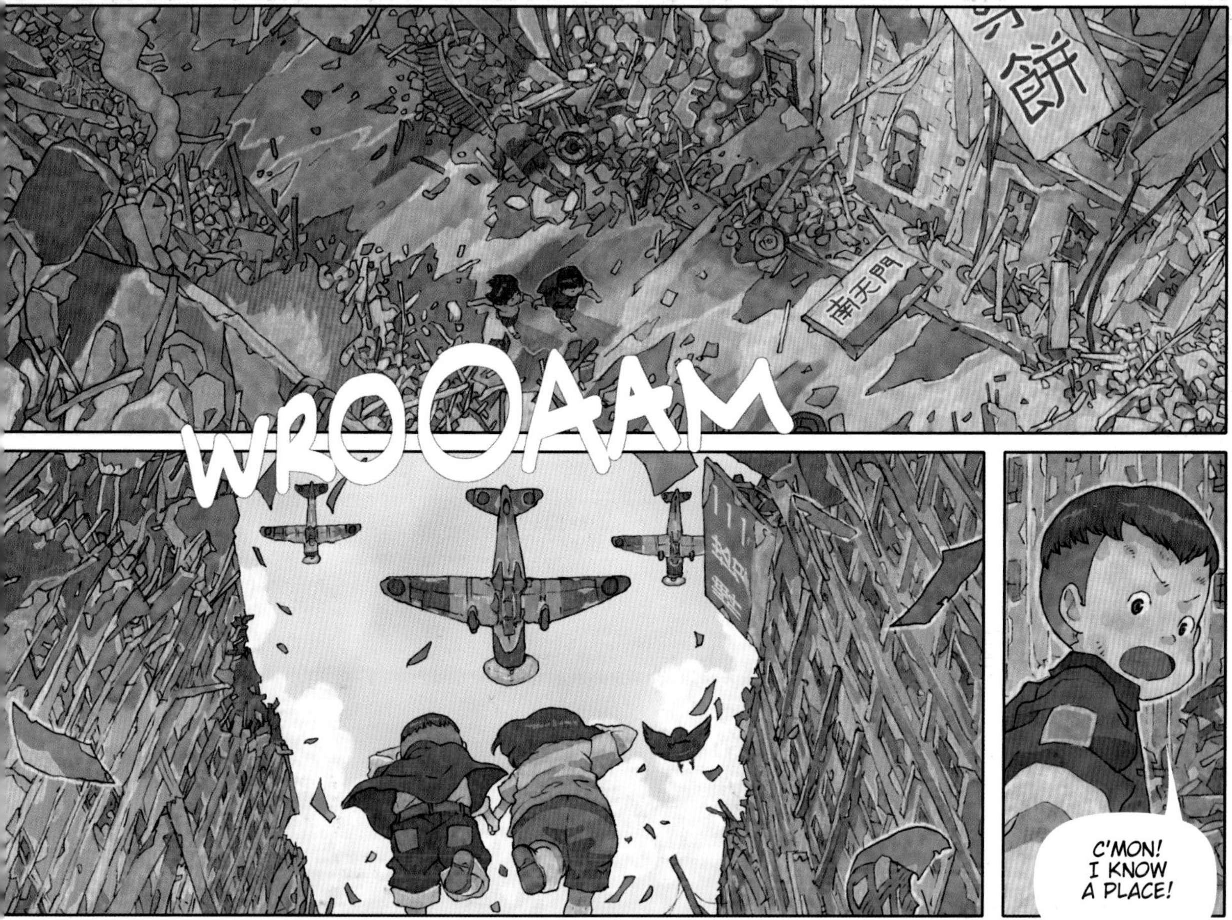
WROOAAM
C'MON! I KNOW A PLACE!

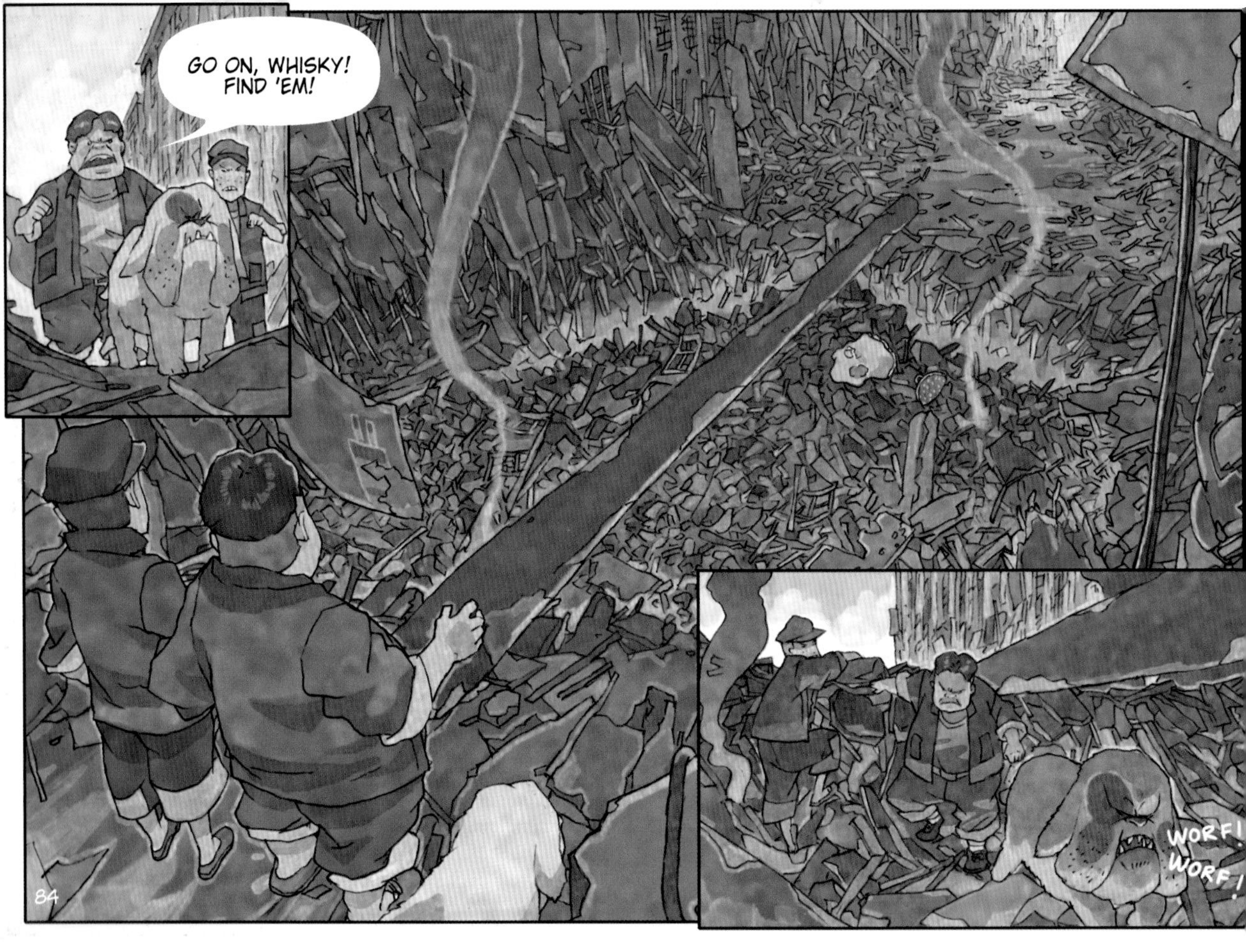
GO ON, WHISKY! FIND 'EM!
WORF! WORF!

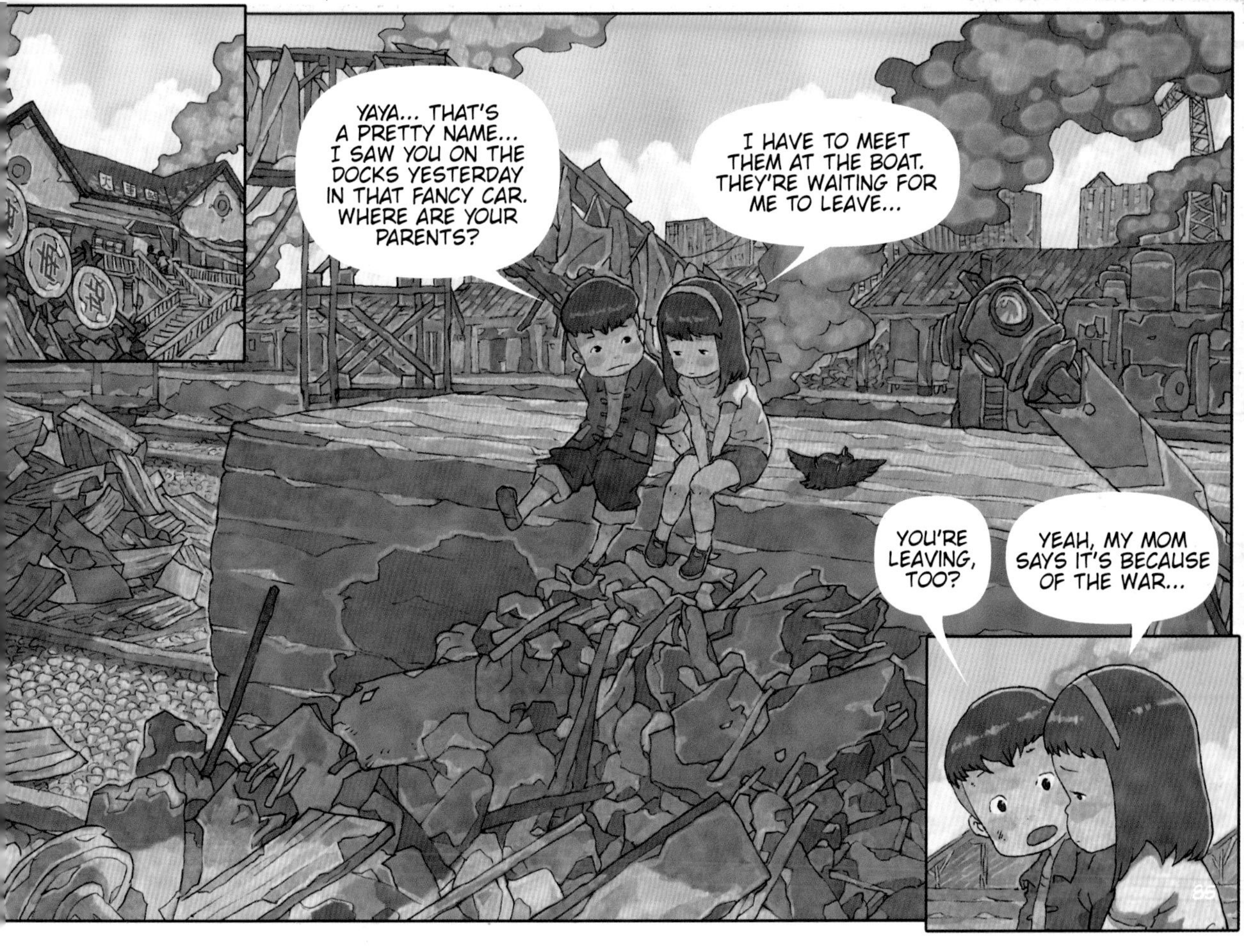
YAYA... THAT'S A PRETTY NAME... I SAW YOU ON THE DOCKS YESTERDAY IN THAT FANCY CAR. WHERE ARE YOUR PARENTS?
I HAVE TO MEET THEM AT THE BOAT. THEY'RE WAITING FOR ME TO LEAVE...
YOU'RE LEAVING, TOO?
YEAH, MY MOM SAYS IT'S BECAUSE OF THE WAR...

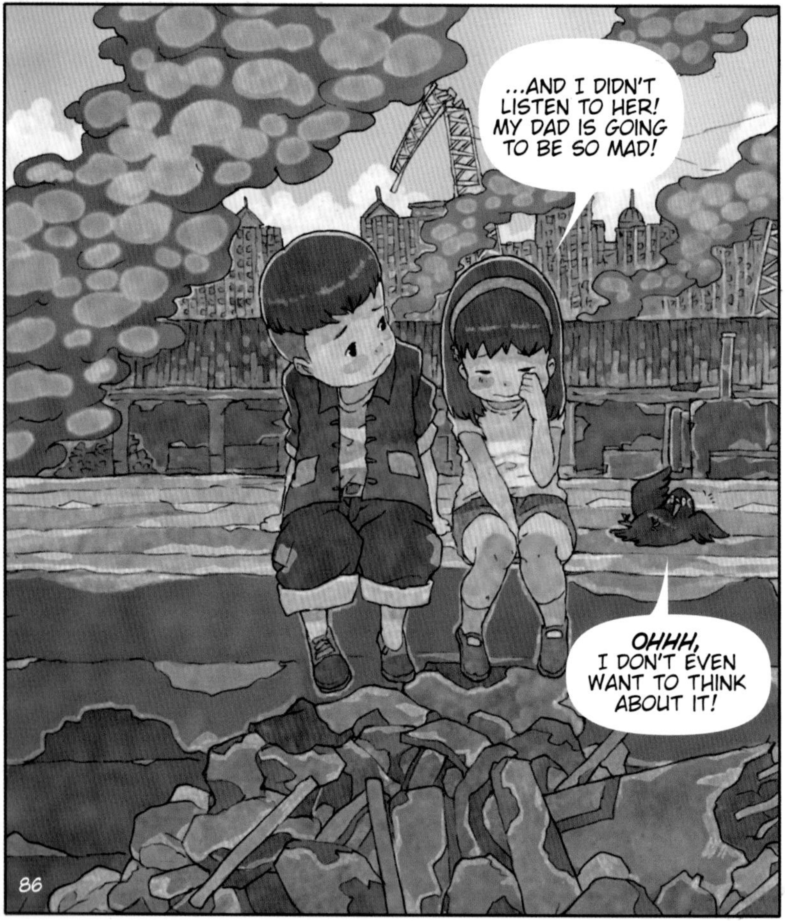
...AND I DIDN'T LISTEN TO HER! MY DAD IS GOING TO BE SO MAD!
OHHH, I DON'T EVEN WANT TO THINK ABOUT IT!

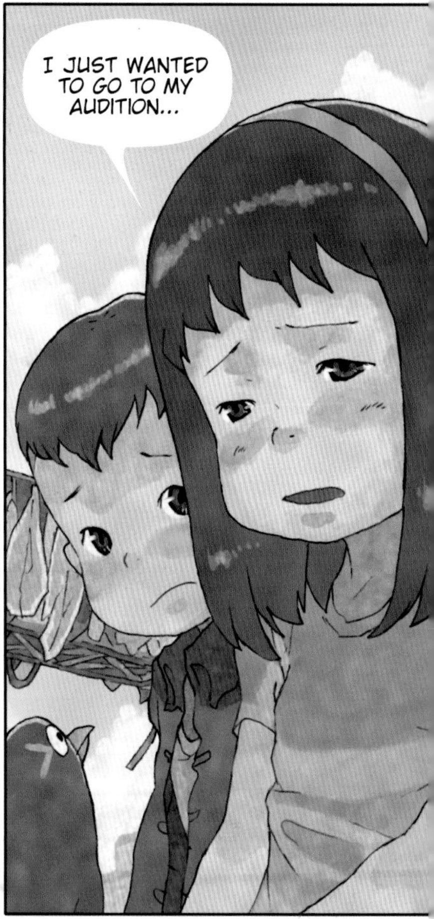
I JUST WANTED TO GO TO MY AUDITION...

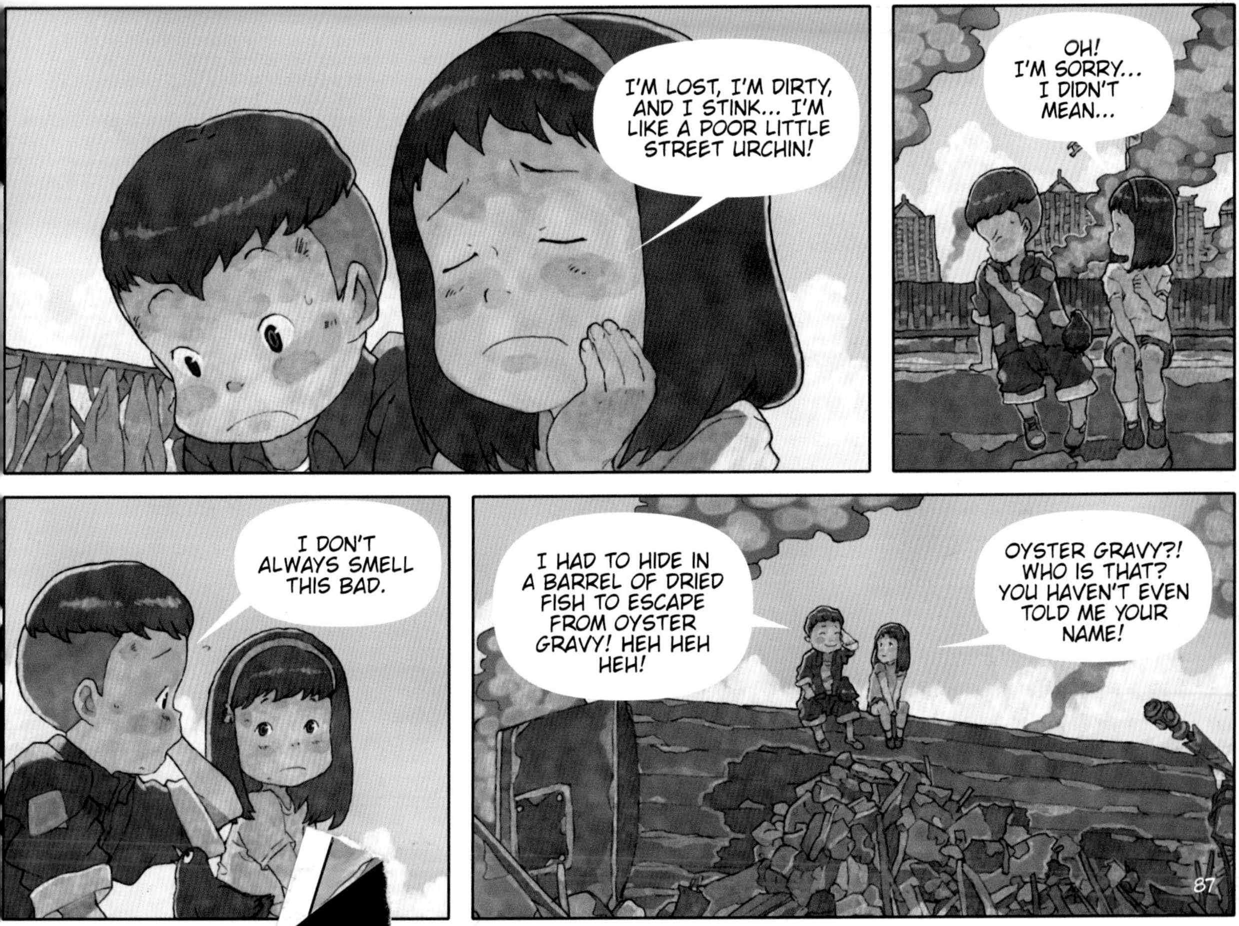
I'M LOST, I'M DIRTY, AND I STINK... I'M LIKE A POOR LITTLE STREET URCHIN!
OH! I'M SORRY... I DIDN'T MEAN...
I DON'T ALWAYS SMELL THIS BAD.
I HAD TO HIDE IN A BARREL OF DRIED FISH TO ESCAPE FROM OYSTER GRAVY! HEH HEH HEH!
OYSTER GRAVY?! WHO IS THAT? YOU HAVEN'T EVEN TOLD ME YOUR NAME!

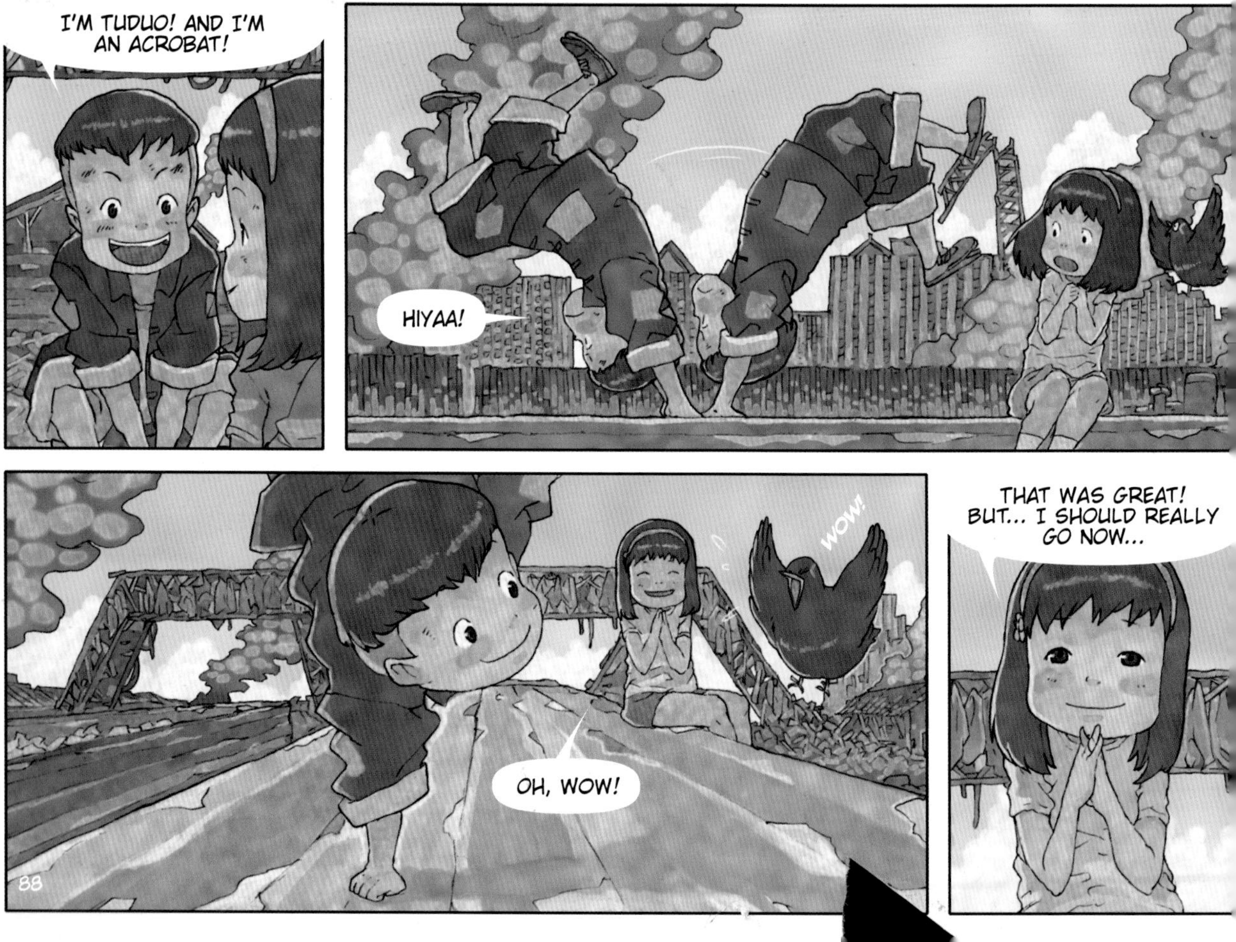
I'M TUDUO! AND I'M AN ACROBAT!
HIYAA!
OH, WOW!
WOW!
THAT WAS GREAT! BUT... I SHOULD REALLY GO NOW...

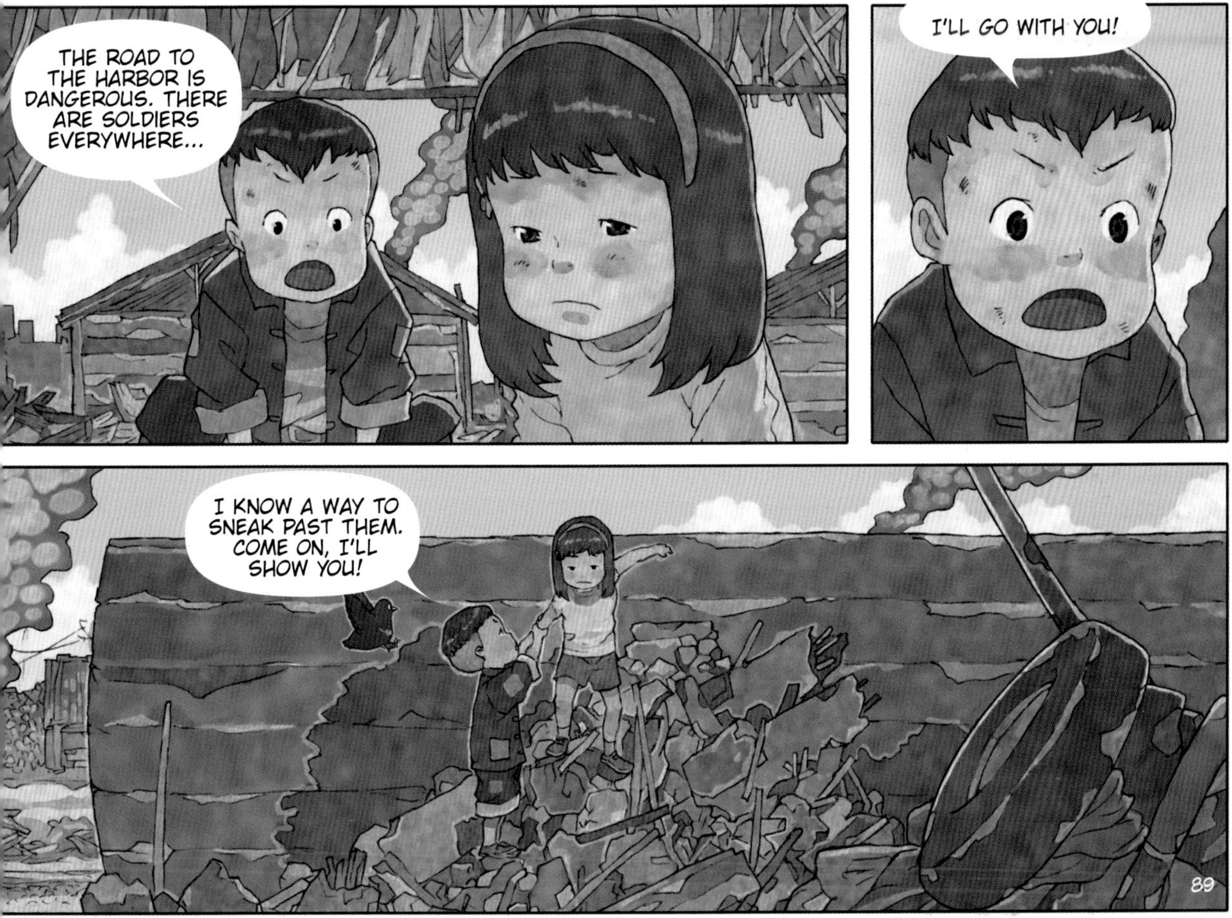
THE ROAD TO THE HARBOR IS DANGEROUS. THERE ARE SOLDIERS EVERYWHERE...
I'LL GO WITH YOU!
I KNOW A WAY TO SNEAK PAST THEM. COME ON, I'LL SHOW YOU!

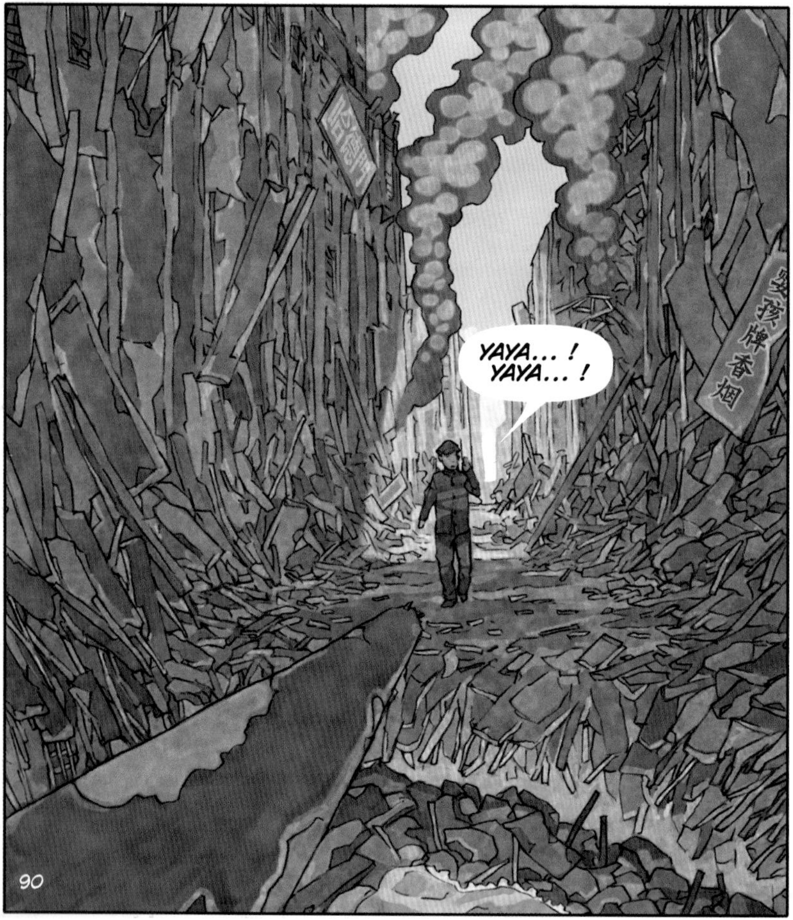
婴孩牌香烟
YAYA... !
YAYA... !

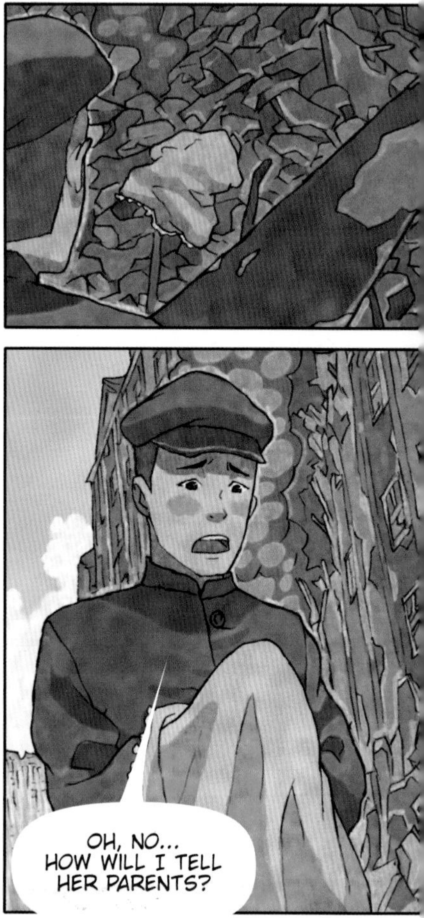
OH, NO...
HOW WILL I TELL
HER PARENTS?

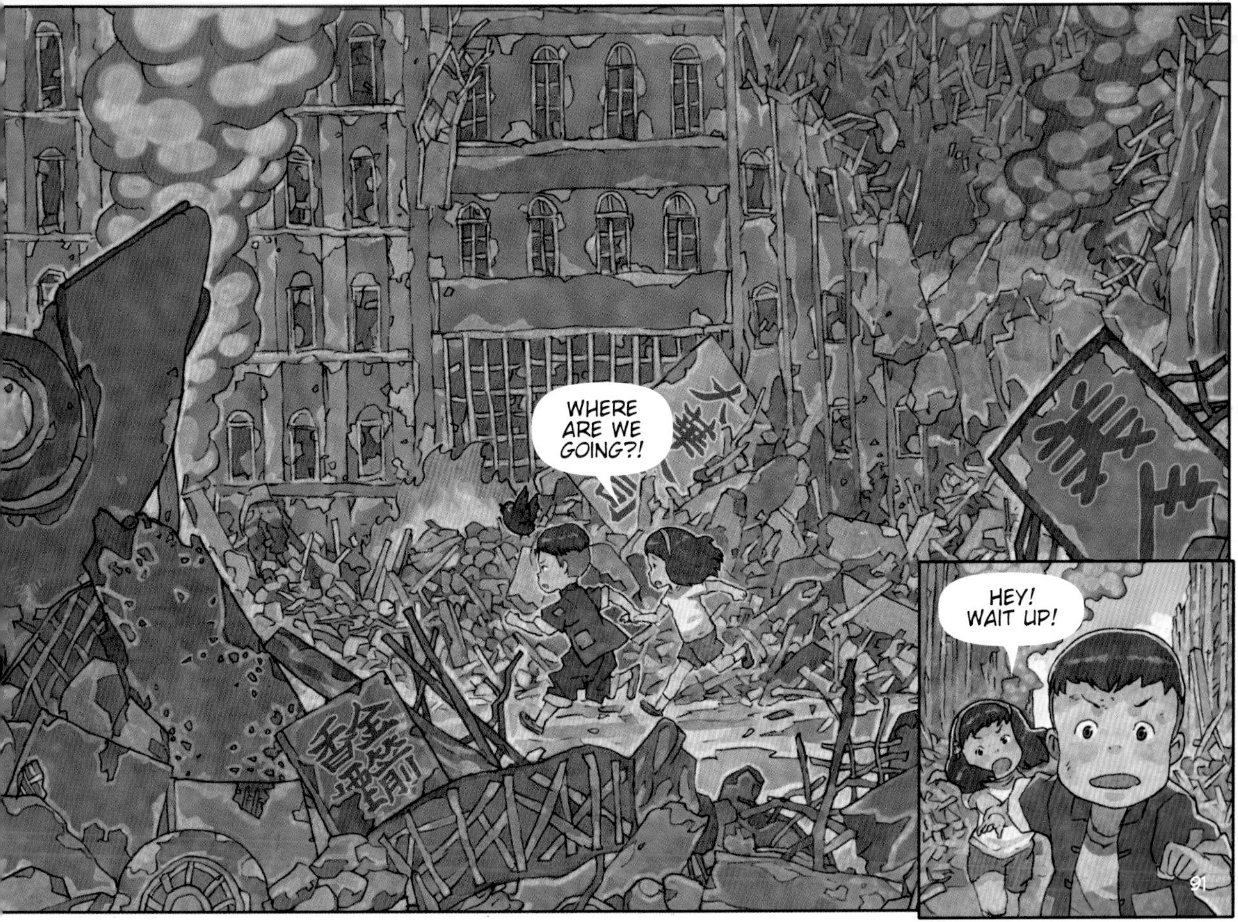
WHERE ARE WE GOING?!
HEY! WAIT UP!

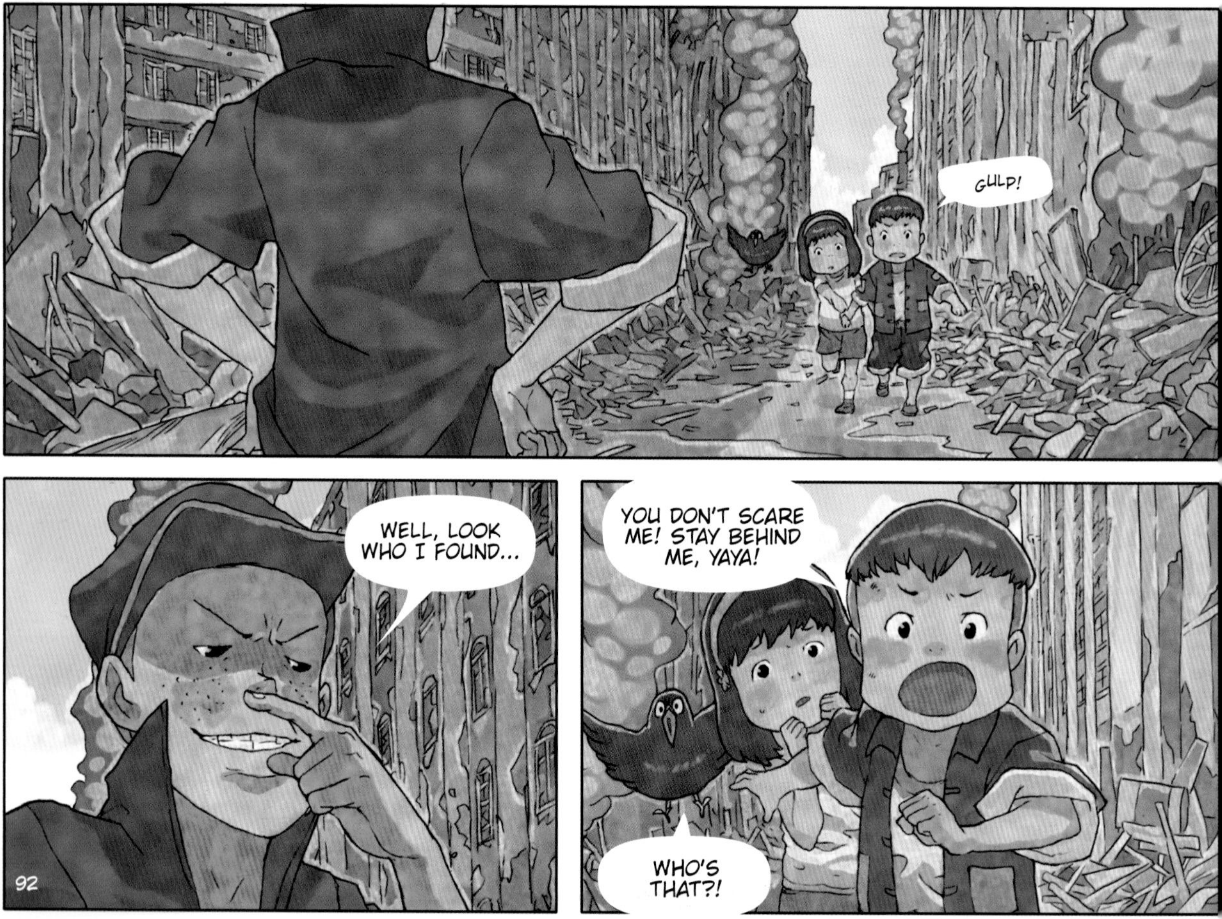
GULP!
WELL, LOOK WHO I FOUND...
YOU DON'T SCARE ME! STAY BEHIND ME, YAYA!
WHO'S THAT?!

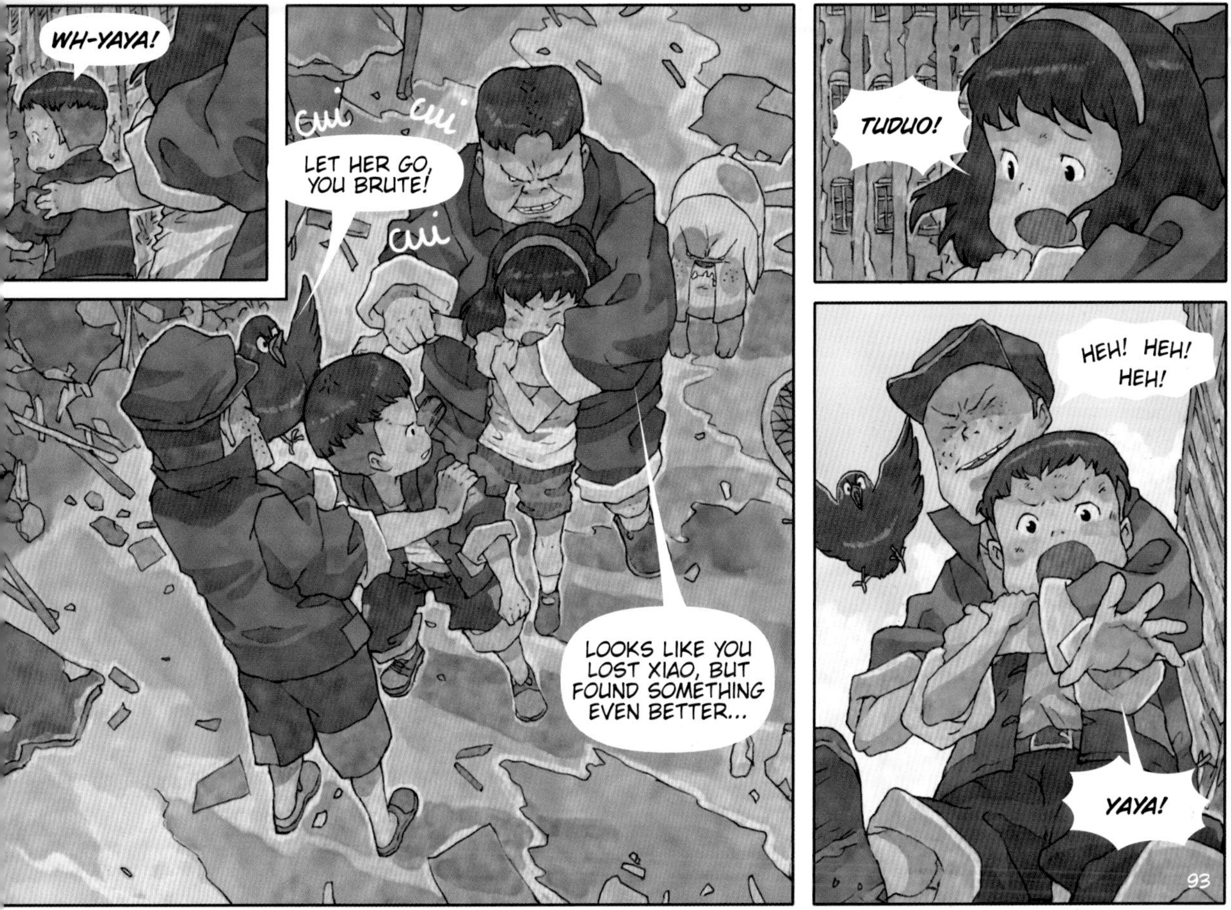
WH-YAYA!
cui cui
cui
LET HER GO, YOU BRUTE!
LOOKS LIKE YOU LOST XIAO, BUT FOUND SOMETHING EVEN BETTER...
TUDUO!
HEH! HEH! HEH!
YAYA!

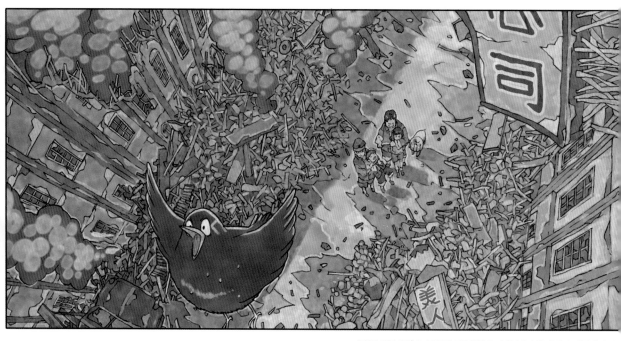

...AND THAT'S HOW YAYA'S ADVENTURES BEGAN...

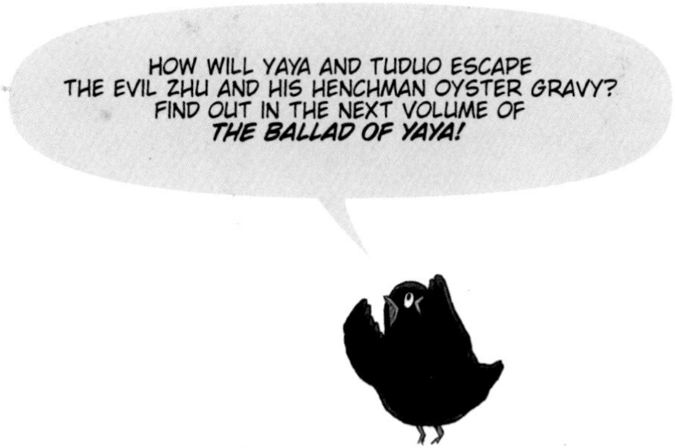
HOW WILL YAYA AND TUDUO ESCAPE THE EVIL ZHU AND HIS HENCHMAN OYSTER GRAVY? FIND OUT IN THE NEXT VOLUME OF ***THE BALLAD OF YAYA!***

ISBN: 978-1-942367-64-2
Library of Congress Control Number: 2018932766

The Ballad of Yaya, Vol. 1: Fugue, published 2019 by The Lion Forge, LLC.

10 9 8 7 6 5 4 3 2 1